SORRENTO GIRL

Dawn Klinge

Copyright © 2020 by Dawn Klinge.

All rights reserved. No part of this publication may be reproduced, distributed or transmitted in any form or by any means, including photocopying, recording, or other electronic or mechanical methods, without the prior written permission of the publisher, except in the case of brief quotations embodied in critical reviews and certain other noncommercial uses permitted by copyright law. For permission requests, write to the publisher, addressed "Attention: Permissions Coordinator," at the address below.

Dawn Klinge/Genevieve Publishing
dawn.klinge@gmail.com
www.dawnklinge.com

Publisher's Note: This is a work of fiction. Names, characters, places, and incidents are a product of the author's imagination. Locales and public names are sometimes used for atmospheric purposes. Any resemblance to actual people, living or dead, or to businesses, companies, events, institutions, or locales is completely coincidental.

Book Layout ©2020 BookDesignTemplates.com

Cover design by Evelynne Labelle of Carpe Librum Book design
https://carpelibrumbookdesign.com/

Sorrento Girl/ Dawn Klinge. -- 1st ed.
ISBN 978-1-7346434-0-4

Dedication

This is for my daughter, Grace, a courageous woman who inspires me.

"For the Spirit God gave us does not make us timid, but gives us power, love and self-discipline."

– 2 Timothy 1:7 (NIV)

One

"Adventure is worthwhile in itself."
– Amelia Earhart

February 1933

Ann Brooks waited on the wooden platform at the train station in Wenatchee with her father on a dark, early Friday morning. She was anxiously listening for the sound of a whistle or the rumbling of wheels on the tracks. A biting cold wind whipped loose several dark curls from the single braid she'd hurriedly made that morning. Ann had taken her gray leather suitcase and left her little home on Hawthorne street well before the sun was up.

When Ann had opened the small piece of luggage from her father last Christmas, she'd discovered a train ticket nestled inside the red satin interior. Printed on the ticket—"Empire Builder, Wenatchee to Seattle, February 3, 1933, 5 AM boarding time."

Her father's face had softened, as it only did for her, and a smile had played at the corners of his eyes as he'd explained. Fourteen-year-old Ann was going to see her Aunt Rose for a few days. The surprise got even better. Amelia Earhart, famed aviator, would also be in Seattle. She would be speaking at the Civic Auditorium to a crowd of Girl Scouts, Camp Fire Girls, members of the Women's Century Club, reporters, and aviation fanatics. Ann and Aunt Rose were going to see the woman they both admired.

The weeks between Christmas and the Seattle trip had seemed endless, but the anticipated day was finally here. In the distance, down the tracks, a single beam of pale light began to grow brighter. Ann squeezed her father's hand in excitement.

"It's coming!" She glanced up at her father with a smile. "Thank you for letting me do this." Her father nodded.

Calvin Brooks was a man of few words, but Ann knew he loved her, and she knew the magnitude of the sacrifice he'd made to provide this adventure for her. It had been just the two of them for as long as she could remember. Life hadn't been easy, and money was tight.

Now Ann could hear the rumbling as the train approached from the east. It was almost here. Her father took an apple and a piece of cheese wrapped in paper from his coat pocket and gave it to Ann, something he did each morning when they parted ways. He on his way to the orchards—she on her way to school. Only this morning was different. She'd never been to Seattle nor had she ridden a train. It would be her biggest journey yet.

Something—perhaps fear, perhaps excitement—made the apple and cheese unappetizing for the moment. She stashed the food in her case and checked to make sure she had everything for the trip ahead—though there was little she could do now if she'd forgotten anything. The book, *For the Fun of It*, by Amelia Earhart, sat on top of her belongings. It was waiting (hopefully) to be signed by the author. Beyond that, the remaining items of her case included one other dress, a nightgown, a change of underclothes, stockings, a toothbrush, comb, one round-trip train ticket, a small coin purse with three dollars in it, and a brown felt hat. She was ready. Her father pulled out the hat and placed it on Ann's head as the train pulled into the station. Ann took out her ticket and fastened the clasp on her case one last time. She and her father were the only people on the platform.

"Your Aunt Rose will be waiting for you. You'll be there in just a few hours, and I'll be here on Sunday night to pick you up. Take care."

And with that, he handed Ann's gray case to the conductor and patted her back, gently pushing her toward the waiting train.

***

A few hours later, Ann was at King Street Station in Seattle. It was a stark contrast to the sleepy little station in Wenatchee. She scanned the crowd for any sign of her Aunt Rose.

A brick clock tower dominated the view, dwarfing everything else around it. At the base of the tower, an archway opened into a large room where all the other passengers seemed to be coming and going from. Ann followed the crowd, marveling at the room's grandeur. From the giant globe chandeliers to the inlaid marble floors, and the elaborate plaster reliefs that covered the walls and ceilings, the decor took her breath away. Ann stopped in her tracks and gazed at her surroundings, causing a traffic jam as busy travelers tried impatiently to move around her.

"Ann, Ann! Over here!" Rose yelled while waving her arms around excitedly.

"Aunt Rose!" Ann ran toward the woman, then wrapped her arms around her in a boisterous hug.

From the time Rose was sixteen, she had taken a particular interest in her niece. Lily, Ann's mother, had died of influenza when Ann was just a baby. Ann's father, Calvin, had insisted on raising her by himself amongst the orchards in Wenatchee, but Seattle was where Ann's mother's family lived. Calvin Brooks was a good father. Ann had an independent spirit and an intense thirst for adventure, just like her mother. Rose often told Ann that her mother would have been proud.

In spite of the miles and the mountains between them, Rose had stayed involved in Ann's life, mostly through letters, drawings, and books. After the Great Northern Railway began its service through Wenatchee in 1929 on its route from Chicago to Seattle, Ann was able to see her aunt more frequently when Rose started making a summer trip for a week each year. Rose was a history professor at the University of Washington. She hadn't yet found the time nor the inclination for marriage or children of her own, but she was the closest thing to a mother Ann had.

"You won't believe what you missed. Guess who just came through the station!"

Ann laughed. "I don't know, Aunt Rose. Who?"

"Ms. Earhart, herself! The mayor was here too, along with a lot of other important people and a bunch of reporters. They were just leaving when I got here."

"I thought she was flying into Boeing Field ..."

"Not in this weather. She had to take the train instead. She's here! She's in Seattle, and we'll see her soon! Are you hungry?" Rose didn't wait for an answer. "Let's get some lunch."

Ann followed her aunt out of the station onto a slush-covered street. They quickly caught a streetcar going toward the Civic Auditorium. Through the fogged glass windows, Ann watched as they rode along the waterfront of Elliot Bay. The city buzzed with activity. They passed rickety shacks, stately tall brick buildings, and street vendors selling everything from fish to newspapers. On one corner stood a wooden pole, at least fifty feet high, with animals carved into it. Ann recognized it as the Tlingit totem her aunt had sketched in one of her letters.

The streetcar was crowded with other passengers, many of them young girls. Some wore their green Girl Scout uniforms. The buzz in the city made it feel like a holiday. They reached the corner of Mercer and Fourth Street, and Aunt Rose reached up and pulled a cord near the ceiling of the car that made a buzzing sound. It was time to get off.

A sideways rain quickly soaked the pair as they made their way across the street toward a small diner. Inside, the smell of coffee permeated the air, and Benny Goodman's band could be heard from a radio in the corner. Every booth was filled with what appeared to be fellow Amelia Earhart fans, so Ann and Aunt Rose found themselves a table at the counter. Clam chowder and grilled cheese sandwiches were quickly brought out to the ladies after they ordered. Ann sighed with happiness as she bit into the gooey warmth of the cheese.

Aunt Rose grinned. "I think I'm just as excited as you are to see Ms. Earhart, but I want to hear from you. What is it about her that makes you admire her so much?".

"She's a trailblazer, Aunt Rose." Ann loved that word. "You know she was the first woman to pilot a plane across the Atlantic. Right?"

Of course, Rose already knew this. Ms. Earhart was a national celebrity who was breaking down barriers for thousands of women.

"Do you want to fly someday?"

"I already have!" said Ann proudly.

Rose's eyes widened with a look of surprise. "You have?"

"Yes. Marty, my neighbor is a crop-duster. He takes me for rides in his plane. He's even let me take the controls a couple of times."

"Wow, that's great!"

"But I don't want to be a pilot, Aunt Rose. I want to be a teacher ... like you." Ann paused. "Maybe for younger kids."

Rose smiled. "You'll be a wonderful teacher." She glanced at the menu, then winked. "Do you want some cake before we go?"

***

Two days later, Ann's father was waiting for her as the train pulled into the station in Wenatchee, just as he'd promised. This time, the train was coming from the west. Once again, it was dark, and the platform was empty. Ann was the only person who got off, and her father was the only one waiting. She set her case on the ground, then smiling with newfound confidence, reached out for a hug. "The best adventure of my life!"

The two walked up the hill toward home. Ann talked nonstop as she described the train ride, Seattle, her aunt's house on Queen Anne Hill, what Amelia wore and said, and how long Ann had waited in line to get Amelia's book autographed—two hours. Her father nodded along in his usual quiet way.

Normal life would resume tomorrow. Dad would return to work, grafting new trees in the orchard, and Ann would attend school.

"I missed you!" Dad gave her a quick side hug. "It's good to have you home."

"I missed you too. Thank you for sending me." She would never forget the past couple of days. She wanted to be a strong independent woman like Amelia Earhart or her aunt. They were fearless. Neither one of them let society's expectations regarding a woman's place in the world dictate their choices. Amelia didn't allow marriage to stop her from continuing to fly and do what she loved, and Aunt Rose had foregone a husband altogether. And though she loved her home in Wenatchee, she was determined to one day return to live in Seattle. The big city suited her. There, anything felt possible.

Two

August 15, 1938

King Street Station, Seattle, WA

"Hotel Sorrento, please," Ann said to the taxi driver as she handed him her suitcase. Getting into the back of the cab, she moved aside the newspaper a previous passenger had left behind, placing her handbag on top. She wanted to take her things to the hotel first, find her room, and get some lunch before walking over to her new school for a meeting with Mrs. Prouty, the Dean of Women at Seattle College. The two had first met a year ago when Aunt Rose insisted on introducing Ann to her friend.

"Where are you going to college?" Rose had asked Ann last summer.

"I'm not." Though Ann wanted to continue her education, it wasn't within her reach.

"Why not?"

"I can't afford it." She didn't want to dwell on the disappointment.

Rose, knowing her niece well, hadn't accepted that answer. "Nonsense. You're going to come to Seattle, and I'll help you. We'll figure it out. I think I know just the right place." And figure it out, they did. Ann could hardly believe it. Not only had the money for tuition been provided for, through a combination of scholarships and a small inheritance left behind by her maternal grandparents, but she also had a job and a place to live.

She would be working as a mother's helper for a family with four kids, and her new home would be a room at Hotel Sorrento. One wing of the hotel had been temporarily leased as a women's dormitory for the college.

Seattle College was a small Jesuit school on First Hill. A College of Education had recently been established within the school after some controversy over admitting women. It was a fight that had gone all the way to the Vatican. Ann would be among one of the first groups of women to graduate from the new program when she finished. According to Aunt Rose, it was a place for trailblazers.

After being assured that Ann would attend college, Rose had taken off on a six-month sabbatical from her teaching job at the University of Washington to conduct some research on cathedrals in England. She would be home soon, and Ann was anxious to catch up with her.

The cab lurched along cobbled roads, and the scenery changed from dusty city streets to a quieter, more genteel neighborhood called First Hill. Stately homes with vast green lawns and iron gates lined the road. Then Hotel Sorrento came into view. The Italian oasis-style building reached seven stories high. Its red-brick L-shape gracefully curved around a large front driveway and formal garden area. A smartly dressed doorman in a red suit with gold buttons stood attentively near the entrance. Ann said a quiet prayer of gratitude and awe as she took in the building's beauty. "Welcome to Hotel Sorrento, the crown jewel of the Northwest!" said the man as he opened Ann's door.

Inside, the rich mahogany paneled walls, chandeliers, and thick oriental rugs gave the lobby a feeling of warmth and luxury. Ann had never stayed anywhere so lovely before. After she checked in at the front desk, a bellhop escorted her to her new home—room 302 in the east wing. Ann entered the room, and her breath caught! The view was striking! Through a large window, framed by thick gold-colored drapes, she could see Puget Sound and much of the city.

Two twin beds with mahogany headboards and white matelassé coverlets took up most of the space in the simple and elegant room. A desk with a banker's lamp sat under the window, and a low bureau with an attached round mirror was near the door. The empty wardrobe indicated Ann's new roommate must not have arrived yet.

She was alone. After the rush of the last few hours, the solitude felt good. Her suitcase and purse rested on the top of the bureau where the bellhop had left it. There was also a copy of the *Post Intelligencer*, the newspaper she'd seen in the cab earlier. Would she have enough time to get some lunch before her meeting with Dean Prouty? Ann glanced at her watch. Thirty minutes. The apple and cheese her father had given her before she left Wenatchee on the train that morning would have to do.

Ann brought her lunch and the newspaper over to the desk and sat down to read.

"'Working Wife' Loses U.W. Faculty Berth." The headline caught her eye. It went on to say that a semi-secret "Anti-Nepotism" resolution had been put in place at the University of Washington to address the financial woes of the Great Depression. The university administration said that "those married women who were on the payroll whose husbands were able to support them should be dismissed from their positions." At the request of Governor Martin, a list had been compiled of "married women and relatives" and "married couples" at the university.

Eager to keep the new policy as quiet as possible, University President Sieg had only informed the department chairmen. A favorite tenured professor from the art department, Lea Puymbroeck Miller, had been away on sabbatical the past fifteen months, studying abroad. During that time, she'd married zoology professor Robert Miller. She'd been unaware of the resolution and was promptly fired upon her return. It caused an uproar among the staff and students who loved her.

A chill ran through Ann's body as she took a bite of her apple and continued to read about the ridiculous and unfair resolution. She wanted a career and a family someday. Hopefully, the situation at the university was an isolated case. Why couldn't a woman have both? Aunt Rose was unmarried, and therefore safe, but how would she react to the news?

For now, Ann had to get to a meeting with Dean Prouty. She was excited to learn which classes she would take that fall and get settled into college life. She tried to put the disturbing article out of her mind as she looked in the mirror and carefully applied her favorite red lipstick.

She wore a brown silk dress with white bands on the cuffs and collar. Her slim figure was enhanced by the feminine style of the dress—a nipped waistline and tea-length skirt. Two-tone, high-heeled Mary Jane's completed the ensemble. Her dark wavy shoulder-length hair was pulled up with a tortoiseshell comb on one side, and the only jewelry she wore was a gold Cartier wristwatch that had belonged to her mother. She'd traveled in the same outfit, but there was no time to change. Hopefully, it would do.

***

Later that afternoon, Ann walked into the lobby of Hotel Sorrento and sighed with pleasure. This stunning place would be home for an entire year!

The meeting had gone well, and Ann was smiling. Classes would start in two days. Some of the other women were arriving now too. Maybe her roommate was here. What would she be like? Would they become friends? The concierge stepped out from his podium to hand her a piece of paper with a phone message from Aunt Rose. She was back in Seattle and wanted to meet Ann in the Fireside Room of the hotel at seven that evening.

***

After a much-needed time of rest in her room, a change to evening clothes, and some time spent exploring and marveling at her new surroundings, it was time for Ann to meet her aunt downstairs.

"Hello, darling. I have someone I want you to meet!" Aunt Rose waved to Ann as soon as she stepped into the Fireside Room. A tall, handsome man stood beside her. Ann approached the couple, and leaned toward her aunt to kiss her cheek. Rose beamed as she turned and placed her hand through the crook in the man's arm.

What was that sparkling diamond doing on her aunt's left finger?

Three

Ann slept late the next morning. A soft pink hue of late summer sunlight spilled across the bare wood floor. The other bed—still empty. Saturday. The rest of the women would arrive today. What would it be like to live with so many women? Perhaps it was like having sisters. She and everyone else would also be meeting their House Mother, Ms. Patrick, and presumably, learning about coed life at the Sorrento. Her aunt had warned Ann that she'd have to get used to strict rules.

The news of her colleague's release from her teaching position had concerned Aunt Rose, but she'd seemed determined to hold off on any worry regarding her own job until she'd learned more. She hadn't known about the "Anti-Nepotism" resolution, and as far as she knew, she'd be teaching again that fall at UW.

One thing was sure. Aunt Rose was happier than Ann had ever seen her before. She was in love with Dr. Gary Francis, her new husband. They were both professors at UW, a situation that was alarmingly similar to the one Ann had read about the day prior. They'd fallen in love while studying at Oxford. After a whirlwind European romance and a short visit with his family in New York City, they'd decided upon a quick courthouse marriage there. Ann had been surprised at the sudden wedding, but she liked Dr. Francis. He was intelligent, charming, and sweet —perfect for Rose. Ann had always enjoyed a good love story, especially now that it involved her aunt. Hopefully Rose's job would be safe. Taking that away from her would be like removing part of her identity.

Breakfast was in an hour. Ann had cooked all the meals for her father and herself for the past five years. Cleaning, gardening, shopping, and laundry were chores she had done on her own while her father worked long hours as a foreman with the Northern Fruit Company. Now, she would be provided three meals a day on fine china in a beautiful dining room on the top floor of the hotel, and a maid would clean her room and do her laundry. What wasn't there to enjoy about this new life?

Ann opened the small closet and took out a pale green cotton day dress with tiny white polka dots. The room already felt warm. The short sleeves would be perfect for today. She didn't have very many clothes to choose from, but she was an accomplished seamstress, and what she did have, she hoped, would help her fit in with the other girls.

After dressing and tidying the room, Ann was almost ready to go upstairs for breakfast when someone knocked on the door.

"Hi. Are you Ann?" asked the girl in the hallway.

"Yes."

"I'm Helen West. I guess we're sharing this room? So nice to meet you!"

"Helen! I'm pleased to meet you too. Come on in! Have you had breakfast yet? If not, you're just in time."

Helen was followed into the room by two bellhops, each carrying a large trunk. "I'm famished!" she said dramatically.

She handed each bellhop a coin before they left, then spun around, arms outstretched, before she flopped on the nearby bed. A petite girl with delicate features, Helen wore a bright smile and a jaunty navy beret. Her red hair was pulled into a chignon. The white drop waist dress she wore had navy buttons running the length of one side. It was somehow smooth and unwrinkled, in spite of her travels. Her appearance was chic and her manner confident. But it was Helen's exuberant spirit that told Ann she was probably going to be a fun roommate.

***

Four women sat on the two beds in Ann and Helen's room later that evening, listening to Nora read aloud from the *Seattle College Co-Ed Code* they'd received earlier that day. Nora Andrews and Peggy Monroe lived across the hallway. Nora was from Tacoma, like Helen, and Peggy came from Olympia. Like Ann, Helen was planning on being a teacher, and Peggy and Nora were both planning on becoming nurses. They'd been at the same table for breakfast, and they'd hit it off as friends. The rest of the day had been spent in a meeting with Ms. Patrick, their House Mother, exploring the nearby campus, and unpacking their belongings.

Nora continued reading. "Part 4, Gentleman Callers ..." She took a deep breath. "Young men may be entertained in the public spaces of the Sorrento after 3:00 p.m. except on Saturday and Sunday when the hour shall be 1:00 p.m. Gentlemen callers are expected to leave the residence by 7:30 p.m. on all evenings on weekdays, on Friday, and Saturday at 11:00 p.m. and on Sunday at 10:30 p.m. No student shall try to evade these rules by entertaining callers outside of the residence or in the gardens at any time before the afternoon calling hours. Gentlemen are to be received in the public areas only."

Helen laughed as she listened to Nora's reading of the code. "What happens to the evaders?"

"Doesn't say ..." said Nora.

The conversation brought Ann's thoughts back to the professor at UW and to her aunt's recent marriage, so she told her friends about it.

"Why would she want to work now if she's married to a doctor?" Peggy asked in a tone of surprise.

How should she respond? Ann didn't know these women very well. She chewed her lip and fidgeted with her sleeve as she considered her answer. Peggy sprawled across one end of the bed. "So, tell me, ladies, what do you all think of Ms. Patrick?"

Ann sighed with relief. Apparently, Peggy's first question was rhetorical because she'd moved on to another before Ann could defend her aunt's decision to work.

"I don't think she's someone you'll want to cross. Evasion might be your best bet!" Nora laughed.

Ms. Patrick was a stern woman of indeterminate age and who reminded Ann of a hawk. The woman's small black eyes seemed to notice everything. Her hair was pulled severely off of her thin, tight face into a low bun, and she had worn a long black wool skirt and a buttoned-up black blazer in spite of the heat that day. She never smiled. Though the women lived in a hotel, off-campus, their status as coeds meant Ms. Patrick would supervise them. She also lived at the hotel, and she would be watching their comings and goings, reporting directly to the dean.

"Ms. Patrick can't stop us from having fun this year!" Helen grinned.

They all hoped she was right.

***

On Sunday morning, the friends went to Mass together at St. James Cathedral. Ann watched the people around her to know when to sit, stand, and make the sign of the cross. She didn't understand how everything worked, but she liked being there. Though different from what she was used to, in many ways, she felt the same peace and the warm sense of belonging she'd often felt when she and her father attended the little Presbyterian church together in Wenatchee. Soaking in the beauty of the sanctuary—the soaring ceilings, the exquisite stained glass windows, the soothing refrains of prayers, and the sweet honey-scented beeswax candles—Ann released a deep sigh of contentment.

The choir sang "Adore te Devote" in Latin as the congregation went forward for the Blessed Sacrament. Ann recognized the melody and remembered the words in English that she had learned as a child. As she stayed behind alone in her pew, she prayed it silently.

I devoutly adore you, o hidden Deity,
Truly hidden beneath these appearances.
My whole heart submits to You,
And in contemplating You, it surrenders itself completely.
Sight, touch, taste are all deceived in their judgment of you,
But hearing suffices firmly to believe.
I believe all that the Son of God has spoken;
There is nothing truer than this word of Truth.

***

Later that afternoon, Ann double-checked the address on the letter she had received from Mrs. Delzer and headed up Spring Street to meet her new employer. The Victorian-style home that matched the address was large and imposing. A child's tricycle was parked on the carved pathway that led through the front garden, softening the initial impression one might have of such a place. Ann had agreed to meet with Mrs. Delzer and her family before officially becoming their "mother's helper" tomorrow.

This job was a kindness extended to Ann on behalf of Aunt Rose, a friend of Mrs. Delzer. Ann would earn a little money to help with expenses, and Mrs. Delzer would have some extra help each afternoon taking care of her children.

Not sure whether to go to the front or back door, Ann paused in the garden.

Just then, a woman stepped out onto the porch, spotting her. "Hello there! Are you Ann?"

"Yes, ma'am, I'm Ann Brooks. I'm here to see Mrs. Delzer."

"That's me. Well, aren't you pretty? Come on up to the porch, dear. We can talk out here where it's quiet before I take you in to meet the children." Mrs. Delzer was different than Ann expected, a welcome contrast to the severity of Ms. Patrick. Shoulder-length blond waves framed her young face. Tall and willowy, she wore a pink silk bias-cut dress with a belted waist and puff sleeves. The porch was elegantly furnished with rattan furniture and soft green cushions. Large terracotta pots with red geraniums and a fat gray tabby resting on a wide windowsill provided a touch of homey comfort. "Please, sit down," said the young mother. "Lemonade?"

"Yes, please, and thank you." Ann smiled and made herself comfortable in a nearby chair.

"Your timing is good. Three of the children will be in school this fall, and I no longer require a full-time nanny. I just need someone to help me around the house and keep them busy between school and supper. Your aunt told me you're going to school to be a teacher?"

"Yes, ma'am, that's right." The two women sipped lemonade and talked. Ann learned that Mrs. Delzer had been a history major at UW before meeting her husband, and Aunt Rose had been her professor. After a while, the discussion returned to the job at hand. Ann would be paid twenty-five cents an hour, and she would work ten hours each week— more when Mr. and Mrs. Delzer needed an evening sitter.

"Margaret and Billy, the twins, are the oldest. They're eight. David is six, and Sally is four. David is deaf. Did Rose tell you?" She hadn't. "Do you know any sign language? It's okay if you don't. You'll learn—and the children will help you. Are you ready to meet them?"

Ann eagerly nodded. "Oh, yes!"

Mrs. Delzer set her glass down and stood. "Come with me. They're in the parlor right now, listening to the radio."

Inside the house, Mrs. Delzer led Ann through the front hallway to the parlor. All four children were quiet and sprawled out on a Persian rug in front of a console radio. The youngest boy, who must have been David, was coloring, and the other three were listening to The Lone Ranger.

Mrs. Delzer introduced the children to Ann, using signs as she spoke. They were adorable, and Ann was taken with their sweet charms.

Mr. Delzer, a tall skinny man, wearing a crisply starched suit, who had been reading a newspaper in a wingback chair near the window, stood and shook Ann's hand. "How do you do?"

"Excellent, sir. Thank you."

Mr. Delzer quickly returned to his paper, nodding to Ann. He was aloof, but Ann was used to men like him. The children asked if they could take Ann on a tour of the house, and Mrs. Delzer went into the kitchen to begin dinner.

"When are you coming back?" Sally's blue eyes sparkled as she twirled a blond curl around her finger and hopped up and down on one foot.

"Tomorrow!"

"I start school tomorrow."

"So do I. I hope we all have a good first day!"

Four

"Women must try to do things as men have tried. When they fail, their failure must be but a challenge to others." Aunt Rose paused. "Do you know who said that first?"

"Amelia Earhart?"

"Yes, dear." Rose paused. "This is a temporary setback, not a failure. Let it be a challenge for you. If you want to be a teacher, you can do it. If you want to be a wife and a mother, you can do that too. If you want to be a teacher, a wife, and a mother, all at the same time, try your hardest! Don't let what happened to me scare you. I'll be fine. Don't worry about me."

"It's a stupid policy." Ann let out a deep sigh. "I understand there aren't enough jobs to go around, but what will they do now? Put a man in your place who isn't as qualified? You're the best! How does this help anyone? How does this help the students? I heard the hospital now has a crisis on its hands, a shortage of nurses because the county fired all the ones whose husbands had jobs. They didn't think that one through very well," Ann said in a bitter tone.

School had been in session for a week now, and it was Ann's first day off. She was having lunch with Rose at a diner across the street from the Sorrento. Ann wanted to cheer up her aunt, who'd lost her job, much to their horror—but it was Rose who was encouraging her niece.

"No, they didn't think it through very well. Now, tell me about school!" Rose said, changing the subject.

"I like my classes—they're interesting. There's a fall "Floral Informal" with an orchestra and dancing tonight at the Olympic Hotel. I hope I don't have to dance—I don't know how to." Ann took a sip of her iced tea. " I'm going with a few of the girls on my floor. They call us the Sorrento Girls around the school. I think it's funny." She paused. "Some of them seem to be here just to get a husband."

"Ah— yes. I'm glad you're placing a high value on your education." Rose smiled. "So, what are you going to wear?"

"I'm not sure yet. I was hoping to get your opinion."

"Do you have time for a quick browse through Frederick and Nelson?"

***

The shopping trip was more than a browse— which was usual with Rose. She loved fashion almost as much as she loved teaching history. She had closets full of beautiful clothes at home.

Ann was ensconced in a dressing room on the second floor of Seattle's most elegant department store with sales girls bringing dresses back and forth for her to try on.

She pulled an emerald silk party dress over her head and gazed in the full-length mirror. The short-sleeved dress with the stylish fishtail skirt fit perfectly. Ann didn't want to know the cost— it was probably more than what she could afford. It was the most beautiful dress she had ever worn.

"This one is stunning." Rose grinned and her eyes twinkled. "We'll take it!"

Ann felt a mix of delight and guilt. "Aunt Rose, I can't ..."

"My treat, dear. I insist."

Feeling like Cinderella, Ann thanked her aunt. How would she ever repay the woman for her kindness?

***

Nora and Peggy crowded into Helen and Ann's room as the four women excitedly got ready for the first social event of the school year. Nora, very much resembling Mae West with her glossy blond curls, tried on a pair of Helen's low-heeled dancing shoes to see if they felt better than the ones she had been wearing. Peggy looked pretty— her dark hair freshly set in a loose finger wave in the front with an intricately braided chignon in the back. Woefully nearsighted but vain, she had decided to leave her eyeglasses in her room that night.

Helen sat in front of the mirror and powdered her nose while warning Nora about the pain she would likely feel in her feet if she decided to go with the borrowed shoes. "Those shoes are a pair of torture devices!"

Ann was ready and wearing the new emerald dress. The girls had raved about how flattering a fit it was for her. She felt good, though she did have a slight touch of nerves. "I don't know how to dance!"

"Let's practice then." Nora slipped off the shoes. "We can teach you. Turn on the radio!"

Ted Weems and his orchestra were playing "What a Day!" over the airwaves, and the girls laughed as Helen began doing the jitterbug, grabbing Ann's hand and pulling her up from a chair. "Just move to the music and have fun! Here—left foot forward, right foot forward, left foot forward, step back with your left foot ..."

***

For the second time that day, Ann caught a ride downtown. This time, with a group of carefree coeds, squeezed into the back of a Buick Eight belonging to Joe McMurry, a senior science major. Outside, it was a crisp but clear evening. Ann had only seen the Olympic Hotel from the street, until now, but she'd admired its beauty. The Olympic was newer and even more grand than the Sorrento. She couldn't wait to see the inside.

Inside, Ann surveyed a scene of merriment. From the Spanish Ballroom's soaring high ceilings hung impressive sparkling crystal chandeliers. Large arched windows ran along the outer wall, giving a view of the city outside. Floral arrangements decorated tables, and a sweet perfume filled the air. A ten-piece orchestra was playing "Over the Rainbow." It was magical.

Spotting an empty chair at a table near a window, Ann introduced herself to the group of students already seated. She recognized the woman sitting directly across from her, the one with a permanent air of boredom from her math class. Even a glittering party like this couldn't bring a smile to Eunice's face. Next to Eunice sat an equally unenthusiastic man who must have been her date. The others—two women and one man—were in high spirits.

"Sit down, join us! I'm Paul Lewis." He stood up and pulled out the empty chair next to his for Ann, smiling broadly.

The two unfamiliar women eyed her coolly, and each nodded her way before returning to their conversation. Eunice said an uninterested hello and introduced Ann to her date, Kenny. He waved toward Ann, then signaled a nearby waiter to come to the table..

The room was loud, not ideal for conversation—a good thing for Ann since she suddenly felt shy sitting next to Paul. He was the kind of man around whom many women suddenly became either very shy or overly flirtatious. But he seemed unaware of the effect he had on women, which only added to his charm.

Tall, broad-shouldered, and athletic-looking, his short dark hair was combed back with Brylcreem, and his handsome face was clean-shaven. He wore a black double-breasted dinner jacket with a black bow tie and a red scarf in his front pocket. A boyish smile and sparkling blue eyes added to his classic movie-star appearance.

"Can I get you a drink?" he asked.

"I'll have one of those, thank you," Ann replied, nodding toward the martini in Paul's hand. As if on cue, a waiter came by the table, proffering a silver tray of martinis to Ann. She felt so grown up. As she took a sip, she tried her best not to betray the fact that this was the first martini she had ever tasted.

"So, Ann, where are you from, and what brings you here?"

A long way from this place. What would he think of her being an orchardist's daughter from the country? She wanted to appear sophisticated and urban, like the other women at the table. But she'd go with the truth, come what may.

"I'm from a small town in Central Washington, Wenatchee. I came to Seattle College to study education." *Keep it simple.* She had yet to meet anyone else at Seattle College from her hometown. She was probably the only one.

"Wenatchee, you say. I've heard it's beautiful, though I've never visited it. I'm from Tacoma, but I've lived here for the last three years. This will be my final year at Seattle College. I'm a journalism major. How are you enjoying everything so far?"

Just then, Helen walked over to the table, grinning and out of breath. She had been dancing the whole time they'd been there, and she was ready for a break. She pulled a chair over from a nearby table and joined the group.

"Hello, everyone!" Helen was the kind of girl who never seemed to meet a stranger. She was at ease anywhere. Her presence was a welcome relief, as Ann had a feeling that Paul was going to ask her to dance—any minute—and she didn't know what to say or do. Hopefully, Helen would offer a distraction.

Introductions were made, once more. Helen's enthusiasm was infectious. Soon, even Eunice and Kenny were laughing and talking with the group. Betty and Joyce, the other two women at the table, joined in the conversation too.

But Paul was focused on Ann, alone. "Would you like to dance?"

The dreaded question. Not because the person asking was dreadful. Quite the contrary. She wasn't immune to his charms, but Ann liked to feel competent and in control. Dancing was not going to make her feel that way.

"I don't know how, but if you'd like to teach me—yes!" Ann's breath caught. Had she actually agreed to dancing with him?

Paul was a patient teacher, and Ann was a quick learner. They danced several songs together before returning to the table. Ann was having fun. Betty, suddenly paying more attention to Ann, quickly asked Paul if he would like to dance with her. Had Paul come to the dance with Betty? She hoped not. It was rude to monopolize someone else's date, and Ann didn't want to be guilty of that blunder.

Ann searched for Peggy, Nora, and Helen. Spying Nora across the room, she made a beeline for her friend.

Nora was visiting with several other women from the Sorrento but turned to Ann with a wink when she approached. "Who's that man you were dancing with? And hey, I thought you couldn't dance. You both moved great out there —he's very handsome!"

Ann smiled. "His name's Paul, and I couldn't dance until tonight—but he's a good teacher." Ann didn't see Paul for the rest of the evening, much as she'd hoped to catch another dance with him. She told herself it didn't matter, and she reminded herself that she wasn't at college to meet a man anyway. Ann was there to study. She didn't need any distractions.

***

At school the next Monday, when she saw the sign-up sheet on the bulletin board in the administration building, Ann added her name to the list of students interested in learning more about writing for the student newspaper. It was called *The Spectator*. At the dance, Paul told her he was the editor. There would be a meeting for potential new writers in Room Six that Wednesday at two o'clock. She'd always enjoyed writing. It couldn't hurt to find out more.

On Wednesday, at three o'clock, when Ann arrived for work at the Delzer home, the children remarked at how pretty Ann's hair was.

Usually a low-maintenance kind of girl, Ann had taken extra care that day when getting ready, and she was wearing perfume.

She had another activity to fit into her busy schedule. Ann was now a writer for *The Spectator*.

Five

September passed quickly, and the warm days that greeted Ann when she first arrived in Seattle gave way to the cooler ones of October. Gray skies and a non-stop drizzle had settled into the city, making the Fireside Room at the Sorrento a favorite gathering spot for students—those who resided there and those who wished they did. The luxurious room had a grand piano in one corner and a commanding fireplace surrounded by emerald green pottery tiles. Mahogany paneled walls and an abundance of cushy couches and chairs gave the place a feeling of warmth and comfort.

Ann loved Seattle even more than she had in those first late-summer days. The blanket of gray that had descended served as a dramatic contrast to the oranges, reds, and yellows of the autumn foliage. The city had never seemed more beautiful to her than it did now.

It was mostly dark in the mornings when Ann walked up Madison street for her first class of the day, and it was dark in the evenings when she returned from work. She was enjoying a full and busy life with school, meeting people, writing for the school newspaper—a favorite part of her days—and helping out with the Delzer household. The days were flying by. Evenings were often spent in the Fireside Room, reading, studying, chatting with friends, playing board games, or having a drink. Sometimes live musicians performed for them, and other times they listened to poetry readings.

That evening, Helen and Ann were seated at a table near the fireplace, ostensibly doing homework, but mostly talking. "There's a nightclub in Chinatown I've wanted to check out called The Black and Tan. They have the best jazz music in town. I think we should go this Saturday," Helen said.

"I've heard of it." Ann glanced around the room. No one was paying attention to their conversation. "It sounds like a great idea, but we're going to have to figure out a way to sneak past Ms. Patrick. We'll be out way past curfew." She chewed on her lower lip. "Do you think we can pull it off?" She didn't want to get in trouble.

"Of course! We're here to have fun, not to stay in our rooms every night. Let's invite Peggy and Nora too. We can pool our coins to pay for a cab." The Black and Tan was a club on the corner of Twelfth and Jackson. It had started as a speakeasy during the days of Prohibition. It was called The Black and Tan because it was a place where all people were welcome—black white, and Asian. The trendy nightclub, known for hosting musicians such as Duke Ellington and Lena Horne, was located under a Japanese drugstore. Many Seattle College students had been to The Black and Tan. Attendance by the women required maneuvering around their house mothers' regulations. Sanctioned social events mostly revolved around formal events, dances, and official student clubs.

The "Coed Codebook" had an extensive list of rules for the women to abide by, and Ms. Patrick's imposing presence had, so far, deterred the Sorrento Girls from testing the limits. Every night, she knocked on each door throughout the east wing of the hotel where the college women were housed. She did this to assure that the ladies were in their rooms by curfew. The men didn't have such rules in their dormitories. This was something that chafed at Ann's independent sensibilities. Though, until now, she had never had reason to push back.

"What are we doing this Saturday?" Peggy asked as she took an empty seat and plopped her books on the table. "I was hoping I'd have a date that night, but I don't think it's going to happen," she said gloomily.

"You, me, Helen, and Nora—let's go listen to some music at the Black and Tan." Ann paused and observed her friend. "What happened to your date, Peggy?"

"Ethel is what happened. Look over there." Peggy turned her gaze toward a couple standing near the bar. Ethel was flirting voraciously with Fred, a junior whom Peggy had met at the Floral Informal. They had gone on a couple of dates since then. Fred was a bore. Peggy would be better off without him, but Ann nodded sympathetically toward her friend.

Helen shook her head. "Ethel flirts with all the guys. Don't worry about her."

"The Black and Tan will be fun. I'm in. Ethel can have Fred. I'm not interested anymore." Peggy didn't sound very convincing with that last statement.

***

Saturday night came, and Ann, Helen, Peggy, and Nora found their way to the club on Jackson street. As they'd heard from others, nothing much happened until after twelve o'clock, so they'd had no problem getting around Ms. Patrick's curfew. They hadn't even left their rooms yet when she did her nightly door checks. They waited until the woman had completed her rounds, then they quietly crept down to the lobby and walked out of the Sorrento. They quickly found a cab and squeezed into the back together, laughing and delighted that they'd met success in the first part of their venture.

The part of the city where the club was located was alive with music and activity. The sidewalks outside were filled with a diverse crowd of merrymakers. A rainbow of colors originating with the neon lights above were mirrored on the dark wet streets below. The aroma of mince pies and hot peanuts from street vendors made Ann hungry. Music poured through various doorways as they walked past.

When they arrived at The Black and Tan, they had to hike down three flights of stairs to enter the smoky, dimly lit club. People gathered around the glass block bar and at the small tables scattered around the perimeter of the crowded dance floor. A marquee sign on the wall announced that night's featured musicians—Lionel Hampton and his band.

Saxophone, drums, bass, piano, vibraphone, and trumpets were being played with a passion Ann had never quite observed before. Loud, fast, and skillfully performed, the band members seemed to be magically connected to the audience. The more the musicians gave to the music, the more the audience responded. It was a continuous, glorious loop that felt magical.

Pure joy—that's how the music sounded to Ann. The propulsive rhythmic feel made it impossible to hear and not want to dance. So, she did.

She grabbed Nora and spun her around. The two of them kicked up their feet, moving to the beat and laughing at their lack of finesse on the dance floor. It didn't matter—they were having fun. Peggy and Helen joined in. There were no barriers here between race, class, or age on this dance floor, and Ann loved the camaraderie and freedom. They danced with anyone and everyone. Strangers were suddenly friends. They danced until they were breathless, and their feet couldn't take anymore.

When at last they left the dance floor and found a place to rest, they realized it was two thirty in the morning—time to get back to the

Sorrento. The women walked out of the club and up to the now quiet street.

Peggy yawned. "Do you think there will be any cabs still out this time of the morning?"

Several minutes passed with no sign of any passing cabs. It was chilly, and the rain was starting to come down in fat droplets. None of the women had thought through this part of their adventure very well. The four of them stood on the sidewalk, huddled together, as they pondered the unwelcome possibility that they might have to walk back.

A red Plymouth turned the corner, and the vehicle slowed down as it approached the women. The driver rolled down the window. Paul poked his head out the window, and his friend from school, Joe McMurray, waved from the passenger seat. Paul grinned. "Hey, you girls need a ride home?"

"Yes!" Helen said, raising her hands. "Thank you. Wow, we thought we might have to walk. I'm glad you showed up."

"Hello, Paul, Joe." Ann said, shyly. "Thank you for the ride."

"No problem!" Joe got out of the car and held the door open for the ladies to pile into the backseat. Though Ann had been writing for *The Spectator*, her path had rarely crossed Paul's in the past few weeks since she'd met him at the Olympic.

Joe climbed back into the front seat, then turned around and grinned. "I'm glad we saw you. We were just at the Green Dot and were headed back to campus."

Everyone was in high spirits, joking and singing as they made their way back to the First Hill neighborhood. When they reached the Sorrento, Paul got out and walked the women to the front door of the lobby—locked!

Nora stamped her foot. "Oh, applesauce!"

Ann laughed at the funny expression she had never heard before. Peggy merely raised her hands up and shrugged. They were all in too good of a mood to really care. It was all part of the adventure.

"What are we going to do now?" Nora asked, laughing at their predicament.

"We're going to have to wake someone up to come downstairs and let us in," Ann said.

Paul and Joe stayed nearby as the women crept around the east side of the building. Peggy picked up some small pebbles and began throwing them toward the second-floor windows. After a few tries, Ethel opened a window and peered out.

"Can you let us in?" Helen whispered as loudly as she could.

"Just a minute, I'll be right down." After a few minutes, Ethel was at the front door, wearing her bathrobe and a sleepy expression. "You owe me now," she said with a wink. Ethel went back to her room, and the women said their goodbyes to Paul and Joe. But before he left, Paul pulled Ann aside.

"I'm glad I got to see you again tonight," Paul whispered to Ann.

"Me, too."

"Would you like to go out to dinner with me next Saturday?"

Ann tried her best to act cool while she nodded and smiled sweetly. "Yes, I'd like that."

"Great. I'll pick you up at seven." And with that, Paul waved goodbye.

Ann closed the front lobby door and caught up with her friends. They all stared at her questioningly as she grinned.

"We're going out next Saturday!" whispered Ann.

Was this really what she wanted?

***

The four women missed breakfast the next morning. The dining room was already closed by the time Peggy, Nora, Helen, and Ann made their way up to the seventh floor. Being Sunday, many of the nearby stores and restaurants were closed as well. They were hungry, but it was a small price to pay for the fun time they'd had the night before.

Helen's stomach growled, and she gave her friends an embarrassed grin. "I think Bartell's drugstore is open. Let's see if we can get some coffee and cookies and bring them back here."

The morning sunlight glistened against a frost-covered world outside the Sorrento as the women walked along Madison. Not all of First

Hill was opulent. There were certain areas of the neighborhood the women had been told to avoid. The Depression had touched everyone. Even many of the rich had found it necessary to cut back and make sacrifices, and some had lost everything. Not far from the mansions, homeless people slept in doorways. A vast shantytown called Hooverville existed near King Street Station. Malnourished children, barefoot and wearing rags, played in the streets.

Though Ann had grown up poor, she'd always had enough to eat, unlike some. She had a comfortable home, and her father had consistently worked. Ann recognized her blessings, even before coming to Seattle. She was grateful, but she also worried a lot, craving a certain out-of-reach control over her life that she could never quite grasp. Not for the first time since arriving at school, Ann felt like an imposter, as if this life could be taken away at any moment.

As a child, she'd been unaware of the inheritance waiting from her mother's side of the family. To call herself an heiress, like the three other women with her right now, would be a considerable overstatement. There was just enough money— if she was careful— to get herself through school. She didn't share the same sense of expectation and ease regarding her future that her friends had.

Ann was at school because she wanted to be self-sufficient. She desired to work as a teacher and have a career. She was different from many of the other women at school. Most of them were there to have a good time and to meet a husband. Walking through the south end of First Hill was a reminder to Ann of what she wanted and what she didn't want—and what she wanted probably didn't include marriage.

Six

Paul Lewis treated his job as editor of *The Spectator*, the school's newspaper, as seriously as if he were the editor of the *New York Times*. TENACITY, PASSION, CURIOSITY, and HONESTY were four words that he'd had painted in large letters on the wall over the door in the office, a constant reminder of the values he prized in his writers and strove for himself. Ann wanted to make a good impression on her editor, but so far, she'd only been assigned to cover a few social events. It was hard to be passionate about the topics or demonstrate her abilities when writing about teas and dances, but she did the best she could.

She visited the office each day at lunchtime to eat, check on any new assignments that might be available, turn in drafts, and get feedback on those projects. Many of the students ate lunch at the office, bringing sandwiches and work so they could fit in their schoolwork, their activities, and still have time for a social life.

The newspaper office was in a large busy basement room on the corner of Broadway and Marion street. It was filled with typewriters, phones, desks, a couple of couches, messy cabinets, bulletin boards, and full bookshelves. The radio in the corner was usually tuned to a jazz station during lunch. She liked it when Paul was there. He had a way of making her feel special— like she was the only girl he noticed.

Ann had done her homework regarding Paul. She wasn't the kind of woman who'd agree to a date without due diligence. So far, she knew he was both funny and kind, and he drove a red Plymouth. He was from Tacoma, had played football in high school, had a lot of friends, was a good dancer, and he was an excellent editor. He produced a paper that students loved to read and had received several awards. He was also undeniably handsome. Ann was anxious to know more.

It was lunchtime on a Tuesday. Ann was reading the week's paper at her desk and drinking a Coke when Paul came over to say hello, pulling up a chair beside her. "Did you get back to your room okay on Saturday? No angry chaperone in the hall?"

Ann grinned. "We made it. Ms. Patrick is none the wiser."

"Good to hear." He wiped his brow and winked. "Hey, we want to include a weekly column with three or four thumbnail biographies of various students around campus, two hundred words, tops. Think you'd like to take it on?"

"Yes, I'd like that. Thank you!" She was excited about the opportunity. "Do you want me to start right away?"

"Sure thing." Paul stood and pushed his chair aside. "All right then, I'll see you around. I'm excited about our dinner on Saturday."

***

On Friday night, Ann washed her hair and asked Helen if she could put her hair in pin curls. She was planning on wearing her hair in a finger wave the next day, a hairstyle she'd yet to master on her own.

"I'd love to help you with your hair." Helen grabbed the box of pins from the top of Ann's dresser. "What dress are you wearing tomorrow?"

Ann considered her wardrobe. "Do you think it would be all right if I wore the emerald silk again?"

"Of course! You are beautiful in that dress."

"It's not too formal? I don't want to presume anything. What if Paul takes me somewhere casual? I'll be overdressed."

"Honey, Paul Lewis isn't taking you to some 'greasy spoon.' You'll be fine," Helen said with a laugh. She'd been on a few dates in the past weeks, though none of the boys had been exciting enough to hold her interest. However, because she had more experience with dating, Ann valued any advice Helen could give concerning romance.

Earlier that evening, and for the first time since she'd come to Seattle, Ann had finally been able to call her father. They'd agreed to a monthly long-distance phone call before Ann had left Wenatchee. She had been feeling homesick, and the sound of his voice had lifted her spirits.

One phone, located off the lobby, was shared by all students and guests staying at the Sorrento. After waiting for what seemed an eternity on their scheduled night to talk, Ann was able to secure the line and get through to him. Ann had done most of the talking, telling him about the Sorrento, the Black and Tan, her classes, and her upcoming date.

Every once in a while her father responded with a few words. "Uh-huh. Good, good." He wasn't much for conversation, but he loved her, and it felt good to connect with him. "The apple crop is good this year. We got them all picked just in time. Seems like we could have snow tonight." He paused. "Okay then, it was nice to talk to you. It's really quiet here at home without you. We'll talk again soon. Good night."

Ann loved her father, but she was sure thankful to have Helen, Nora, and Peggy around for conversation. They liked to talk as much as she did. When the four of them were together, which was often, the chatter was nonstop. It was a significant change from what Ann had been accustomed to, living alone with her father at home. They'd enjoyed a calm companionship together over the years. Was he lonely without her?

***

The lobby of the Sorrento was in a flurry of activity on Saturday night, as usual. From the adjacent Fireside Room, one could hear live piano music. People came and went at such a pace that the front door was never really shut. A cold breeze whooshed through the room every few seconds. It was a young crowd, and college students filled the space. Some women waited for their dates to arrive, others gathered with friends, finalizing plans for an evening out and organizing transportation. Ann was among those who were waiting.

Paul arrived promptly at seven, looking like he had no intention of taking Ann anywhere but the most elegant restaurant in town. He smiled as if he were the luckiest man in the room when he saw Ann standing near the elevator.

"Good evening, Paul," she said, approaching him.

"Ann, how are you? You're lovely." His approving gaze relayed more than his words. "Shall we go?" Paul escorted Ann out the front door and to his waiting car, then opened the passenger side door for her. "We're going to the Terrace dining room at the Mayflower Park Hotel." He glanced inside the vehicle as Ann settled into her seat. "Are you comfortable?"

"I am, thank you. I'm looking forward to dinner." Being in the car together was the first time Ann and Paul had ever been alone. Ann felt shy and nervous, and her heart was racing, but she was also delighted to be there. She didn't know what to say to him.

The Mayflower Park Hotel was on Fourth and Olive, not far from Hotel Sorrento. Paul parked the car on the street and walked around to open the door for Ann.

She stared up at the tall building. It was much bigger than the Sorrento. She felt like a princess as she walked into the beautiful lobby on Paul's arm.

The staff greeted Paul by name and led the couple to a small round table near the window. The darkened room was lit by soft glowing lamps in the center of each table. A tuxedo-clad waiter handed each of them their menus before asking what they would like to drink. Paul ordered martinis for both of them. After the waiter left, Paul regarded Ann and smiled. She loved that smile.

In the corner of the room was a small stage with a piano and a microphone. A woman in an evening gown sang a slow, sad, jazz song, accompanied by a man at the piano. Ann and Paul studied their menus. Steak for Paul and salmon for Ann. Relaxing, finally, Ann sat back in her chair and peered out onto the street below.

"So, Ann, I never asked you what first brought you to Seattle College?" Paul asked, drawing her attention.

"My aunt Rose lives here in Seattle. She suggested attending the school and helped me apply." Ann didn't know how much she should reveal, so she kept it simple. "What about you?"

"My parents live in Tacoma, but I went to high school at Seattle Prep and lived with my grandmother during that time. Seattle College just felt like the natural next step. My grandmother wasn't too keen on my decision to major in journalism. She wanted me to be a priest, but she came around, eventually."

A priest? "Do you have any brothers or sisters?" Ann asked.

"No, I'm the only one. How about you?"

"I'm the only one too. It has always been just my father and myself. My mother died when I was young, and my father never remarried. My aunt Rose has been like a mother to me, though."

Paul seemed focused on Ann and interested in everything she shared about herself. "What was it like growing up in Wenatchee?"

"The town is a great place to live—lots of orchards, much smaller than Seattle and a lot less rain."

Her date was easy to talk to, so Ann decided to be candid. She told him everything about being an orchard foreman's daughter, about floating down the Wenatchee River on hot summer days, her first trip to Seattle to see Amelia Earhart, and why she wanted to be a teacher.

Paul was equally honest with Ann. His father was a real estate investor who had suffered some significant losses over the past years. It had been hard on the family. Living with his grandmother in Seattle during his high school years had been Paul's reprieve from a home filled with strife.

They talked through dinner, dessert, and long after that. All too soon it was time to leave. Ann couldn't miss her curfew.

A short time later, Paul walked Ann to the door at the Sorrento. His warm, strong hand grasped hers, and he gazed into her eyes.

Ann stopped breathing for a moment, but her heart raced on ahead.

Smiling, he squeezed her hand gently. "Ann, would you do me the honor? Could I call on you again?"

Seven

November first was the day Ann would get to find out where she was assigned for her math teaching practicum. Finally. Her classes were interesting, but she was excited to get some experience teaching in the classroom.

She walked to class with Helen that morning. The sidewalks were icy, and the two of them stepped gingerly, holding on to each other, trying not to slip.

"What grade did you request?" asked Helen.

"I asked for anything from fifth to eighth grade." Ann shivered as the cold wind penetrated her coat. "I'm getting experience with younger children already when I watch the Delzer kids, so I thought it would be good to get some experience with the older ones."

"I'm hoping I get a kindergarten class.. They're so cute," said Helen.

As the two women walked along in quiet companionship, Ann's thoughts went back to her own time in fifth grade.

Her fifth-grade teacher, Miss Roberts, was the reason Ann had decided to become an elementary teacher. She was the first teacher in Ann's life who'd challenged her. Miss Roberts was strict and deeply knowledgeable about a wide range of subjects. Ann admired her, thinking Miss Roberts was the smartest person she'd ever met, other than her Aunt Rose, of course. Miss Roberts's assignments were hard, but Ann had wanted to please her teacher, so she'd worked more diligently than ever before in school, and in the process, proven to herself how much she was capable of doing.

Before Miss Roberts, Ann had found school easy and boring. She didn't feel like much was expected of her because she was a girl. That all changed in fifth grade. Miss Roberts had always treated the boys and girls the same. Her expectations were high for everyone.

When Miss Roberts presented Ann with an "outstanding scholar" award in front of the whole school, Ann had never been more proud in her entire life. That day, Ann learned a truth that changed everything for her. Ann realized she was smart. She knew this deep in the heart of her soul—and it wasn't something that made her prideful. No, it was just a matter-of-fact thing she understood about herself. Since then, she had carried within her a quiet confidence that she could achieve whatever she wanted in life—if she set her mind to it and worked hard. She aimed to help other children find that same confidence in themselves. That's why she wanted to be a teacher.

Helen and Ann reached their building and hurried inside. They were freezing, but they had both made it to their class without slipping on the ice.

At 8:00 a.m., their teacher, Ms. Danson, began. "The practicum is for those interested in going into teaching. The idea is to get a taste of what it's like before you commit to this field of study. You will be responsible for creating and teaching a unit plan for your assigned class throughout two weeks." The teacher walked up and down the rows. "You will need to meet with the classroom teacher and submit your unit plan for approval by next Friday. Each of you will spend ten classroom hours at your school teaching your math unit. This is after you have *first* spent ten hours *observing* the class during math instructional time." She paused to emphasize her next point. "Additionally, you will be responsible for correcting assignments and grading quizzes and tests within your unit plan. Your grade for this practicum is based on the teacher's evaluation of how well you taught the unit plan."

As Ms. Danson finished, she began passing out slips of paper to each student with their assigned class information. Helen was placed in a first-grade classroom at Seattle Day School.

"You'll be teaching at the school the Delzer children attend," Ann said.

Helen grinned. "What class were you assigned to?"

"Eighth grade at Seattle Prep. It should be fun." What Ann didn't admit was that she was also a little nervous. Seattle Prep was a private, all-boys school associated with Seattle College. She had no idea what to expect.

It wasn't easy juggling everything required for school. Ann needed to meet with Mr. Ferguson, her assigned classroom teacher at Seattle Prep. Of course, he could only be reached after school, since he was busy teaching during the day. But Ann had an after-school job at the Delzer household, so this presented a problem.

Ann loved working for the Delzer family. Mrs. Delzer treated her like a younger sister and companion more than an employee. Her duties were light—pick up the older children from school and walk home with them, help them with homework, and help prepare dinner. Usually, the two women worked side by side. Ann always arrived back at the Sorrento in time for the evening meal. She was grateful for the job and enjoyed being with the young family.

She'd walk over to the Delzer home today during her lunch hour and request the afternoon off. If Mrs. Delzer approved, Ann would visit Seattle Prep after school and meet with Mr. Ferguson.

***

Later that afternoon, Ann rode the streetcar over to Seattle Prep. She arrived just as school was ending. The hallways were bustling with activity and intense boyish excitement as a crowd of students was leaving for the day. Most of these boys were bigger than she was— and not much younger. She took a deep breath, pulled herself up as tall as she could, and did her best to appear the part of a professional rather than the young schoolgirl she still felt like.

She found the main office and was soon being led by a stern and stout secretary toward Mr. Ferguson's room. The teacher was seated at his desk, grading papers, when the secretary introduced Ann. "Mr. Ferguson, this is Miss Brooks, your new student teacher from Seattle College."

Mr. Ferguson raised one eyebrow, then stood and gestured toward a vacant chair in front of his desk. "Miss Brooks, please—come in and sit down."

"Thank you for taking the time to help me, Mr. Ferguson," Ann said, attempting to sit gracefully in the chair.

A tall, thin, elderly gentleman, Mr. Ferguson wore round wire-rimmed glasses that gave him an owlish appearance. The blackboard behind him was covered with complex equations written in chalk, and his messy desk was piled high with books and papers. Empty student desks were lined up in neat rows. A flag, a clock, and a wall of windows opening out onto a grass field were the only adornments in this dedicated place of learning. Ann knew, right away, that she was going to like Mr. Ferguson.

The teacher moved a stack of papers to the side of his desk. "Can you teach a two-week unit on percentages and fractions?"

Ann smiled with confidence. "Yes, sir."

"Good. Can you be here from eight to nine each morning?"

"Yes, sir."

"Uh, huh...okay. Well then, be here tomorrow at eight for your observation, and then you can teach your unit in two weeks."

Ann nodded. "Yes, sir." She was grateful there would be time to prepare.

"Any questions?"

"No, sir, I'll be here tomorrow morning."

"Very well. I'll see you then." Mr. Ferguson stood, offering a handshake. The meeting was over, and he smiled for the first time. He reminded Ann of her father. She didn't want to let him down.

***

The phone in the hallway at the Sorrento wasn't in use when Ann walked by that evening, a rare occurrence, so she decided to take advantage of the opportunity and make a call. "Aunt Rose! How are you?"

"Ann! Thank you for calling, dear. I'm doing all right." A note of sadness filtered into Rose's voice.

"You're missing your job?" Of course, she was —teaching meant everything to her aunt. "I'm so sorry."

"I am. Gary is wonderful, and I love married life. No regrets there. I'm not complaining, but yes, I do miss teaching—very much. It isn't right, what happened. I appreciate you and all the other people who have stood up and spoken out against the school's decision. There's a student protest on Saturday at UW. There have been several other women, like me, who've lost their jobs recently. I have some hope that things could change, but I also understand what led us here. These are hard times we're living in." Rose paused. "We should have you over to dinner soon," she said, switching topics. "I need to hear all about school and what you've been up to."

"I would like that—thank you! I'll be at the protest on Saturday. I wouldn't miss it." Ann twisted the phone cord around her finger. Should she bring up the other thing on her mind? "By the way, I met someone at the dance. We went on a date last weekend. I like him, but I don't know if it will go anywhere—or if I even want it to."

To Ann, it seemed absurd to think about anything serious with Paul. Dating for fun was all she wanted at the moment. *And who am I to say that it isn't what Paul wants too?* She was here for school, and she was here to become a teacher—and she didn't want anything else to get in the way of that.

"I understand, darling." Rose's empathetic tone confirmed that she could relate to Ann's situation. "Tell me everything when you come to dinner. How about this Friday?"

***

Dinner was always something to anticipate at the Sorrento. Ann enjoyed the sweeping views of Elliot Bay from the dining room up high on the top floor. From there, she could see the city spread below, and in the distance beyond, the majestic Olympic Mountains—at least on cloudless days.

Now that it was getting dark by dinner time, the picture outside had changed to twinkling city lights—a beautiful sight. The food was good, but she especially appreciated that she didn't have to shop, cook, or clean up afterward. Tonight, the chef was serving meatloaf, potatoes, and Jell-O salad. Ann never had to dine alone, either, as she had done so often at home when her father was working late. Now, she usually had dinner with Helen, Nora, and Peggy—as she was doing tonight.

"Did you get to meet with your mentor teacher today?" asked Helen as she picked up her fork.

"Yes, I did. He was quiet, but I liked him. He reminded me of my father. I'll go back tomorrow and observe." Ann draped a napkin across her lap. "I never imagined that I'd be teaching an all-boys class. It should be interesting."

"Yeah? You'll do great. I met with my teacher today too. Twenty-five first graders." Helen grimaced. "I'm a little nervous."

Nora laughed. "It will be like herding kittens!"

"I've got to get started studying for my anatomy test, so I should probably hit the books," Peggy said. Peggy and Nora left together after that, leaving Helen and Ann alone at the table.

Helen gave Ann a teasing smile. "So ... are you going out with Paul again this weekend?"

"I don't think so. He hasn't asked. I'm going to have dinner with my Aunt Rose and Gary. Excuse me, I guess he's *Uncle Gary*." Ann smiled. "That's on Friday night, and on Saturday morning, I'm going to go to a protest at UW—it's in support of my aunt and all the other women who lost their jobs because of that stupid 'anti-nepotism' rule. Want to come with me?"

***

Ann sat near the back of Mr. Ferguson's classroom the next morning with a notebook and pen in hand, ready to take notes. The boys were loud and teasing each other as they came into the room and found their desks. Every one of them did a double-take when they saw her sitting there. Some smiled and nodded, but all of them seemed confused as to the reason for her presence. Other than the stern secretary, Ann knew of only one other woman in the building—an art teacher.

"Good morning, boys," said Mr. Ferguson. The students quickly settled into their desks. "Miss Brooks will be with us for the next four weeks. She's a student teacher from Seattle College who'll be observing, and later, teaching you gentlemen a math unit. I expect you to help her feel welcome, and I expect you to give her your full attention and respect when she's teaching. Say hello to her."

"Good morning, Miss Brooks," said the boys.

Ann smiled and returned the greeting. *I like this.* It was the first time a class had given her that kind of reception.

Mr. Ferguson grabbed a small stack of papers from his desk. "Now, take out a pencil. We have a quiz this morning."

There wasn't a whole lot to observe when the boys were taking their quiz, but Mr. Ferguson gave Ann a textbook to examine while she waited. Her thoughts drifted as the clock ticked slowly through the hour. Paul had told her that he'd gone to this school. Did he have Mr. Ferguson as a teacher? Had he sat in this very room? Ann sighed. She shouldn't be thinking so much about Paul. *Push those thoughts aside, Ann, and concentrate on becoming the best teacher possible.*

Eight

"How about coming to Madison Park with me on Sunday after Mass? It's cold, I know, but it's still a great place to visit. We could get some lunch there," Paul said.

"Yes, I'd like that. I've never been there— but I've heard about it." Madison Park was a Seattle neighborhood on the western shore of Lake Washington. The fairgrounds were there, and it was a favorite recreational spot for college students.

Ann and Paul were both working and eating lunch in the newspaper office that Wednesday afternoon when he brought up the idea. Ann smiled and thought about the weekend ahead. It was going to be full but good.

"Do you want me to pick you up at the Sorrento, or would you like to go straight from St. James?" Paul handed Ann a bottle of Coke.

"We can go straight from Mass."

"So, how's school going lately?"

"Great! I have a student teaching practicum at your alma mater—eighth grade math with Mr. Ferguson." She took a bite of her sandwich.

"Really? Mr. Ferguson is still teaching?" Paul popped the top off his Coke bottle and took a drink. "Huh, that's great! I like him."

Lunch was over too soon, and Ann had to get to her next class. She would have liked to have stayed and talked with Paul all afternoon. It felt good when they were together.

Was he dating any other girls? Or was she the only one?

***

Aunt Rose and Uncle Gary—she'd still have to get used to the uncle part—lived in a little bungalow on Queen Anne Hill. It wasn't too far away from where Ann lived, and she was sorry that she hadn't yet made an effort to visit them since she'd been at school. Gary had offered to pick her up in his car, and she was grateful, as it was already dark by four o'clock that afternoon.

Ann loved her aunt's cozy little house. It was as warm and inviting as its occupants. Situated on a steep slope, the backside of the house had windows that offered an expansive view of the city. Rose's poodle, Mimi, greeted Ann first, with a wagging tail and nose nudges when Gary and Ann walked in together. The welcoming scent of freshly baked bread filled the air, and a crackling fire beckoned the new arrivals to come in and get warm.

"Ann, darling! Welcome!" Aunt Rose hugged her niece and took her coat.

"Aunt Rose, thank you for your invitation. Your home is so lovely."

"Thank you. We have a roast for dinner. Nothing fancy, but we're happy to have you. Come in! You can help me with the salad." Rose waved Ann toward the kitchen in the back of the house. "My garden is still producing some lettuce. I think it will be too cold soon for it to continue, but I put covers over the plants at night, and I'm pleased that they're still holding on." Rose pointed to the sink. "Do you want to wash the lettuce?"

Riding in the car on the way over, Ann had been able to chat with Gary and get to know him a little better. She was happy for her aunt. He was a kind man, and the two of them seemed well suited for each other. She'd told him about her visit to the Black and Tan Club, and he, being a musician himself, had been excited to hear all about it.

Gary walked into the kitchen just then. He had turned on a record, and the house filled with the sounds of jazz. "Can I pour you ladies something to drink?"

The three of them laughed and talked late into the evening. Rose burned the roast, but it was no matter, there was plenty of salad and bread to go around. Aunt Rose had lived alone for years as a single woman, rarely cooking for herself, so she was still learning. Ann was seeing a whole different side of her aunt tonight—one she hadn't known before.

Aunt Rose told Ann about her plans to start writing, now that she was out of a teaching job. Rose did her best to smile and remain positive, but Ann knew it wasn't easy for her to have something that had been so important to her taken away—and so unfairly, at that. Ann told Aunt Rose about the math practicum and a little bit more about Paul.

When Uncle Gary and Aunt Rose drove Ann back to her home at the Sorrento, she sat quietly in the back seat. The protest would take place tomorrow. She didn't know if it would help to get her aunt's or anyone else's jobs back, but she would be there.

***

After Mass on Sunday, Ann waited for Paul on the front steps of the building. She had been sitting with Helen, Peggy, and Nora. There was no sign of Paul yet, but Ann knew he was somewhere among the crowd. She still hadn't entered into the catechumenate process to prepare for church membership, and she wasn't sure if she would— but St. James was a welcoming place, and she attended Mass most Sundays.

"Hi, Ann!" Paul gave a short wave, then hiked down the steps.

"Hello!" Just seeing him made her feel warm inside.

He smiled and held out his arm for her. "Ready to go?"

"I am. I'm glad the sun is out. The lake will be beautiful today."

Paul led Ann toward his car, which was parked on the street, and opened the passenger side door for her. A small bouquet of pink roses lay across her seat.

She looked at Paul with a shy smile. "Thank you! These are lovely."

"As are you," Paul said with a wink. Ann's heart skipped a beat, and her face grew warm. "Would you like to take the ferry from Madison Park to Kirkland? It's a short ride over. We could do that after lunch if you like."

Paul drove the car toward the lake and found a parking spot near the dock. Ann felt the warm sun shining on her through the window. She was completely comfortable and at ease now, and the afternoon stretched in front of her like a gift she couldn't wait to open.

Paul led Ann toward a small diner across the street. The two of them found a booth in front of the window. Paul handed her a menu that was tucked behind a napkin box on the table, then grabbed one for himself. "This place has the best fish and chips I've ever tasted."

"Well then, I'll have to try them." The smell coming from the kitchen was enticing.

"How did it go yesterday at UW?" Paul asked, focusing on her.

She'd told him earlier about her plans to attend the protest, and now she observed him for his reaction as she relayed the story about the crowds, the speeches, and how she felt about all of it. She wasn't sure what his views were on working wives and mothers and where he stood on the issue of the new and controversial *Anti-Nepotism* policy at UW.

Ann wanted to ask him, more than anything, but awkwardness stopped her. She could feel herself falling for Paul, and she loved being with him. Naturally, her presence at the protest had made her position clear, and he didn't seem to have a problem with it. That would have to satisfy her—for now.

"I don't think we changed anyone's mind, but now more people are aware of what happened, and I'm glad I could be there to support my aunt. It was encouraging to see so many people marching—both men and women," she said.

"Mm, hmm." Paul clasped his hands in front of him on the table and leaned forward. "Would you like to do a short write up about it for The Spectator?"

Ann grinned. "Yes, I'd be happy to."

The fish and chips arrived at their table, hot, crispy, and flaky-tender. Paul was right. This meal was amazing. Ann dunked her fries in the tartar sauce, and Paul dunked his in ketchup. Outside the window, they watched the ferry pull up to the dock and heard the loud, low honk of the horn announcing its arrival.

"I've never been on a ferry."

His eyebrows raised. "Really?" Paul sat back in the booth and smiled. "I'm glad I get to be with you on your first trip. It's a great way to get around."

They finished eating and made their way to the dock. The ferry was a large white and green vessel with the name Leschi painted on the stern. A few cars drove onto the lower deck. Paul and Ann boarded with about twenty other walk-on passengers. They were only going to walk around downtown Kirkland for an hour or so, then get back on the boat and return.

The sun sparkled on Lake Washington as the boat crossed the lake. Paul and Ann stood close at the bow, huddled against the cool breeze, as the ferry passed house after house on the shore. The water was mostly smooth, but Paul put a protective arm around Ann. She loved the way it felt to be so close to him and how he smelled clean, like shaving cream.

The boat pulled up to the Kirkland dock after a short thirty-minute ride. There weren't many businesses open, and Kirkland was a small town, but the pair had an hour to explore before another ferry would take them back to Madison Park. The lakefront area was beautiful. Paul had chosen a fun way for them to spend a Sunday afternoon.

He pointed to a building nearby. "Let's see if there's a soda fountain inside that drugstore." They were both happy to find one there.

"I'll have a Cherry Lemon Sour." Ann said when they were seated at the bar.

"So, are you dating anyone else right now?" Paul asked with a twinkle in his eye.

"No, why?" Was he dating someone else?

Paul leaned in close. "Because I don't want to date anyone else but you," he said, then drew back and grinned.

"I don't either," Ann said with a smile. She was ready to throw caution to the wind.

On the boat ride back to Madison Park, Paul and Ann were in a world of their own, oblivious in their happiness to anything else happening around them. It didn't matter that it had started to rain or that the cold wind made choppy waves on the lake, making the boat bob around like a little cork. All that mattered was that they were with each other.

When Paul dropped Ann off at the front door to the Sorrento that evening, he leaned in and kissed her. His breath smelled like a cherry-flavored LifeSaver. Ann's mind went blank for a moment. Her heart was beating faster than the wheels on a runaway train. Her toes were tingling. And then, she kissed him back. It was slow and sweet—and she never wanted it to end.

***

It had been an eventful weekend. Ann was alone in her room, getting ready for bed, thankful to have some quiet time to think about all that had happened. Less than three months ago, she had been living a quiet life in Wenatchee helping her father in the orchards. Everything about this new life of hers was different and uncertain. Uncertainty made Ann nervous.

Ann applied some Pond's cold cream to her face and let it sit while she brushed out her hair. Carefully placing the dress she had worn that day on a hanger, she returned it to the closet. She was too wound up to sleep, so she chose a book from a small pile on her nightstand. It was her old signed copy of Amelia Earhart's book, *For the Fun of It*.

Amelia was gone now—or so they said. The search for her missing plane had been called off more than a year ago. There wasn't a clue as to where she had disappeared. Ann liked to think, maybe her heroine had found her way to an exotic island in the middle of the South Pacific and was living with the natives, happy and at peace.

She opened the book to a familiar spot she'd marked long ago and read the words from Amelia Earhart that had become so meaningful to Ann. "Courage is the price that life exacts for granting peace."

Nine

On Tuesday afternoon, Ann stopped by Seattle Day School, like she usually did every day after finishing her own classes. She picked up Margaret, Bill and David Delzer, and they all walked home together, talking about their day as they went.

And, as usual, little Sally was the first to greet the group upon their arrival, and she ran to the gate. "Guess where we're going today!"

It was unusually warm for a November afternoon, and if Sally's enthusiasm was a hint, Ann guessed they were probably headed to Sally's favorite place, Monkey Island, at Woodland Park.

"Umm ... we're going to the dentist?" Ann teased.

Sally laughed. "No!"

"We're going to the bank?"

"No, silly. We're going to Monkey Island today!"

Ann picked up Sally and spun her around. "Monkey Island! I can't wait!"

The other kids excitedly ran into the house to see their mother and to find out if it was true. Mrs. Delzer was in the kitchen, and she was busy packing food into a basket. Mrs. Delzer hugged each one of them and told them they would leave as soon as she was done packing the snacks to take along. Ann greeted Mrs. Delzer and busied herself with helping by putting away the dishes that were on the drying rack.

They had been on this outing several times already in the short time the family had employed Ann. Woodland Park was Seattle's zoo, and the children loved to visit. They had recently moved the monkeys out of their old cages and put them on a concrete "island" that had a few trees and was surrounded by a moat of water. It was a popular attraction, and with seventeen monkeys, there was usually some drama unfolding. Not all of the monkeys got along with each other. Sometimes, they were downright mean. They reminded Ann of naughty children in need of a good teacher to put them in line.

After a bumpy streetcar ride, they arrived at the zoo. Ann carried the picnic basket, and Mrs. Delzer led the group to a gazebo in the rose garden where they could sit and eat before visiting the monkeys. The children devoured their sandwiches and ran off to play while Mrs. Delzer and Ann sat and talked.

Mrs. Delzer was the kind of mother Ann wanted to be someday—warm fun, and involved in the daily lives of her children. Mrs. Delzer had wanted to become a high school history teacher before she was married. After all this time, how did she feel now about putting her dreams aside for her family? It seemed like too much of a personal question to ask.

Sally came back over to where they were sitting. "Can we go see the monkeys now?"

"Yes, sweetheart," Mrs. Delzer said, packing up the basket. "I think we're ready. Tell your brothers and your sister that it's time to go."

Sally skipped along the dirt path toward the exhibit while the rest of them tried to keep up with her. A crowd stood, watching and laughing at the monkey's antics, but Sally wasn't deterred. She just pushed through until she was at the front. The monkeys were in high spirits, climbing the trees and swinging on the ropes. A zookeeper stood nearby as he prepared to give them some food. Sally observed him, completely enthralled.

"I don't want to be a mommy when I grow up. I want to be a zookeeper instead," Sally said when they were on the way home.

"You can be both if you want," Margaret said. Mrs. Delzer smiled at her girls.

Billy scowled. "Girls can't be zookeepers!"

"Yes, they can too. Just because you haven't seen one yet, doesn't mean it isn't possible. Your sister is a smart girl. She can do anything she sets her mind to," Mrs. Delzer said gently. Sally and Margaret gave each other satisfied smiles as if that settled it.

Margaret tugged on Ann's sleeve. "Are you going to be a teacher and a mother?"

"Yes, I'd like that," Ann said. *Would it be possible?* She kept the question to herself.

"I want you to be my teacher," David signed. He had been reading their lips, something he was getting better at.

"I'd like that too," Ann signed as she kissed David on the top of his head. David could read lips reasonably well with the children's help, and Ann had also learned some sign language.

When they got home, it was nearly dinner time. Ann made biscuits and chicken noodle soup for the family while Mrs. Delzer ran around and tidied up the house. When Mr. Delzer arrived, Ann quietly gathered up her things and left for the day.

The Sorrento's windows glowed with a welcoming light as Ann approached after her long day.

Ann greeted Mr. Frank, the doorman, as she came through the entrance.

"Message for you at the front desk, miss."

She opened the note.

I'll come by the Sorrento tonight for the poetry reading.
I look forward to seeing you.
Love, Paul.

Love? Ann's heart skipped a beat, and she walked upstairs with the biggest smile on her face.

***

Ann found Helen, Nora, and Peggy at their usual table in the dining room upstairs and sat down.

"Hey, Ann. How was your day?" Nora looked up from her plate of spaghetti and meatballs.

"Full. I had teaching practicum, school, the newspaper, and work. But it was good. I took the Delzer children to Monkey Island."

"I don't know how you do it all," Nora said.

Peggy almost bounced from her chair. "Hey, Ann, did you hear? Emily and Matthew got engaged."

"I heard she's leaving school after this semester," Helen said with a shrug.

Ann sat quietly as she took a bite of spaghetti. The news gave her an uneasy feeling in the pit of her stomach. Emily was another one of the Sorrento girls. She had been training to become a nurse, so why would she leave after only one semester?

There weren't any women students at Seattle College, that Ann knew of, who were already married. *Why?* It seemed to be an unspoken rule that once a coed became engaged, it was time to quit school. Ann didn't like that, and she didn't appreciate the feeling that there didn't seem to be much choice.

"I don't see why she should quit school just because she's engaged," Ann said, with a tone that relayed her disappointment.

Helen laughed. "She accomplished what she came for."

"There's no reason she couldn't be a wife and a nurse," Ann said.

"True, but Matthew comes from a traditional family." Helen reached for her glass of water. "I'm guessing they wouldn't like that."

The conversation changed to a lighter note after Peggy mentioned the chocolate cake for dessert. Ann pushed aside her concerns and got herself a piece of cake.

The cake was moist, and the creamy chocolate frosting melted in Ann's mouth. "Are any of you going to the poetry reading tonight in the Fireside Room?"

"I'm going, and I have a poem to read," Nora said. "Bobby mentioned he might come by tonight."

"Oh, good. Paul is coming too." She was excited to see him.

"You and Paul have seen a lot of each other lately," Nora said with a wink.

"Yes, he asked me to go steady with him last Sunday." Ann replied shyly.

"And you said, yes?"

Ann nodded. "I did."

"Swell!" Nora said with a twinkle in her eyes. "You two certainly make a cute couple!"

***

There were only two weeks left until Ann would be able to go home for Thanksgiving. She was excited to see her father again and just as happy to have a few days off from school. It would feel good to be back in Wenatchee and to see the valley during one of her favorite times of the year. Today was Saturday, and Ann was running a few errands around the city on her own. She thought she'd stop by King Street station and purchase her ticket home. She didn't want to take any chance of having the train sold out when the time came.

It was nice to have some time alone with her thoughts as she walked. She had finished the observation portion of her math practicum, and on Monday, she would be teaching twenty-five eighth grade boys for the first time. She'd written the plans, and Mr. Ferguson had signed off on them. The boys in his class were respectful and listened well, but was that because Mr. Ferguson was the kind of teacher who naturally commanded respect? How would they be when she was in charge?

Strolling up Fourth Avenue, Ann watched the people around her with curiosity. She loved living in the city because there was activity happening all around. It infused her with energy. There were also a lot of beautiful buildings, which she never tired of seeing. But other things she observed broke her heart. Soup kitchens with long lines of hungry people outside, waiting for what might be their only meal of the day, were a common sight.

As she walked past one such kitchen, she glanced inside. Mr. Ferguson—the very person who had been on her mind—stood with apron on, ladle in hand, serving soup on his day off. He glanced up at that moment, saw her, and waved. Ann waved back and smiled. She would have liked to have gone in and visited a while, but he was busy, so she continued on her way. She continued to think about Mr. Ferguson in the soup kitchen long after. Maybe she could do something like that.

She wanted to stop at the Bartell Drugs store and buy some new lipstick. Paul was taking her to the movie, *Angels with Dirty Faces*, that evening.

Should she have invited Paul to come to Wenatchee with her for Thanksgiving? When was the appropriate time to do something like that? She didn't know. She hadn't even told her father about him yet. She knew Paul well enough to know that he, like most of the other students at Seattle College, came from a very different world than she had, one of relative wealth and privilege.

She hadn't hidden anything about herself from him, but how would he react when he saw her humble roots? She wasn't ashamed. That would be the wrong word. Ann loved her home, and she was proud of her father. But would Paul's opinion of her change? He hadn't yet offered to take her to meet his grandmother, who lived in Seattle—so maybe it was too soon.

A bell on the door of the drugstore rang a greeting as she entered. The smell of fresh coffee wafted in from the back where the soda fountain was located. She'd rest awhile and warm up with a hot coffee before heading back into the rain and returning to the Sorrento.

Ann sat down at the counter and pulled over a newspaper that had been left behind. She read about how things were getting bad for the Jewish people in Germany. All the Jewish owned businesses had been closed per a new decree excluding Jews from German economic life.

"Coffee, miss?" a young girl behind the counter asked.

"Yes, thank you." What was happening to this world? She was thinking about the Jewish people in Germany and what it would be like to suddenly have one's livelihood ripped away for no good reason. Ann had become more adept at pushing away uncomfortable thoughts lately. These things didn't seem suitable to bring up in the type of social settings she now inhabited. But sitting alone at the counter that Saturday morning, her mind lingered on the inequalities around her. She thought again about Mr. Ferguson in the soup kitchen, only a couple of blocks away. He was doing something good for people. She wanted to do something useful too.

On her way home, Ann saw a man selling apples on the corner. The boxes said, Northern Fruit, Wenatchee, WA. That was her father's employer. This little reminder of home made her feel happy. "How much for a whole box?" she asked.

"Fifty cents, miss."

"I'll take it." Ann had one more stop to make. She doubled back the way she had come earlier, carrying the heavy box in her arms, returning to the soup kitchen where she had seen Mr. Ferguson. There was still a line of people stretching out the front door. Ann passed out the apples to anyone who wanted one. They were gone quickly. It wasn't much, but it was something.

Ten

"My grandmother would like me to bring you to dinner at her house on Sunday," Paul smiled as he sat down next to Ann.

"Oh? Well, that's very kind. This Sunday?" Ann was taken by surprise. She bit the lower corner of her bottom lip.

"Yes, one o'clock, right after Mass."

"Okay, yes. I'd like that." It was a big deal. Ann wasn't quite sure what to think. Paul's grandmother, Elizabeth Lewis, was well known among Seattle society. A wealthy widow, she lived in a big old house on the lake in the Laurelhurst neighborhood by herself, and, as Ann already knew, it was considered a big honor to be invited to one of her tea parties.

Ann and Paul were working on homework together in the library that Wednesday evening when he'd asked. She'd missed him while being away in Wenatchee over Thanksgiving break, and she had, until a minute ago, been feeling content, relaxed, and happy to be near Paul once again as they worked side by side. Suddenly, her shoulders tensed.

"What should I wear?" Ann asked.

"You're always beautiful. Don't worry. Grandmother will love you. Wear the dress you were wearing when we first met—the green one," Paul said as he reached over and squeezed her hand.

It was getting late. Paul offered to walk Ann back to the Sorrento. Light snow was falling when they exited the library—the season's first. Barely visible, except under the glow of the streetlight, but there, nonetheless. The tiny flakes kissed their faces as they gazed up with excitement.

"I hope it sticks!" Ann twirled around with her hands reaching toward the sky.

"Ann," Paul said, grinning at her, "I love you."

Ann didn't hesitate in her response. "I love you too!"

***

The next morning, Ann woke up to the sound of Helen's delighted exclamations as she peered out the curtains onto a sparkling white world below them. Their room felt cold, and Ann struggled to push the warm covers off of her and get up. She loved the snow too, but she had to get across town to Seattle Prep. Hopefully, the streetcars would be running on their regular schedule. She'd need to bundle up and dress warmly.

She had finished her unit plan with the eighth-grade boys, who had been a pleasure to teach, and all she needed to do was return one more time with the corrected tests and the grades, then say goodbye. Ann would get to pick up Mr. Ferguson's assessment of her teaching as well, and hopefully, have a chance to talk to him. She had loved her time in his class, and she was eager for her future career in teaching.

After a quick breakfast of oatmeal, Ann was out the door. Thank goodness she'd given herself some extra time, because the first streetcar that came along was on time, but it was full. She had to wait for the next one. Nobody wanted to drive in the snow. Finally, another trolley arrived, and she was on her way to Seattle Prep.

When Ann walked through the crowded hallways of Seattle Prep this time, she did so with confidence. Now, the students were used to seeing her around, and her presence was no longer a novelty. She arrived at Mr. Ferguson's classroom several minutes before the first bell.

He was sitting at his desk. "Hello, Miss Brooks. Last day, huh? We're going to miss you around here." The teacher leaned back in his chair and smiled. "Maybe you should take my job when I retire."

"Yes, last day. I'm going to miss all of you too." A brief wave of sadness washed over her. She really was going to miss them. How kind of Mr. Ferguson to share his confidence in her. "The class did wonderful on their last test. Thank you for having me these past few weeks."

Mr. Ferguson handed Ann an envelope with his assessment and smiled. "You're a fine teacher. I gave you high marks in all areas."

"Thank you." Ann's cheeks warmed at the compliments. It felt good to hear that. "I learned a lot from watching you."

The students were coming into the classroom now, and they were finding their seats. The first snow had brought a high level of excitement, and though she knew she would be sorry to say goodbye, Ann was somewhat relieved that Mr. Ferguson would be the one who'd need to try and hold their attention that morning. It certainly wouldn't be easy.

***

Paul pulled his red Plymouth up to the front of the Sorrento on Sunday, and Ann met him at the door. She carried a small box of chocolates as a hostess gift.

"Are those for me? How'd you know the secret to my heart?" teased Paul.

"I'm hoping they'll be the secret to your grandmother's heart."

"She loves chocolate, and she'll love you."

Ann hoped he was right. Paul drove slowly along the icy streets, and she was grateful for the extra time alone with him. He had a way of calming her nerves and making her feel better.

They arrived and parked in the circular driveway in front of the home. Ann placed her hand in the crook of Paul's arm as they walked up to the front steps to his grandmother's old Tudor-style mansion. She tried her best not to gape, open-mouthed, at its grandeur. Before they reached the door, it opened, and a friendly gray-haired older man wearing a black suit greeted the couple, welcoming them into the front hall.

"Hey, Pepper!" Paul said, helping Ann with her coat. "How're you, old guy?"

"Mr. Lewis! I'm doing fine, thanks. It's good to see you. And you, lovely lady—you must be Miss Brooks! Let me take your coats for you." Pepper took both and draped them over his arm.

"Thank you, sir, so nice to meet you," Ann said, appreciating the warm welcome.

Just then, an elderly, elegant lady approached the group. Dressed in black, she wore a stern expression, and her white hair was pulled into a tight chignon.

"Paul, dear, thank you for coming tonight."

"Grandmother, it's a pleasure. I'd like you to meet my friend, Ann Brooks. Ann, my grandmother, Elizabeth Lewis."

"Welcome, Ann. I'm pleased to make your acquaintance."

"It's a pleasure to meet you, ma'am. Thank you for having me. These are for you." Ann gave Mrs. Lewis the chocolates, and though the woman was perfectly polite, it was difficult to ascertain how she felt about the gift—or Ann.

She examined the home Paul had lived in throughout his high school years. A glittering chandelier dominated the space in the front hallway.

Mrs. Lewis set the box of chocolates down on an antique credenza next to a crystal vase of roses. "Come, let's go into the dining room. Dinner is ready."

The evening went pleasantly, and Ann was reasonably satisfied that she hadn't embarrassed herself by breaking any rules of etiquette or offending Paul's grandmother. Paul adored her, so it was essential to Ann that she made a good impression on Mrs. Lewis.

***

Christmas break was the following week. Ann would be returning to Wenatchee on the train. It would only be for a few days because Mr. and Mrs. Delzer had asked Ann to come back to Seattle early. She would stay with the children while the two of them went on a New Year's holiday ski trip.

When she'd called her father on the Sunday after the dinner at Mrs. Lewis's house, Ann had finally told him about Paul. He hadn't seemed as surprised as Ann had expected him to be but said he was pleased for her—*as long as Paul was a good guy, and Ann was happy.* She'd reported on Paul's admirable qualities and assured her father that she was happy. Paul would be spending Christmas at his grandmother's house, and he would be spending a few days skiing in the mountains too.

Paul and Ann were having lunch together in the newspaper office on a Thursday afternoon. "I know you have plans for Christmas already, but if you'd like to come to Wenatchee for a day or two before, I'd love for you to meet my father, and I could show you my hometown," Ann said.

"I'd like that. Thank you! Maybe I could ride over on the train with you and keep you company." Paul put his hand over the top of Ann's.

Ann didn't know why she'd been so nervous to ask, but she was relieved and excited that Paul had accepted her invitation. She thought about what she would like to show Paul while he was in town. Maybe he would want to go sledding on Badger Mountain. That was one of her favorite activities to do at Christmastime.

***

Calvin Brooks was waiting on the platform at the train station when Paul and Ann arrived. She ran straight toward him and gave him a big hug and kiss on the cheek. "Father! Merry Christmas!" Ann took a step back and grabbed Paul's arm. "I'd like you to meet my friend, Paul."

The two men shook hands and said their greetings. Ann was happy to have the two of them finally meet and even more pleased when her father told her that he would be able to join them when they went to Badger Mountain for sledding the following day.

Her father took Ann's suitcase from her and led the group toward his truck. "Have you two had dinner yet?"

"Yes, we had dinner on the train," Ann said.

The streets were covered in snow, and the town resembled something from a Christmas card. Paul commented on how pretty it all looked, and Ann felt proud. In no time at all, her father was parking the car in front of the little Cape Cod-style cottage on Hawthorne street that she had always called home. Her old cocker spaniel, Noel, was waiting at the front door to greet them.

Paul stayed for two days, sleeping on a cot in the basement. Ann took delight in cooking for both Paul and her father—and in introducing Paul to her friends and neighbors. Paul and her father seemed to enjoy each other's company, and Paul was gracious, seemingly oblivious to the stark contrast of the simple life Ann and her father lived to the opulence of his grandmother's home.

He helped Ann and her father cut down a Christmas tree in the woods, bring it back, and decorate it. Before his departure, Paul and Ann exchanged gifts. She gave Paul a silver money clip, and he gave her a beautiful pair of pearl stud earrings.

Ann wanted to know what her father thought about her relationship with Paul. Did he think they were getting too serious, too fast? He didn't say anything, and Ann never asked.

***

It had been a whirlwind holiday season full of fun and activity. Ann had done her best to keep the Delzer children busy while their parents were gone. The more downtime they had, the more mischief they seemed to find. They had gone ice skating together, had visited parks and museums, baked cookies, and read countless stories. Ann loved the children, but she was ready to say goodbye and return to the relative peace of the Sorrento when Mr. and Mrs. Delzer came home.

Tomorrow, a new semester of classes at Seattle College would begin. For now, she was resting in the Fireside Room with a hot cup of tea and a book. Paul had told her he would stop by and say hello that evening. She hadn't seen him since they had been in Wenatchee together, and she was excited to hear about his vacation. Just then, he breezed through the entrance with his usual confident smile, seemingly brightening the entire room.

"Hi, Ann," Paul said, kissing her on the cheek. He had a bronzed face from his ski trip, appearing more handsome than ever to Ann.

The two of them sat by the fireplace, talking about what they'd been doing the past week when they'd been apart.

"Would you like to go for a drive?" he asked.

Yes, she would.

A short while later, they were at Smith Tower. The beautiful white tower dominated the Seattle skyline and was famous for being the tallest building on the west coast. "We're going up to the Observatory if that's all right with you," Paul said, leading Ann across the marble floor toward the elevator.

Ann took in a sharp breath when the elevator door opened on the thirty-fifth level. They could see the city below them through the floor to ceiling windows. She was in awe at the beauty of the twinkling lights that glittered far below them. They stood together in silence, holding hands. "It's beautiful! Thank you for bringing me here."

"Ann, I've missed you this past week. I want to spend next Christmas together—and every Christmas after that. Will you marry me?" Paul asked, taking a velvet box from his front pocket.

He opened the box and revealed a sparkling diamond ring.

She didn't hesitate. "Yes!" Ann kissed him. Everything about the moment was perfect. Would their lives always be this wonderful?

Eleven

Ann lay awake in bed for most of the night, thinking. Helen was already asleep when she'd returned from Smith Tower, and it was too late to call Aunt Rose or her father. She'd have to keep the big news to herself a while longer.

She replayed the events of the evening as she stared up at the ceiling. Romantic, sweet Paul had surprised her, for sure. Impetuous, that's what she was. They needed to talk. Paul would be graduating in a few months. What were his expectations? And why hadn't they talked about these things first, *before* she said yes? She was upset with herself for not being more honest.

The alarm woke her up while it was still dark outside—6:00 a.m. Had she slept at all? It felt like the middle of the night. The room was cold, and Ann wanted to stay under her warm quilt. A bedside lamp switched on. Helen was awake.

"Good morning," her groggy roommate said as she headed toward the bathroom.

"Morning." Ann stared at the sparkling diamond engagement ring. Now wasn't the right time to tell her friend. She quickly slipped it off and put it in her nightstand drawer before getting up and putting on her bathrobe.

***

Nora, Peggy, Helen, and Ann were together again, at last. They were having breakfast together in the dining room on the first day of the new semester—pancakes, eggs, and coffee. They hadn't seen each other over the winter holidays, and there was a lot of catching up to do.

"Too bad, we don't have more time to talk." Nora poured a generous amount of syrup on her pancakes. "I want to stay here all morning and catch up with my sisters."

Peggy finished her orange juice. "I've missed you all! How about we meet for ice cream this evening at Jack Frost?"

"Sounds good. I've got to get to class." Ann dropped her napkin on her empty plate and stood. "I'll see you all then. Seven o'clock?"

She left her friends and stopped by her room to grab her books and coat, then walked toward the campus. It was a return to a familiar routine, and it felt comforting. Ann needed to call her father and Aunt Rose too, but the morning was rushed. She'd find time to call them later.

This semester, her first morning session was a literature class held in Garrand Hall, a ten-minute walk from the Sorrento. Ann's feet were numb with cold by the time she arrived.

Father McGoldrick introduced himself to the students as their teacher. Ann already knew who he was, and she was happy to be in his class. The teacher was well known, not just at school, but in the city. He was the person who had pushed for allowing coed classes at Seattle College. She owed a debt of gratitude to this man for the simple fact that she was at this school, because of his willingness to speak out for what was right. The teacher got straight to his lecture as soon as the big hand on the clock said eight.

"'Act as if everything depended on you. Trust as if everything depended on God.' Who said that?" Father McGoldrick raised his eyebrows and scanned the classroom.

A man in the back row raised his hand. "Saint Ignatius of Loyola."

"Yes, Saint Ignatius, founder of the Society of Jesuits. For this class, we're going to read a wide variety of literature I think you need to be acquainted with, and we're going to start with the writings of Saint Ignatius, specifically, his Spiritual Exercises. You'll need to purchase the book."

Ann breathed in deeply and exhaled. She hadn't heard that quote from St. Ignatius before. It was something she'd be thinking about for a long while.

***

Paul glanced down at Ann's hand. "You're not wearing your ring."

"No, I want to tell a few important people first, and I haven't had a chance to yet."

"Oh, okay. Your story about the protests at UW over the recent firings goes to print today. I thought it was good."

"Thank you! Hey, so I was thinking, I've never heard you tell me what your plans are after graduation," Ann said.

"I'll find a job wherever I can. Something to do with journalism. It's not easy right now. Newspapers are laying people off in many cases—not hiring."

"No, it isn't. I was just curious." She didn't want to push, and the newspaper office was hardly the place for a talk like this, so Ann left it at that.

Paul and Ann were sharing lunch—the usual—ham sandwiches brought over in a brown paper bag from the campus dining hall, and hot coffee, brewed right there in the newspaper office. The office always smelled of coffee and ink.

"Some people might think you live in this office," Ann teased.

Paul kept a change of clothes hanging near his desk—a necessity, he said, for when he had tight deadlines and not enough time to run back to his dorm. The couch often doubled as a place to nap after all-night writing and editing sessions. "Yeah. I might need to work late again tonight."

"Okay. I'm meeting up with Peggy, Nora, and Helen at Jack Frost after dinner tonight. That's when I plan on telling them about us." She knew they'd be happy for her, but telling them made it seem so real.

Paul smiled, took Ann's hand, and kissed it. "Have I ever told you I love you?"

"Not today, you haven't," she teased.

***

"Paul asked me to marry him." Ann was using the phone in the hallway near the front desk at the Sorrento during dinner. She would have to skip dinner and be content with ice cream alone.

It was the only way she could fit in a moment to call her dad.

Her father cleared his throat. "He talked to me when he was here before Christmas. You found a good man. I could see that you were happy together." He sounded excited. "I gave him my blessing. When are you two getting married?"

"We haven't set a date yet." Ann was surprised at her father's enthusiasm.

"Will you still finish school?" That was the question she had circled, all the last sleepless night.

"Of course," Ann said.

"And he knows this?

"Well, we haven't talked about it yet." Ann twisted the phone cord around her finger.

"You two need to talk."

"I know." Ann was finishing up the conversation with her father when Peggy, Nora, and Helen stepped out of the elevator.

Helen waited for Ann to put the receiver on the hook. "Ann! We missed you at dinner! Are you ready to go to Jack Frost with us?"

"Yes, let's go!" Ann needed some sugar. The women joined arms and left the Sorrento together, off to their favorite ice cream shop, just up the street. The brightly lit shop was full of college students, but Nora managed to snag the last table for her friends.

"I've got some news," Ann said when they were all seated. She paused and looked down. She felt like the least likely candidate of the bunch to be sharing this particular piece of news, but here she was. Her friends waited expectantly for her to continue.

"Paul and I are engaged!" Ann pulled the ring out of her pocket and placed it on her finger at that moment.

Peggy grabbed her hand and gasped. "Ann! Wow! This is exciting! Tell us all about how he asked you!"

Ann loved telling the story of how Paul surprised her by taking her to the top of Smith Tower. Even as she spoke, it felt like it had happened to someone else, like something out of a movie.

Helen clutched her hands in front of her dramatically. "He's such a romantic!"

"You're a lucky girl," Nora said, then offered Ann a warm smile.

"So, when is the big day?" Peggy scootched closer.

"We haven't talked about that yet." Ann was delighted that her friends were so excited for her, but she was growing more uncomfortable as the questions continued, so she tried to change the subject. "Enough about me! Who else wants to tell us about their Christmas vacation?"

Helen sat up straight and grinned. "I can't beat your news, but I did something rather exciting. I traveled to San Francisco with my parents—and we took an airplane!".

"What was it like?" Peggy asked.

"Loud—but thrilling, and we had a good time in San Francisco."

Ann's thoughts immediately went to her childhood hero, Amelia Earhart, and the plane crash. She tried not to shudder at the thought of something happening to Helen. Lots of people flew on commercial planes today. When did she become such a worrier?

Twelve

Father McGoldrick's assignment of St. Ignatius's Spiritual Exercises had intrigued Ann. She had been doing more than reading the text as a piece of literature. Though the exercises had often been used as part of a thirty-day silent retreat for Jesuits, Ann had been using them for her current life at school by praying and meditating on the words and the Scripture readings daily—ever since she had purchased the book. She didn't understand a lot of it, but she did her best. It felt like clean water drenching her parched soul. She was thirsty for more.

Today, Ann had woken even earlier than usual so she could complete the daily exercises before school. She sat with her Bible, and the book spread out on her lap, coffee in hand, downstairs in the Fireside Room, on her favorite brown leather sofa, in front of the warm fireplace. Helen was still asleep when Ann had crept out of bed and dressed in the dark. She could hear distant activity as staff members at the hotel worked quietly in preparation for the day ahead, but for now, she remained alone.

Ann had never read the Scriptures on her own before. She wasn't a stranger to them, having heard them read aloud each Sunday in church, but her experience with them had always been as part of a communal ritual. Now, in this quiet time, she experienced them differently, as if God were speaking directly to her.

She had a lot of questions right now, and Ann thought, maybe, she could find some answers if she applied herself to the exercises outlined in this ancient text. The words from Psalm 27:1 seemed to pop off the page. "The Lord is my light and my salvation; whom shall I fear? The Lord is the strength of my life; of whom shall I be afraid?"

Paul would be traveling with the school's basketball team to Oregon the following weekend, mostly because he loved Chieftain basketball. Also, so he could write an article for *The Spectator*. He and Ann had both been busy during the month since their engagement, and they still hadn't gotten around to having any serious talks about a wedding date or any other essential details.

"Do you have any fun plans for the weekend while I'm gone?" Paul stopped to pet an orange cat who'd crossed in front of him on the sidewalk.

"Not yet. Helen is going to Spokane to meet her sister's new baby, so she won't be around either."

It was an unusually warm day for February in Seattle, a Sunday afternoon, and Ann and Paul were taking advantage of the good weather by taking a walk around the neighborhood. They sat down on one of the benches in a local park. Children played nearby on a merry-go-round, and an older gentleman sat under a tree, feeding the ducks from a paper sack full of breadcrumbs. When Ann studied closer, she saw that it was Mr. Ferguson.

She walked over to greet him. "Mr. Ferguson, hello!"

He looked up, smiling. "Miss Brooks! How are you? And Paul? Well, what do you know! What are you two kids up to?"

Paul offered a handshake, and Mr. Ferguson accepted. "I'm graduating in June, and Miss Brooks and I are engaged. I heard you're still teaching math at Seattle Prep!"

"Yes, sir, they're still keeping me around. Congratulations on the engagement. It couldn't have happened to two nicer kids. I'm glad to hear it." Mr. Ferguson focused on Ann and smiled. "By the way, that was a kind thing you did a few weeks ago with the apples. The folks there sure appreciated them."

"It was nothing—though I have wanted to talk to you. I'm glad we ran into you. Do you volunteer at the soup kitchen regularly?"

"Yes, it's my honor to do so."

"I was thinking, or wondering—if maybe there was any need for more volunteers?"

"Always! Why don't you join us this Saturday morning at eleven? I'll show you the ropes."

Ann smiled and nodded. "I'd like that. Thank you, I'll be there." She was excited.

"You're welcome to join us, as well, Paul." Mr. Ferguson threw some more breadcrumbs toward the ducks, who were now squawking at him.

"Thank you. I'd like that very much. I'll be out of town this weekend, but maybe the next?"

"Very well. You're welcome anytime."

Paul and Ann sat with Mr. Ferguson a while longer, enjoying their time with the old teacher, before heading back toward the Sorrento. The snow had all melted, and a few of the trees showed the earliest signs of spring, with the tiniest of green buds adorning their branches. Ann looped her arm through Paul's and smiled.

He kissed the top of her head. "So, when should we get married? We haven't talked about that yet."

He'd finally brought it up. Ann felt relieved. She didn't know why she had been so afraid to broach the subject. Paul loved her—and the feeling was mutual. She could be frank about her concerns. "I still have three years left of school after this semester. Do you want to wait for me to finish first?"

"Three years, huh. That's a long time. You know, I'll provide everything you need once we're married. We won't have to live off my salary alone. There's a trust fund ..." Paul frowned.

Ann felt like she had inadvertently insulted Paul. "I don't want to wait three years, either—but I do want to finish school. It's important to me. I want to teach, even if we don't need the money."

Paul seemed surprised. "Oh, okay. I understand." *Did he understand?* She wasn't sure. "We can talk more about it later," Paul said. They were back at the Sorrento.

"Do you want to have dinner here with me tonight?" Ann asked, placing her hand on his arm, hoping her touch would assure him that despite her desire to finish school, she wanted to be with him.

Did he still believe that?

***

On Saturday morning, Ann and Peggy took a streetcar to the soup kitchen on Fourth Avenue. Ann had invited Peggy along at the last minute, and she was glad to have her friend with her. The kitchen was run in an old storefront. A large sign above the front entrance read, *Soup, Coffee, and Donuts for the Unemployed*.

Though it wouldn't open for lunch service for another half hour a line of people already waited at the front door. Peggy and Ann went around to the side door in the alley and knocked as Mr. Ferguson had instructed. A middle-aged woman wearing an apron and a friendly smile answered.

"Hello, I'm Ann Brooks, and this is my friend, Peggy Albright. I'm a friend of Mr. Ferguson, and we're here to help."

"Oh! Hello. Come on in, ladies," she said, waving them inside. "Nice to meet you both. My name's Mrs. Johnson. Thank you for coming. It's always nice to have a few extra pairs of hands. Put on some aprons and follow me."

Mrs. Johnson took two aprons from some hooks on the wall in the hallway and invited Ann and Peggy to leave their coats there. Then she led them into a large, brightly lit room with long tables. A makeshift kitchen was at the back of the room, with two sinks for washing dishes, a long table for chopping vegetables, and a large wood stove. Several crates of carrots, cabbage, and potatoes were stacked against the wall. Along one wall, shelves were filled with serving dishes.

"This place is run by the parish. Mr. Ferguson is here every week—a good man. He'll be back in just a moment. I believe he's outside, meeting the bread delivery truck. What you ladies can do now is make some coffee. First, you'll need to fill these percolators with water from the sink. Think you can do that?"

Peggy nodded. "Yes, ma'am."

Between the two of them, Peggy and Ann got the coffee going, and they kept at it for the next two hours. Because of the limited electrical outlets, they could only make two pots at a time. Once the doors opened and people started coming through the line, the coffee carafes were emptied and refilled countless times.

Most of the people coming through the line were men, though a few had their families with them. Some smiled at the women, thanking them, and others looked down quietly, seemingly not wanting to make eye contact.

There wasn't time for people to linger or visit over their soup after they ate. The diners ate quickly, depositing their used dishes in large tubs when they left to make room for more people, who were still coming through the line.

Volunteers ladled soup into bowls, poured coffee, and washed dishes, nonstop. The time passed quickly. When finally the doors were closed, Ann and Peggy guessed that they had served several hundred people that day. Mr. Ferguson spotted the two women across the room and came over to say hello.

"Mr. Ferguson, hello! This is my friend, Peggy," Ann said.

"Nice to meet you, Peggy. Thank you both for coming and helping today. Will we see you again next week?"

"Yes, I think so. I'm glad we came," Ann said.

Ann and Peggy were quiet as they walked out of the building that day. They were tired but satisfied. It felt good to serve other people in this way. Ann thought about the book by St. Ignatius that she had been reading for her literature class and the idea that her fundamental vocation in life was to be who God made her to be—to love and serve as God desired.

Maybe she didn't have to know precisely what God's plan was for her—*yet*. Perhaps, what God wanted was for her to say yes to the opportunities he placed right in front of her—to love others and to trust, in faith, that he had a good plan for her. She was glad she had said yes to that nudge felt last Sunday in the park when she had asked Mr. Ferguson about volunteering at the soup kitchen.

***

Helen was in their room when Ann came back from the library on Sunday evening. She was lounging on her bed, reading.

"Hi, how was your trip home?" Ann sat on the edge of her own bed.

"It was good," Helen said, putting her book down. "My sister is doing well, and little Annabelle, her daughter, is adorable."

"Is this her first child?"

"Yes, she's two years older than me. She was part of the first group of women here at Seattle College to be part of the College of Education a few years ago, but then she got married, and now she has Annabelle."

"Oh! Good for her. Hey, I was wondering, do you know of any women students here, right now, who are married?"

"Not that I know of, but who says you can't be the first? Is that what you want?"

"Yes, I think so, but I'm not sure about what Paul thinks." Ann took off her shoes.

"You two need to talk!" Those were the same words Ann's father had said to her.

"You're right. I think I'm going to go downstairs and see if the phone is available. I'll be back in a little while." Ann tried to call her Aunt Rose, but she wasn't home.

Who says you can't be the first? Helen's words stayed with Ann long after she had crawled under the covers that night and tried to go to sleep.

There were married women at the University of Washington—but then again, the administration had just fired several of their women professors for nothing more than being married to other faculty members. Women who wanted to work—not out of necessity but just because they enjoyed it—were seen as suspect, their character questioned. It wasn't fair.

Ann remembered the words her aunt had used to describe Seattle College. It was a place for trailblazers.

Thirteen

Ann glanced at the calendar hanging near the desk in her room. Monday, February 13, 1939—which meant tomorrow was Valentine's Day. How fun to share it with Paul this year—her very own Valentine. Maybe she could help the Delzer children make cards after school this afternoon, and she could make one for Paul while they were at it.

It was time to get ready for school. Ann chose a navy wool skirt and her green sweater, then quickly dressed. She pulled her hair up into a chignon and applied a swipe of red lipstick. She'd barely have time to run upstairs and grab a piece of toast from the dining room before heading outside to walk to class. The days were speeding by, and she and Paul still hadn't decided on a wedding date.

Nora and Peggy were in the lobby when Ann came downstairs, holding her toast in one hand and her books in the other. The three women walked up Madison street toward the school together, catching up on the latest gossip and doing their best to avoid any deep puddles that might soak their feet.

Peggy shifted her books from one arm to the other. "I've got a date for tomorrow night with Paul's friend, Joe."

"He's cute! Where are you going?" Nora asked.

"I don't know yet."

"I don't know where Paul and I are going yet either," Ann brushed some toast crumbs off her scarf. He hadn't given her any clues, insisting he wanted to surprise her.

***

"Have you thought any more about when you'd like to set a date for the wedding?" Paul asked.

They were having dinner together at Murphy's, a restaurant near the waterfront that featured the best seafood in Seattle. When it was light outside, the place also shared some great views. At this hour, it was already dark, but it didn't matter, because inside, the atmosphere felt cozy with candlelight, soft music, and the smell of freshly baked sourdough bread.

"What about June, after you graduate?" Ann asked. "I've been thinking, though." She paused and took a sip of water. "I want to continue with school after we're married. I have a small trust from my grandparents. It will cover my tuition."

"It's not tuition I'm concerned about." Paul's serious gaze held hers. "What if I get a job somewhere away from Seattle?"

Ann had thought about that too. She didn't know what to say.

Their waiter came by the table at that moment, saving Ann from the awkward moment, for the moment. "Are you ready to order?" he asked.

"Yes, sir. I'll have the salmon, please," Ann said.

After the waiter had finished taking their orders, a silence fell over the couple as they sipped their drinks and ate their breadsticks. Finally, after a couple of minutes, Paul reached for her hand and gave it a gentle squeeze. "I'll do my best to find something right here in Seattle. I want you to be happy."

"I want you to be happy, too, Paul," Ann smiled with gratitude. "What places are you applying to?"

"*The Seattle Daily Times, The Seattle Post Intelligencer, The Oregonian.* I haven't heard back from any of them yet," Paul seemed unconcerned. "I think June sounds good for a wedding. Why don't we begin with our plans and see what happens?"

"Okay, then. Well, we're making progress!" Ann laughed. She put on her best smile and took a drink of her wine. She didn't want to think about what would happen if *The Oregonian* was the paper that hired Paul, but it was not worth worrying about now.

"I have something else to ask you," Paul said, picking up his glass of wine. "Would you like to come over for Sunday dinner again at my grandmother's this weekend? My parents are going to be there, and they'd like to meet you."

***

"Aunt Rose, it's Ann."

The phone had been sitting in the hallway, unused when Ann had been on her way upstairs for dinner, and since that was such a rare occurrence, she'd decided to seize the opportunity and use it. Ann didn't care if she missed dinner. She needed to hear her aunt's voice.

"Ann, sweetheart, how are you?"

"I'm good." Ann twisted the phone cord around her finger. "I don't know. I just wanted to talk to you and hear your voice." She'd been thinking about her mother a lot lately, missing her, wishing she could have known her, and Aunt Rose was the closest person she had to a mother.

"I'm glad you called. It's always nice to hear from you. Did you and Paul set a wedding date yet?" Rose asked.

"We've narrowed it down to June. I want to continue with school after we get married. What do you think about that?"

"I think that's a great idea. There's no reason you can't be married and be a student at the same time. What's Paul going to do after he graduates?"

"He's not sure yet. One of the places he applied to work was *The Oregonian*, but he says he wants to make it work so I can stay in school."

"Have you met his parents yet?"

"I'm going this Sunday."

Aunt Rose was quiet for a moment. "What do you want to do...stay in college? Work—particularly when you don't need to—it's something you know I support, but prepare yourself, dear. Even if Paul supports you in this decision, you'll likely face some opposition. You're going against the grain of expectations, and there will be people who will try to stop you. Stay true to what you know is right for you and stand firm. I know you're strong, Ann, and I probably don't even need to say this. I just want you to know that I'm here for you, and I'm on your side."

***

The tea was getting cold. Ann had brought it to her room with her to sip on while she got ready to go to Paul's grandmother's house for Sunday dinner. But she forgot the tea as she nervously sat in front of her mirror and worked on her hair. She wanted to make a good impression on his parents.

Paul would be by to pick her up in thirty minutes. Maybe she should have picked up more chocolates to bring along as a gift. It would be the first time she would see Elizabeth Lewis since the engagement, and the first time ever that she'd meet his parents.

What would they be like? Paul had, after all, moved out of their home and into his grandmother's house because of "difficulties." And, he was one of the most easy-going people she had ever met. How onerous were his parents? She should have asked for more information.

Nevertheless, they were still his parents, and they must have some redeeming qualities—though Paul had never mentioned any. Ann picked up a nail file and inspected her hands.

They were fine. She took a sip of tea and nearly spat it out. *Lukewarm.* It was time to go downstairs. Gathering together her coat, a hat, and her handbag, Ann gazed around the room one last time. It was a comfortable room. She was looking forward to coming back to it at the end of the evening.

Paul was waiting for her in the lobby when she came out of the elevator. "You are beautiful. Are you ready?" Despite his kind words, he sounded tense.

"Thank you, I'm ready." Paul drove through the Washington Park Arboretum on the way to his grandmother's house. Dusk was settling in. "When it warms up a little more, I'd love to come here for a picnic," Ann said.

"I'd like that. We could plan something here, along with some friends, for your birthday."

He didn't forget! Ann's birthday was in two weeks. It would probably still be too cold and wet for a picnic in the park at that time, but Ann was impressed that Paul remembered. She'd only mentioned her birthday once—a long time ago.

Smiling, Ann reached across the seat and kissed Paul on the cheek as he drove. "Do your parents know I'm not Catholic?" It had just occurred to her that maybe they didn't. Would that be a problem?

"Not yet ..." Paul paused as if trying to find the right words. "Listen, my mother, she's, um ... opinionated. Don't let her intimidate you. I listen to her, but I don't always agree with her."

As they pulled up to the house, Ann peered at Paul and breathed in deeply, shoring herself up for what lay ahead. She wanted to remember everything about this moment—the warmth of Paul's hand on her own, the clean smell of his cologne, and the sunshine on her face coming in through the window. *I can do this.*

Paul walked to the side of the car and opened the door for Ann, leading her toward the front door. This time, since it was still light, Ann could see and appreciate the beautiful landscaping leading up to the mansion. A few early rhododendrons were already beginning to show off their pink blooms.

The friendly face of Mrs. Lewis's butler, Pepper, greeted them. "Good evening, Mr. Lewis, Miss Brooks. Please come in. May I take your coats?"

Mrs. Lewis, Paul's grandmother, came into the foyer, followed by a black cocker spaniel. "Paul, darling, so nice to see you," she said, holding out her arms to accept a kiss on the cheek from her grandson. Then, turning toward Ann, she did the same. "Ann, it's good to have you back. Welcome."

The epitome of politeness, the elder Mrs. Lewis was, as ever, difficult to read. She led Paul and Ann into the front sitting room where a middle-aged couple sat stiffly together on a settee. Paul's parents, Frank and Gloria Lewis. Frank resembled Paul, except his face was deeply creased, and what little hair he had was white. Gloria, a large woman with a sour scowl, held onto a cane in one hand and a cigarette in the other. Neither of them got up when Paul and Ann came into the room.

Paul walked toward them. "Hello, Father. Hello, Mother," he said in the most formal tone Ann had ever heard him speak. "It's good to see you. I want to introduce you to Ann Brooks, my fiancé. Ann, these are my parents, Frank and Gloria Lewis."

"How do you do? It's lovely to meet you," Ann said, stepping forward. Whereas the elder Mrs. Lewis was challenging to read, Ann had no problem, whatsoever, discerning the feelings of Gloria Lewis. Paul's mother did not like her.

"Hello, Ann, so good to make your acquaintance. Paul, how are you?" Frank Lewis finally stood and extended a handshake to his son. His words were polite, but his manner was abrupt.

"Ann. Paul. Hello." Paul's mother remained seated, and she snuffed out her cigarette into the crystal ashtray on the coffee table in front of her.

This was going to be a long evening.

Fourteen

Pepper rolled a cart carrying cake and coffee into the dining room. He winked at Ann when he noticed her watching. The dinner plates had been cleared away, ending what had been a meal eaten mostly in silence. Paul reached for Ann's hand underneath the table and gave it a warm squeeze.

"I thought a cake would be an appropriate way to celebrate Paul and Ann's upcoming nuptials. Don't you agree?" the elder Mrs. Lewis said, looking pointedly at Paul's mother.

"Of course," sniffed Gloria.

By the woman's tone and glare, the awkward dinner had merely been the calm before the storm.

"It would have been nice, however, if you could have told us about your plans before your engagement," Gloria said, directing her words toward her son.

"Yes, Mother." Though respectful, Paul's response lacked enthusiasm.

Gloria Lewis then directed her attention toward Ann. "So, tell me, Ann, since we hardly know a thing about you, where are you from and who are your parents?"

"I'm from a small town in central Washington, Wenatchee. It's mostly known for growing apples." Ann took a deep breath and clutched the napkin in her lap, hoping to calm her shaking hands. "My mother, Lily, is deceased. She died when I was very young. She originally came from Seattle, and her maiden name was Fairbanks. My father is Calvin Brooks. He was born in Kansas, but he came to Seattle as a teenager. He moved to Wenatchee after the war and has been there ever since."

"Hmm ... are you Catholic? I would assume so since you're at Seattle College."

"No, ma'am. I'm Presbyterian, but I've been attending Mass at St. James since I moved to Seattle."

"Of course, you'll need to do something about that."

How was Ann supposed to respond to that comment?

"Paul did I ever tell you where I met your grandfather?" Was the elder Mrs. Lewis trying to steer the conversation in a different direction? "It was in Chicago. He hired me as a florist at Marshall Field's. Did you tell your parents how you and Ann first met?"

Paul smiled, gratefully, and proceeded to tell his parents about the first fall informal at the Olympic Hotel where he and Ann had met.

When they were finally able to say their goodbyes and make their exit, Ann was never more grateful to retreat, sinking into the soft upholstery of Paul's Plymouth, relishing the sound of the engine starting up. She relaxed for the first time since she had left the Sorrento earlier that day.

"Thank you. I know that wasn't easy. My parents aren't easy. Now you know why I lived with my grandmother in high school. You did wonderfully," Paul said in a dry tone.

"I did? I don't think your mother liked me at all," Ann said, hoping for a little encouragement, but he didn't deny it.

"I do my best to be respectful, but it's my grandmother's opinion, not theirs, that holds the most influence over my decisions. I wouldn't worry about it. I love you, and I want to marry you." The muscles in his jaw clenched as he said it.

Ann's heart broke for Paul. His parents were disconnected and distant. She was used to having a father who didn't have a lot to say—but she had always known she was loved. Frank and Gloria were cold, but maybe that was just their way. They were so different from Paul. It seemed hard to believe they came from the same family. Ann tried to give them the benefit of the doubt. Maybe they would warm up to her. She hoped.

***

Sally's mud pies were a work of art. The little girl had carefully prepared one for each of her siblings, one for Ann, and one for her mother. She was using the small tin pans she'd received for her birthday a few days ago, and she had set up a play kitchen in the corner of her backyard, using a tree stump for a counter and a garden hose as her sink. Sally had converted the doghouse to an oven. She was five now and getting more impatient with each day for the time when she would be able to start kindergarten and go to school with Margaret, Billy, and David.

When Ann and the older three children strolled through the front gate together after their walk home from school, Sally was waiting for them with mud streaked across her dimpled face and clothes. "I made you some pies!" she said proudly.

"You did? How nice of you!" Ann grinned and clapped her hands. "What kind of pie is mine?"

"Apple." Sally took Ann's hand and pulled her toward the make-believe kitchen.

"Let me take my things inside first, and let's allow your brothers and sister to put their things away too." Ann slipped her hand from the child's. "They need to put on their play clothes. Then we'll join you for some pie."

The three hours she spent with the Delzer children each day after school was often the favorite part of Ann's day. Their home was full of noise, fun, laughter, and lots of love. As she entered the house with the children, Ann greeted Mrs. Delzer, who was in the kitchen making a real pie.

"Hello, Ann. Hi, kids, how was your day?"

"Hello, Mother—yum, pie! It was good!" Billy said as he ran around the corner and up the stairs to his room.

"Do you have anything you need me to do inside first? Or would it be okay if I ducked outside for a few minutes with Sally? She wants me to join her for mud pie," Ann said.

"Please, go on!" Mrs. Delzer laughed. "She's been waiting all afternoon for someone to play with her outside. But when you come back inside, I have something I want to talk to you about."

***

Filling the tub with hot water and a generous pour of bubble bath, Ann prepared a bath for Sally. Mud covered the little girl from head to toe from her afternoon outside. Mrs. Delzer brought her daughter upstairs and plopped her into the giant claw-foot tub.

"I can take these clothes down to the washroom," Ann offered as she gathered up the dirty items from the floor.

"Oh, thank you. You know, I've been thinking ahead regarding next year. I'm excited for you and Paul and your upcoming marriage—but we're going to miss you when you're gone!" Mrs. Delzer kneeled next to the tub. "Have you two set a date yet?"

"We think it will be in June, after Paul graduates. I'm going to miss all of you too."

"If you have any friends whose names you'd like to pass along as recommendations for another mother's helper, I'd be so grateful."

Ann blinked back unexpected tears. It was a fair question, but the reality of how fast her life would be changing, once again, hit Ann with a force as she thought about leaving the Delzer family.

"I've always wondered what it would have been like if I would have stayed in school after I married Mr. Delzer. I don't know ..." Mrs. Delzer stopped bathing Sally and focused on Ann. "I'm happy with the way things are, but maybe one day I'll go back and finish that degree." She seemed to be thinking out loud as she said the words. Then, she brought herself back to the present. "Alright, we're just about done here. You're free to go, Ann. I don't want you to be late for dinner. We'll see you tomorrow."

Ann had never told Mrs. Delzer that she wanted to stay in school after she was married, so what prompted the woman to bring up her own doubts about not finishing her degree?

***

After returning to the Sorrento, Ann hurried to her room and put on a clean dress for dinner. She glanced in the mirror and laughed. A streak of mud crossed her right cheek. She wiped it off, applied some powder and lipstick, and closed the door behind her as she went to join her friends in the dining room. When she got to the table, everyone else was already there.

"So, how did it go with meeting Paul's parents this weekend?" Peggy poured a glass of water and handed it to Ann.

Ann made a face. "His mother isn't too happy about the fact that I'm not Catholic. And I still can't read his grandmother. I can't tell if she's only polite or if she actually likes me. His father? I'm not sure about either. He didn't seem very pleased to be at the dinner."

"Ah, well ... how's Paul feeling about you not being Catholic?" Helen asked.

"He doesn't mind," Ann said with a shrug. "We both agree on the big ideas. We have more in common with our Christian beliefs than we have differences. We're still figuring those things out."

"I think that's a good thing. Your faith should be personal and meaningful to you—not something you follow to make other people happy," Peggy said.

"Thank you, I agree." Ann smiled and picked up her fork, eager to taste the pot roast in front of her. It was comforting to know that her friends understood. "Anyhow, we're talking about getting married in June."

"Oh, yay!" Nora perked up at hearing that announcement. "You can count on us to help you!

Where's the wedding going to be? Wenatchee or Seattle?"

"I don't know yet. It will probably be something simple."

"Please, let us help, any way we can," Helen said. The Sorrento Girls were a sisterhood. Having them around was the best part of living in this beautiful hotel.

Ann knew her friends would help out anyway they could. Choosing flowers, picking out a dress ... those things would be easy. But she wasn't naive. With Paul's family, navigating through some of the other decisions, like which church, would be a challenge.

***

After dinner, Ann headed to the Fireside Room. She and Paul had made plans to meet there and study, and she found him in a chair facing the fire and reading. Ann paused before going over to him. She just stood there, admiring her fiancé and appreciating what a handsome man he was.

He looked up and smiled. "Hey, how was the rest of your day?"

Ann joined him and set her books down on the table next to Paul. "It was good! This wedding stuff is starting to feel more real each day. The girls were asking me all sorts of questions at dinner, and Mrs. Delzer is asking for recommendations so she can replace me."

"Ah. Well, my grandmother called. She was asking lots of questions too." Paul sounded tired.

"What sort of questions?"

He didn't answer directly. Instead, Paul rummaged through his book bag and pulled out his reading glasses, buying time to think, Ann presumed. "She's from another generation. She's very traditional. It might take her some time." He paused. "I told her that you wanted to continue with school after we got married—and I told her that we hadn't yet decided if we wanted to get married in the Catholic church."

"Oh." How should she respond to that news? She wasn't surprised. She had suspected these issues could cause some problems with Paul's family. Ann twirled her engagement ring on her finger, thinking. "What did she say?"

"She's not happy if I'm completely straight with you. I'm going to see her tomorrow evening for dinner, just the two of us. I'll bring her around. I know she likes you. How could she not? It's just a lot for her to take in."

"She loves you. I know she's important to you. I don't want to cause problems." Ann's voice quavered as she spoke, betraying the hurt she felt.

"Don't worry. You're worth it. I knew you were a different kind of girl when I asked you to marry me—and I love you, exactly the way you are. I don't want you to go and change yourself just to fit in with my family." Paul grabbed Ann's hand and kissed her palm, finally coaxing a smile from her lips.

Paul's words were sweet, and she knew he was sincere. But she was still worried. Would his family come between them?

Fifteen

Spring had finally arrived in Seattle. Ann loved how the breeze smelled like saltwater and sunshine. It was finally warm enough to sit outside on the seventh-floor terrace at the Sorrento. She could see Elliot Bay from there, along with much of the city. The hotel staff had uncovered the lounge chairs after the long winter, and several of the coeds were using them as their new study spot on that Sunday afternoon.

Ann had finished her homework already, so she planned to sit there and enjoy her book. It had been a long time since she'd had the leisure to read, just for fun, rather than for a school assignment. But instead of reading, her mind was wandering.

March was her birthday month. She was turning twenty on Thursday. Ann had found out from Peggy earlier that morning that she shared not only a room but the same birthday as Helen. What could she do for her friend to celebrate?

Helen was an incredibly generous friend, and the two of them were always finding something to laugh about. Ann was grateful that she had such a great roommate. She liked to bake cakes, but that was kind of hard to do when one lived at a hotel. Maybe Mrs. Delzer would allow her to use her kitchen so Ann could surprise her friend with a cake. She'd ask tomorrow.

The other thing on her mind was Paul. He had left for Portland after Mass, as he had a job interview first thing Monday morning with the newspaper editor at *The Oregonian*. "Just a backup plan, in case the Seattle job doesn't come through," he'd said.

Ann picked up her book once more, trying to focus on something else. She was reading, *Gone with the Wind*. She didn't want to think about any need for a backup plan. Maybe June was too soon. That nagging idea had been intruding upon her thoughts lately. It wasn't too late to push it off. They hadn't sent out any invitations yet.

"Is that a good book?" Helen sat down in the chair next to Ann. "Here, I brought you some coffee," she said, as she handed the steaming mug to Ann.

"Oh, thank you! Yes, it's a good book. I'm not getting through it very quickly, but I want to finish it before the movie comes out."

"Peggy just told me that you and I share the same birthday," Helen said.

"Yes—Peggy ... she's the one who always seems to know when someone is having a birthday. What would we do without her?" Ann put on her sunglasses. "Hey, Paul and I were talking about having a picnic in the arboretum next Saturday, if the weather cooperates. It would be even more fun if we made it a party and celebrated both our birthdays! What do you say we invite a bunch of people? I'll make a cake!"

Helen practically bounced in her chair. "I'd love that! Let's plan on it."

***

Mrs. Delzer had informed Ann earlier that week that she wouldn't be needed after school on Friday. The family would be taking a long weekend getaway with the children at Lake Quinault Lodge. Then she had generously invited Ann to use their kitchen for baking the cake while the family was gone—and the picnic baskets stored in the basement.

Helen and Ann had been inviting friends to join them for their Saturday afternoon birthday picnic at the arboretum all week. And now, they were taking the streetcar to Pike Place Market to pick up some supplies for the party. On their actual birthday, they'd been too busy to do much of anything besides school and homework—but still, it had been a beautiful day. The women were excited to visit Pike Place Market and to prepare the food.

Paul had surprised Ann at the newspaper office at lunch on Thursday with roses, chocolates, and a homemade card. They had avoided any talk of the Portland interview. Much to Ann's delight, she had also received a beautiful card in the mail from Paul's grandmother.

The streetcar stopped at First and Pike, and Helen and Ann got off and looked around. The place was crowded, as usual. The smell of fish, the shouts of vendors, and an array of produce greeted the shoppers. The giant red letters next to the big clock said Public Market Center. They towered above the building at the entrance.

"We have fourteen people who have confirmed, so we'll need a lot to eat!" Helen said.

"We could get some bread and eggs and make egg salad sandwiches, but what do we need to make mayonnaise?" Ann asked. Helen just stared at Ann with confusion. She was the wrong person to ask, as she didn't have a lot of experience in the kitchen.

Fortunately, an elderly lady standing nearby had been listening to them. "All you need to do, dear, is combine some egg yolk with lemon juice, vinegar, mustard, and a little salt. Whisk those ingredients together first—then slowly add some oil, whisking as you go, until you've got the right consistency," the woman explained.

"Thank you!" the younger women said in unison.

"Do you want me to write it down?" the lady asked.

"I think I can remember it," Ann said.

"Very well, dears—have a nice day," the lady said as she moved on to a stall that sold cured meats.

"Okay, then. That was nice." Helen grinned and pointed ahead. "Let's go find some eggs."

The women found the sandwich ingredients, apples, cheese, and everything they needed to make a cake. Their baskets were heavy as they made their way back to the corner where they could catch a streetcar back to the Sorrento.

Ann's arms were aching from carrying the load. "We can take all of this food to the Delzer's house and store it there."

"Do you want some help baking the cake? Or maybe just some company?" Helen asked.

It was unusual for Helen to be free on a Friday night. Ann gladly accepted the offer.

***

"The guest of honor isn't supposed to be doing the work for her party!" Nora said as she took a basket from Ann. They were setting out lunch in the picnic shelter.

Ann laughed. "I've had a lot of fun planning this party. I'm just happy that so many could make it today!" The skies were gray, but at least it wasn't raining, and it wasn't too cold. The gathering of those celebrating Helen's and Ann's birthdays included Nora, Peggy, Ethel, and Shirley—all friends from the Sorrento. Paul, his best friend, Joe, Harry, Celeste, David, and Mary (from the newspaper) also joined them.

"I'm going to miss all of this after I graduate," Paul said, glancing around at their friends.

Joe handed Paul a bottle of Coke. "Hey, don't be getting all sentimental yet! We still have a couple more months."

Ann listened and said nothing as she spread out the tablecloth. She tried to push away the irritation she suddenly felt. Paul had enjoyed his four years of college, but Ann was only finishing up her first year. Sure, Paul was doing his best to find a job locally so they could get married and she could still stay at Seattle College. But so far, his only interview had been in Portland. Hopefully, something else would come along—and soon. "I think everything is ready. We can eat now!"

The lunch was a success—and the chocolate cake—even more so. Ann got over her momentary bad mood and enjoyed the time with her friends. After eating, Helen suggested they explore the large park and its trails weaving through a beautiful, tree-filled landscape. Paul held Ann's hand as they meandered through the park, and Ann felt happy and content. They watched in amusement as Peggy and Joe, off in the distance, tried to maneuver a rowboat around the pond.

"Joe told me he's joining the navy when he graduates," Paul said, with a hint of concern.

"Oh? I thought he was going on to graduate school at UW. Are you worried?" Ann asked. Peggy would be disappointed in that news. She didn't hide her feelings well and talked about Joe often.

"Germany seems to be preparing for war in Europe, but we've got the Neutrality Act. We'll stay out of it, I think."

Ann nodded, hoping he was right.

***

On Sunday morning, the sky unleashed its floodgates. Ann peered out the window from her third-floor room. Did she want to go outside in that mess? She usually walked the short distance to Mass at St. James, but it was raining so hard that it was hard to tell if the water was coming down or sideways. *Maybe it will calm down while I eat breakfast.*

In the dining room, Ann ate her pancakes with strawberry jam and enjoyed her hot coffee while watching the scene on the street below. Helen, Nora, and Peggy eventually joined her at the table.

"Ugh— do you think your fiancé might come by and give us all a ride to Mass this morning?" Peggy asked.

Paul lived in a spartan dorm room and shared a phone with an entire floor of men, so there wasn't an easy way to reach him at the last minute on a Sunday morning. Maybe he would come by to pick them up, but there was no way to be sure, so the women decided to take their umbrellas and brave the elements.

Ann finished her breakfast and told her friends that she would meet them in the lobby in thirty minutes. She stopped by her room to gather her overcoat, her hat, and an umbrella, then went downstairs to wait.

When the elevator doors opened, she spotted Paul chatting with the doorman. *What a guy.*

Paul looked up, saw her, and smiled. "Good morning! I thought you might like a ride this morning. It's kind of soggy out there!"

"Thank you—and yes! Do you mind waiting for a couple of minutes and giving my friends a ride too?"

"Of course not." He led her toward the adjoining Fireside Room so they could sit and wait. He seemed like he was thinking about something. "You always come to Mass with your friends and me, which is great, and I appreciate it, but I wondered if you miss attending the kind of church you're accustomed to—the Presbyterians? They have those here in Seattle too." He smiled. "Would you like to visit next Sunday?"

Ann nodded gratefully. "I'd like that, thank you. Don't get me wrong. I like going to Mass—especially with you, but it would be nice. My parents got married at the First Presbyterian Church here in Seattle. My mother and her family attended there until she met my father and moved to Wenatchee."

"Well then, let's go pay a visit—next week."

Helen, Peggy, and Nora walked in at that moment, voicing their relief and gratitude that Paul had, indeed, come to rescue them from a walk to Mass in the rain.

"Oh, good! You're here! I can leave this old thing behind," Peggy said to Paul as she set her umbrella near the door. Umbrellas, Ann had learned since moving to Seattle, were something the locals rarely used—except in the worst downpours.

Nora laughed. "Ann, you've got a good guy here— a real keeper."

Yes, she did, Ann thought with pride. It was true. As they left the Sorrento together, Ann said a silent prayer of gratitude—and then she added a request. *Please God, may this plan not cause problems with Paul's family*

Sixteen

The coffee was ready and so was the soup. It was time to open the doors to the crowd waiting outside. Mr. Ferguson nodded toward Ann, indicating she could do the honors. When she unlocked the front door, one of the regulars, a gentle giant of a man named Sam, was first in line. It was raining again, and his clothes were soaked, but he was smiling.

"We missed you last week, Ms. Brooks! It's good to see you again," Sam said. Then, as if he was telling her a secret, he added, "You make the best coffee of anyone here."

"Thank you," Ann said, smiling. "It's good to be back!"

Ann had been coming back to the soup kitchen on most Saturday mornings, ever since her first visit last December. She had become the person they relied upon to make the coffee, and she took a certain amount of pride in the fact that people were always telling her how good it tasted. She often brought along one of her friends to help, and Paul had come a few times too. But today, she'd come alone.

As usual, the time went by quickly, and Ann was busy the whole time, grinding coffee beans, getting more water, pouring, and chatting with the many people who came through. When at last, when everyone had eaten, and the room was empty except for the volunteers, Ann got herself a cup of coffee and sat down.

Mr. Ferguson walked over, poured a cup of coffee, and joined her. "How are you doing, Ann?" the old teacher asked.

"I'm good, thanks." Ann felt comfortable with Mr. Ferguson. She wanted to get beyond the basic pleasantries of small talk. He seemed like a friend Ann could talk to, someone who would give it to her straight. She needed a person like that right now.

As if sensing this was so, Mr. Ferguson gave a nod toward the kitchen and said, "There's still some soup left. Why don't we sit and have some lunch before you go?"

Mr. Ferguson asked Ann about how school was going, her family, and her upcoming wedding plans. He carefully listened as she explained some of the concerns she had—and more specifically, the concerns Mrs. Lewis had.

"You know, my wife wasn't Catholic. Mary was a Methodist. Sometimes we'd go to Mass, and sometimes we'd go to her church. We've made it work. It's called a *mixed marriage*." He smiled, obviously enjoying the memory of his late wife. "She took some catechism classes before we were married, and I've done my best to learn more about her doctrine. I needed to ask for special permission from the bishop before our marriage, which he gave. It wasn't common practice back then, or even now. We were married for fifty years, and we were happy. We never were able to have children." He paused. "That would have made it more complicated—but you take things as they come. I never thought it was right to force a certain way of thinking on my wife. We both loved God. *That*, I know. Anyway, I don't think there will be labels or denominations in heaven."

Ann appreciated his candor. "Wow, thank you for sharing your story with me. I would have loved to have met your wife. I feel encouraged by what you told me."

"I'm sure she would have loved the opportunity to meet you too. She passed away about a year ago. She used to come to the soup kitchen with me on Saturdays. She did that as long as she could until she got sick."

Ann had never known what it was like to have a relationship with a grandparent, as hers had all died when she was very young, but she imagined that maybe this—talking and receiving wisdom about important things—was something like it. When it was time to go, she gave Mr. Ferguson a big hug. He had given her a lot to think about.

***

The beauty shop was her next stop of the day. She was meeting Helen there at two. She'd have to hurry. Ann had been chatting with Mr. Ferguson for so long that now she was running late. With one minute to spare, Ann, breathing hard from her walk up the hill, walked into the shop.

Looking around, Ann decided she might want to turn around and get out of there before anyone saw her—but it was too late. Her friend had already seen her. Helen had been encouraging Ann to try this salon for months, but Ann had resisted, insisting she could set her own hair in waves.

Tonight, the school was holding a spring social at the Rainier Club, and Ann wanted a new hairstyle, so she'd finally relented to Helen's request to join her at the salon. But now, she wasn't so sure about it.

What was happening? Ann tried not to stare with her mouth open. A lady in the corner was hooked up to the strangest machine Ann had ever seen. She looked like an alien—or an octopus with too many legs. About fifty rods stood straight out of her head. Attached to those rods were thick wires, and those wires connected to what seemed like a light fixture, which hung about a foot over her head. The whole contraption was plugged into an electrical socket. A faint sizzling sound came from it, and steam was wafting from the rods. Was her hair being fried? To top it all off, the foul smell of ammonia permeated the entire shop, and the smell seemed to be coming from that machine.

"Hello, Ann!" Helen said. "Alice, this is my friend, Ann. Ann, meet Alice. She's the best stylist in the neighborhood. You're going to love her!"

"Welcome, Ann. It's good to meet you. Come, sit here in this chair, and we'll talk about what you want to do with your hair," Alice said, directing her to the seat.

Ann sat down cautiously. She continued to eye the lady in the corner. "It's nice to meet you, Alice. I just want a wash and a set, please."

"Sure, darling. But let me tell you about something even better. How would you like it if you could have permanent waves? You would save so much time! See that lady over there? When we take her hair off those rods, she'll have beautiful, permanent waves. All the Hollywood stars use these." Alice pointed at the alien octopus lady.

Helen looked like she was stifling a laugh as she watched Ann. Ann wanted to bolt. It had to be written all over her face."Uh, not today, thank you."

"Okay, not a problem. Just come over to this sink then, and we'll wash your hair."

Ann had to admit, the experience of having someone else wash her hair was amazing. She started to relax. After washing Ann's hair, Alice put her hair in rollers and directed her to sit under the dryer. Helen was already sitting under a dryer in the chair next to her, reading a magazine. Then Alice went over to the octopus lady and started the process of releasing the woman's hair from the rods. Helen and Ann watched with curiosity.

Interest, mixed with a touch of horror, finally turned to relief when they saw that the woman's hair was, indeed, curled and intact. Ann still wasn't convinced she wanted to try the perm machine. Though she *did* decide that regular visits to the salon would be a good idea.

When Ann emerged from the salon that day, she was quite pleased with the way her dark hair had been fashioned into glossy waves, and she felt surprisingly glamorous.

***

Paul, Ann, Peggy, and Joe arrived at the Rainier Club together that night, and the party was already well underway. A jazz band was playing, and people were dancing. The room was sparkling with laughter. It all reminded Ann of the first night she had met Paul at the Olympic Hotel.

"Hello, beautiful," Paul said to Ann as he took her coat and hung it up for her.

"Thank you. Want to dance?" Ann smiled and grabbed Paul's hand, not waiting for an answer.

Someone was singing "Pennies from Heaven" as Paul and Ann stepped onto the dance floor. They had danced to this song on that first night.

Ann listened to the lyrics that spoke about sunshine but also the need for showers in life. She let her thoughts wander, thinking about their future together. She was head over heels in love with Paul. Her feelings hadn't changed. If anything, her feelings had grown stronger—but they'd been dating for only four months when Paul had proposed. There was so much they hadn't discussed yet—and there were still some big questions hanging in the air. It seemed like anytime a storm loomed on the horizon, they diverted to safer topics—how his family felt about her, what that potential newspaper job in Portland would mean for Ann's plans to finish at Seattle College—these were the *storms* they ran away from. But now wasn't the time to talk about these things either. No, not here at the dance, so Ann pushed her concerns aside and focused on how great it felt to be dancing in the arms of the most handsome man in the room.

After the song ended, Paul went in search of some cake. Ann sat down with Peggy and Joe at a table. Peggy seemed to be blinking back tears as she quietly ripped apart a napkin in her lap.

"Umm, I'm going to go touch up my lipstick. Peggy, do you want to come with me?" Ann asked with a smile. Peggy nodded, and the two friends went in search of the washroom. "What's wrong, Peggy?"

"I'm okay. Joe was telling me that he's not going to go to graduate school at UW after all. Instead, he's joined the navy. He leaves in June right after he graduates. I'm just a little disappointed, that's all." Peggy wiped a tear from her cheek. "I don't want to see him go."

"Oh, honey. I'm sorry. I know you'll miss Joe." Putting herself in Peggy's shoes, Ann thought of the sadness she'd feel if it was Paul leaving.

"I'll be fine. I was starting to have deep feelings for Joe, but I guess I was wrong about how he felt about me." Peggy paused. "Hey, do you mind if I use some of your lipstick?" Peggy dabbed at her eyes with a tissue, straightened her shoulders, took a deep breath, and smiled.

"Of course, you may." What could Ann possibly say to comfort her friend? "I don't think his choice to join the navy means he doesn't care for you—but I understand why you're sad." She gave Peggy a few minutes to collect herself. "Are you ready to go back yet?"

When the women returned to the table, smiles were in place, and emotions were in check. But for the rest of the evening, Ann kept thinking about Peggy and Joe. Would they be able to keep a long distance relationship? At least now Peggy would have time to finish school.

Seventeen

It was Sunday morning, and Paul was taking Ann to visit the First Presbyterian church. Ann rifled through her closet, searching for something to wear, and decided on her gray wool suit with a white silk blouse and a simple black pillbox hat. Paul would be at the Sorrento to pick her up in an hour. She had enough time to join her friends upstairs for breakfast.

When Ann walked into the dining room, she paused and took in the beauty of the place and the view outside. Sunlight flickered off the crystal glassware on the tables, casting rainbows on the clean white linen tablecloths. Through the large windows, Ann could see little white sailboats dotted about Elliot Bay's blue expanse. Hotel guests and the women of Seattle College were scattered throughout the room, dressed in their Sunday best, creating a scene of quiet elegance. Helen was seated at their usual table near the window, already enjoying a cup of hot coffee and a plate of eggs and toast.

"Oh, good, you're here! I thought I'd be eating breakfast by myself today. I think Peggy and Nora are still asleep," Helen said as Ann joined her.

"Hmm, that coffee smells good." Ann poured herself a cup. "Did you have fun last night at the dance?"

"Yes! Did you leave early? You were already asleep when I got back to the room."

"I guess we did. We drove with Peggy and Joe —and they were ready to go. Joe told Peggy he was leaving after graduation to join the navy," Ann said.

"Aw, that's rough." Helen sighed. "So, you're leaving us and joining the Presbyterians today, huh?"

"Just a visit. For now. I don't know what Paul and I are going to decide on."

"Actually, I think it's great. I'm just teasing you. It shows that Paul's willing to keep an open mind toward what's important to you. He's a good guy."

***

To Ann, there was a comforting sense of the familiar at First Presbyterian that was reassuring, even though it was the first time she had ever entered its doors. The church Ann had attended all her life in Wenatchee certainly looked very different from the vast sanctuary that she and Paul were now seated in. But once the very first song began, Ann felt like she was at home again, back in the little white-steepled church on Chelan Street. Her heart was filled with gratitude as she sang along.

She tried to listen to the sermon, but instead, Ann's thoughts focused on her mother. Try as she might, she couldn't remember her. She had been too young when her mom had died. All she had were a handful of photographs and the stories she'd heard from her father or Aunt Rose. Ann often filled in the missing pieces with her imagination. In front of her was the altar where her parents had stood when they said their marriage vows. It was a beautiful church, and her mother must have been a lovely bride. Ann tried to picture her mom walking up the aisle toward her father on their wedding day.

Ann knew, from pictures, that she resembled her mother—so much, in fact, that occasionally, Aunt Rose would call her niece by her sister's name—Lily. She'd noticed an older woman staring at her intently. Had the woman known her mother?

Ann's grandparents, Douglas and Agatha Fairbanks, had brought their two daughters, Lily and Rose, to this church each week when they were young girls. The Fairbanks family was highly respected in this city, as they were one of the first families in Seattle. They possessed a small fortune from their various real estate holdings, and they had been quite influential. They expected their beautiful daughters to become society women.

When the Great War broke out, Ann's mother was only eighteen. She began volunteering at the local Red Cross office and trained to become a nurse. Many new people came into the city at that time to work in the shipyards. One of them was Ann's father, Calvin, an orphan from Kansas, who had been living on his own since turning sixteen. From that time on, he'd taken work wherever he could find it, and there was plenty to go around in Seattle once the war started.

Then the Spanish Influenza hit Seattle in 1918—after a trainload of infected navy recruits arrived. The entire city shut down in an attempt to stop it from spreading, but over a thousand people died before it was over. Her father became very ill and ended up in the hospital. That was how her parents met. Lily was a nurse at that hospital. Calvin recovered after a lengthy battle, and her parents fell in love.

Calvin was from a different social class than Lily, and he didn't meet the Fairbanks' approval. After their marriage, Calvin and Lily decided to start a new life in Wenatchee, away from the disapproving interference of her parents. With his savings, Calvin bought a small house on a few acres, and he planted an apple orchard. By all accounts, the couple was happy. A year later, Ann was born. When Ann was only six months old, her mother, the nurse who had managed to stay healthy throughout the entire Spanish Influenza epidemic, contracted the flu and died. Calvin was devastated, but he was determined to give his daughter a loving home, even if he had to do it on his own.

Douglas and Agatha Fairbanks, who had never treated Calvin well, tried desperately to convince him to move to Seattle after that. They wanted their granddaughter near them, but Calvin refused. He'd determined to raise his daughter in Wenatchee. Her mother's sister, Rose, was the only link between Ann and her grandparents, and that was a tenuous one, at best, as Rose had a complicated relationship with her parents. She'd chosen the less traditional path of an academic career over marriage, and they didn't approve.

Ann had met her grandparents only once when she was very young, and they'd both died before she was ten years old. Rose had been unable to maintain the large family home by herself and had chosen to sell it. There were very few links left between Ann and the family she had never known. But this church was one of them. The Fairbanks had been some of the founding members.

Ann had been surprised when she learned that her grandparents had left behind an inheritance for her. She'd never imagined that she would have the opportunity to go to college and live the life she had now. She wished that she could have known her grandparents better. Ann was glad that Paul had suggested visiting this church—but now intense feelings of loneliness, loss, and sadness were overwhelming her. She was feeling homesick.

When the church service was over, the woman who had been watching Ann approached her. She was a plump elderly lady, with cool blue eyes and silver hair, possessing a surety about her that indicated she was rarely contradicted.

"Good morning, dear." She smiled warmly. "My name is Edith Carson. I couldn't help but notice you because you remind me of someone I used to know. You're a Fairbanks girl, aren't you? I'm sure of it."

"It's nice to meet you, Mrs. Carson. My name's Ann Brooks. My mother was Lily Fairbanks. She grew up going to this church. Did you know her?"

"Lily Fairbanks ..." Mrs. Carson paused as if in deep thought. "Of course!" She laughed. "You're the spitting image of your mother. God rest her soul. I was very sorry to hear about her passing. It was too early, and I've missed your grandparents. I knew them well. I taught Lily and Rose in Sunday school many years ago. It's good to meet you, Ann." She reached for Ann's hand and gave it a squeeze. Then, turning to Paul, she introduced herself once more.

Ann stayed and talked with Edith for several more minutes, promising to return soon. When she walked out of the building later with Paul, her feelings about what church she wanted to attend after they got married were even more confused.

***

Nora and Peggy came over from their place across the hall on Sunday afternoon and joined Helen and Ann in room 302. Nora brought a box of chocolates to share, and they were listening to music on the radio. It was dark and rainy outside, but cozy and warm inside.

"Your room is prettier than ours," Peggy said as she surveyed it. "But at least we don't have to live in the dorms."

"We've got a better view, but you've got more closet space," Helen said. Closet space was significant to her.

"Are you all going home for Easter break?" Ann turned down the radio.

Easter break was five days away. All four women talked about their plans. Ann was only going home for a couple of days because Mrs. Delzer had asked for extra help while the kids were back from school. It was a busy time of year in the orchards, so Ann's father would likely have been working the whole time anyhow. Peggy, Nora, and Helen would all be gone for the week. It was going to be quiet around the Sorrento.

"Ann, how's the wedding planning going?" Peggy grabbed another chocolate, then sprawled across Helen's bed. "You need to let us help you!" Ann hadn't done a thing toward wedding planning yet, other than deciding on the last weekend in June. Her aunt kept asking her the same thing. She repeated the line she told her aunt. "We don't even know where Paul will be working, or where we'll live. It all feels a little premature because of those things. But you're right. I should get started."

"How about, Saturday after we get back, we'll go shopping. We need to find you a dress!" Helen said.

"Yes! I'd like that." The surge of excitement over finding the perfect dress fizzled quickly. The bride's family traditionally paid for the wedding, but Ann's father certainly didn't have the means to provide a wedding in the style that her friends and Paul's family were likely expecting. What money she did have—her inheritance—was needed to cover school costs. Ann chewed on her lower lip. What was she going to do?

***

It was Good Friday. Ann had just finished her last class before Easter break. She would be taking the train to Wenatchee in the morning. This time, she was going by herself. She was excited to see her father again. Paul had offered to take Ann to the station, but after that, he would be going to Tacoma to spend the weekend with his parents. She would see him again on Monday. Helen had already left to go home, so Ann had the room to herself.

The gray leather suitcase, the one her father had given her the Christmas when she was fourteen, would be just right for a quick weekend away. It was sitting on her bed. Ann had about an hour to spare before she needed to pick the Delzer children up from school, so she planned to do her packing now. She had dinner plans with Paul later that evening.

Ann was getting better at managing a busy schedule. School, work, a social life, writing for the school newspaper, and volunteering at the soup kitchen. It was a lot. Ann loved those things, but she was also happy to return home for a couple of days. Life there was more straightforward. Wenatchee would be beautiful this time of year. The foothills around the valley would be a deep velvety green, and the apple blossoms in the orchards would just be starting to bloom.

A knock sounded on the door. Ann answered and saw her friend in the hall.

"Hey, Ann, I just wanted to say goodbye on my way out. I hope you have a good visit to Wenatchee," Nora said as she reached out to hug Ann.

"Thank you! I hope you have a nice vacation. I'll miss you!" When Ann closed the door, she thought about how quickly the year had already flown past. She still thought of Wenatchee as home, but the Sorrento had become her home too. The girls who lived there were like a family. How would she feel when she had to say good-bye to them—for good?

Eighteen

The cinnamon rolls were ready. Ann pulled the pan out of the oven and breathed in the delicious scent, then set it on the counter next to the plate of bacon her father had just cooked. It was their tradition. Father and daughter had been making this special breakfast together every Easter morning since Ann was ten years old.

Dad poured coffee into two mugs and brought them to the table. Already on the table, in Ann's spot, sat a small box wrapped in pastel pink paper. It was another tradition, and Ann already knew what was inside. Each year, her father gave her a new pair of white gloves for Easter.

"Thank you," Ann said, smiling as she sat down. They had both woken early, anxious to have some time together before they left for church. They'd enjoy a leisurely breakfast, and though her father never talked much, it was good to be with him in companionable silence.

Ann quietly snuck a piece of bacon under the table, giving it to Noel.

Her father smiled. "Your dog has missed you, but don't be giving her any more bacon. It's not good for her." Then, he noticed the sparkling diamond ring on her left ring finger. "Paul did a fine job picking out that ring. It's very nice."

"Yes, it's beautiful."

"Have you decided where you want to have the wedding? Wenatchee or Seattle?"

"No, we haven't talked about that yet." Would her dad have strong feelings one way or the other? "You know he's Catholic, right?"

"Yes, he told me. It doesn't bother me. How does his family feel about him marrying a Protestant? I'll understand, and I'll support you if you want to become Catholic. I hope you know that." He peeled the shell from an egg as he spoke.

"I don't think they're pleased, and I haven't decided yet what I want to do." She appreciated his support, and felt like a weight had been lifted from her shoulders. "Paul has only had one job interview so far, and it was in Portland."

"Oh?" Her father lifted his cup of coffee and took a gulp. "And how do you feel about that?"

"Worried."

***

"I'll do the dishes tonight," Ann said after dinner that Sunday evening.

"Let the dishes wait," her father said. "I have something to show you."

Ann followed him to the small attic room upstairs and watched as her father moved some boxes around. He uncovered a trunk Ann had never seen before. "This is your mother's wedding dress. I don't know if it's still the style, but if you want to wear it, it's yours now."

Ann reached into the trunk and felt the soft material against her fingers. She'd only seen this dress in a photograph, and her mother had been beautiful in it. Tears pricked at the corner of her eyes as she carefully pulled the dress out, removing the tissue that had been protecting it. The garment was fashioned in the late Edwardian style—tussore silk, with floating silver lace panels down the sides and inserted around the neckline and bodice. "Thank you!"

"You're welcome, sweetheart. I'm sorry she's not here right now. I know it must be hard for you doing all of this without her. You know, I don't think I told you this before, but when your mother first started working for the American Red Cross, during the war, the headquarters were at Hotel Sorrento. And now, that place has played a special role in our family's history twice."

***

Ms. Patrick had called the Sorrento Girls together for a house meeting on Tuesday evening after Easter break. The school year was in its final stretch, and there was one more social event on the calendar. The Sorrento Girls would be in charge of organizing the annual Mother-Daughter Tea.

Helen, Nora, Peggy, and Ann sat together on a couch in the Fireside Room, waiting for instructions. It was a chaotic scene at the moment. Small groups of girls were chatting in various corners, and people were moving in and out of the room.

"Attention! Attention!" Ms. Patrick was trying her best to call the meeting to order. "The Tea will be held right here on Mother's Day. We're going to start the planning by taking nominations for the chair positions."

Ann wanted to disappear. She generally felt this way every year around Mother's Day. It had always been awkward—all through her school years, and even now, into college. She desired neither pity nor any attention called to the fact that she was motherless.

Helen, as if sensing Ann's discomfort, reached over and squeezed her hand. "You can sneak out if you want. I'll cover for you," she whispered.

Ann nodded, gratefully, and made a quick exit to the lobby. Much to her surprise, Paul was there, waiting. "Well, hello!" Ann said.

"Hi. I didn't want to interrupt. I can wait until your meeting is over." Paul kissed her on the cheek. "I was just wondering if you wanted to walk over to Jack Frost and get some ice cream."

"You're not interrupting at all. I didn't want to be there. Let's go!"

The two of them walked, hand in hand, out the front door and down Madison street. Last week, when most of the students were gone, Ann and Paul had been able to spend more time together than usual. Ann had worked each day, helping Mrs. Delzer with the children, but her evenings were free. With no homework, they were able to go for walks around the neighborhood, enjoy picnics in the park, and just hang out together.

Today, Ann was quieter than usual, but she couldn't help it. This time of year, she always felt the loss of not having a mother.

"Is anything bothering you?" Paul asked.

"It's just the Mother-Daughter Tea. That's what the meeting's about in there. I don't want to go, and I don't want to help organize it, but I'm not sure if Ms. Patrick will stand for that. You rescued me, actually," Ann said.

"Ah, glad to be of service!"

"So, I was thinking. I'm going to take the classes, and I'll do what I need to do to become a member of the Catholic Church. I've grown to love and appreciate it since I've been here, and I know it's important to your family—so, it's important to me too. We can still visit the Presbyterians from time to time," Ann said.

"You mean that? Wow. I don't know what to say. Thank you," Paul said.

Ann was happy with her decision. There was still much to work out, so many things to talk about—but at least this was one less thing.

***

The Sorrento Girls voted for Helen as chair of the Mother-Daughter Tea committee. It was a monumental task that occupied all of her free time and also a good portion of the room she shared with Ann. Currently, tissue paper flowers covered both of the beds, a work in progress that was a part of the decorations.

In spite of her initial reservations, Ann had given in and offered to help. Helen was her friend, after all, and she couldn't abandon her now. She still didn't want to go, but she would contribute her efforts toward the planning and execution of the event.

Helen fluffed one of the paper flowers. "Why don't you invite your Aunt Rose to the tea?"

Ann considered it. "That's a good idea. I hadn't thought of that. She has been like a mother to me in many ways." She sat on the edge of her bed. "Do you think it will be okay?"

"Of course!"

"I'm going to go downstairs and call her right now." Ann set the tissue paper flower she had been working on aside and shook out her hands. They were cramped and sore from all the twisting and cutting involved in the project.

A long line of women trailed down the hallway, all waiting to use the phone, but Ann didn't mind. At least she was getting a break from the flower making factory that her room had been turned into. Where were Peggy and Nora? They should be helping too!

When it was Ann's turn to use the phone, she called her aunt. "Aunt Rose? Hello! I wanted to ask you something." Tentatively, she explained the situation to her aunt, as though she were asking for a considerable favor.

"I'm honored you would ask me," Rose said. "I'm excited!"

"Oh? I'm so happy! Thank you!" Ann hadn't expected her aunt to respond with so much enthusiasm or emotion. "By the way, how's your book writing coming along?"

They talked for a few more minutes. It was a conversation that left Ann feeling loved, and it was a good reminder that she wasn't alone. A lot of people loved her.

Ann was encouraged to hear that her aunt seemed genuinely happy with the direction her new career was taking. Aunt Rose was a strong woman. She wasn't surprised about how quickly Rose had recovered from losing her faculty position at U.W. It was the school, and the students there, who had missed out on one of their best teachers. The Mother-Daughter Tea was in two weeks. Ann was looking forward to it for the first time. She couldn't wait to introduce her friends to her aunt.

Nineteen

The lilacs were in full bloom, scenting Mrs. Lewis's back garden with their beautiful perfume. A small bistro table on the lower terrace overlooking Lake Washington had been arranged with a silver tea service for two. The sun felt warm on Ann's skin, and it was impossible not to appreciate the setting in which she found herself in, even if her nerves were on edge. It was the first time she'd been alone with Mrs. Lewis.

Taking a delicate bite from the buttery scone on her plate, Ann listened to her future grandmother-in-law's story about how the garden they were enjoying was designed. Ann smiled and nodded when appropriate, all the while knowing she had not been summoned there merely for small talk about gardening.

Mrs. Lewis had sent an invitation earlier that week to the Sorrento for Ann to come to Saturday afternoon tea at her home. She had even arranged for her driver to pick up Ann and deliver her. Ann was both delighted and nervous. She knew Mrs. Lewis would have questions for her, and she'd want to talk about the upcoming wedding. It was hard to forget Paul's words regarding his grandmother's feelings for Ann. Uttered several weeks prior, the simple "she'll come around" hadn't exactly inspired confidence.

"Would you like some more tea, dear?" Mrs. Lewis picked up the teapot.

"Yes, please." Ann could sense the conversation was about to take a turn toward the real reason she was here. She prepared herself.

"I had reservations initially about this marriage, you know—not because you're not a lovely girl. You are. My concern regarded the differences between your different religious upbringings, but Paul told me that you were willing to convert. I appreciate that." She lifted her teacup and took a sip. "I want you to know that I no longer have those reservations, and I would like to extend an offer to host an engagement party for the two of you. I know we don't have very much time before the wedding, so my thought was to plan a small affair, here at the house. It would be held on the second Saturday in June. You can give me a list of names of people you would like to invite."

It was more than she had ever expected. Ann felt her tense muscles relax. "Thank you. That is very kind, and I'm grateful."

The rest of the afternoon was spent discussing wedding plans. Ann did not want a large wedding. She and Paul had already decided on a private ceremony, with family only, at St. James, followed by a reception in August, which Mrs. Lewis had also insisted on hosting. It was all happening very fast.

When the car dropped Ann off at the Sorrento later that day, Ann decided to go for a walk around the neighborhood instead of returning to her room. She needed to be alone, and she needed time to think.

***

The day of the Mother-Daughter Tea arrived. Aunt Rose gave Ann a hug when she saw her. "It's all so lovely! Thank you for inviting me."

The Sorrento Girls had transformed the seventh-floor dining room. A pink and white confection of flowers and balloons filled the space.

The hours of hard work the women had poured into the preparations now seemed worth it. A string quartet provided music, although it was barely heard above the voices of the women, excitedly making introductions and chatting with each other.

Ann led her aunt toward the corner where Helen and her mother were standing together. Helen smiled as they approached. "Hello, you must be Mrs. Francis. I'm Helen, Ann's roommate, and this is my mother, Gloria West," Mrs. West, who had the same beautiful red hair as her daughter gave a friendly nod and extended a hand in greeting toward Aunt Rose.

Introductions were made, and soon Peggy, Nora, and their mothers were happily chatting together. There were so many in attendance that it was standing room only. Nora was part of the entertainment that afternoon. She sang the song, "A-Tisket-a-Tasket" in the style of Ella Fitzgerald. The women had always thought their friend had some star quality to her, but now they knew for sure. Nora performed as if she were born for the stage. It was a delightful surprise to see her talent on display and hear the applause when she was finished.

The women enjoyed a light buffet of finger sandwiches, cake, and tea. In a quiet moment, when it was just the two of them, Aunt Rose asked Ann about her upcoming plans for the wedding. Ann was relieved to finally have something concrete to tell her, though she still didn't have answers for the more significant questions—those concerning their plans for their life together after the wedding. Paul was still waiting to hear back from the newspapers where he'd applied. And until they knew where he'd be employed, they wouldn't know where they'd be living. Because of that, Ann had delayed in registering for the fall semester at Seattle College.

"You are still planning on continuing school next year, aren't you?" Rose asked.

"Yes, yes, of course," Ann said. She felt uncomfortable with her aunt's question, though she didn't know why. She had been clear with Paul that finishing school was necessary—and he had agreed, offering his support and assurances that it would be possible.

"Good, I'm glad. You're going to be a wonderful wife to Paul. You'll also be an outstanding teacher."

"You're going to come back to school after you get married?" asked Mrs. West, who had just caught the tail end of their conversation. "They let you do that?"

"Yes, that's my plan, ma'am," Ann said with more confidence than she'd recently felt.

Mrs. West's raised eyebrows expressed surprise and she seemed to be searching for her next words, "How very *modern*, dear. Good for you." An awkward silence ensued until Nora and her mother returned to the table, offering a new topic of conversation.

"Nora! I had no idea you could sing like that! You were fabulous!" Ann said.

"Yes, Nora, you really must do that more often!" Helen said.

"Thank you! I was nervous at first, but it was a lot of fun," Nora said.

When the event was over, the Sorrento Girls made quick work out of putting the dining room back in order. It was a lot easier to take down the decorations than it had been to put them up. The tissue paper flowers that had taken over Helen and Ann's room, along with many hours of their time, went into the trash bins. Ann would cherish her memories of sharing a room with Helen, listening to the radio, cutting and twisting tissue paper into flowers, and laughing and talking together late into the night.

She would also hold dear the memory of having Aunt Rose by her side for the tea, not as a replacement for her mother, but as a beloved family member who filled an important role in mothering her over the years. Inviting her had been the right thing to do.

***

It was the last week of school. All that remained were final exams. Ann would be moving into the Delzer's guest room at the end of the week. Mrs. Delzer asked Ann to stay on for one more month to help with the children. It was a beneficial arrangement for everyone, as Ann needed to be in Seattle, making preparations for her new life as a married woman. There was still so much to do.

Ann grabbed the box containing her favorite hat and brought it down from the top of the wardrobe. Arranging the hat carefully on her head, she assessed herself in the mirror, satisfied that she was ready. Paul would be waiting for her downstairs within the next few minutes. They both had a lot of studying to do and had decided to take their books to the park. The evenings were warm now, and it wouldn't get dark for several more hours.

When Ann made her way downstairs, she found Paul using the phone in the hallway off the lobby. She kept quiet during the conversation, trying not to eavesdrop, but he didn't sound happy. Who was on the other end of the line?

Paul finished his conversation and turned toward Ann. "Are you ready to go?" He leaned over and gave Ann a quick kiss on the cheek.

She held his arm and stood fast until his eyes met hers. "Is everything okay?"

"Yes. Everything is fine." He shrugged as if he didn't have a care in the world. "Here, I'll carry those for you," Paul said as he took Ann's books from her. They walked to the park together without saying much.

"I'm moving back into my grandmother's house this weekend—just until we know where we'll end up," he said, finally breaking the silence.

"That makes sense. There's lots of room there." She paused and looked at the ring on her left hand. "It doesn't feel real yet, that we're getting married in a month. Maybe it will once we find a house. The girls are throwing me a party—a wedding shower on Thursday night before everyone goes home for the summer."

"Oh? That's nice of them. My last final is tomorrow. I'll need to make a quick trip to Portland and back before the weekend. We can search for a house next week."

"Portland? Are you meeting with the folks at *The Oregonian* again?"

"Yes, but don't worry. I want to hear what they have to say. I've been talking to people here in Seattle too." They were in the park now. Paul set the books down at a picnic table, and the two of them were soon deep into their studying. They worked quietly, each deep in thought until it was too dark to see the words on the pages anymore.

***

On Thursday night, Ann put on a pretty floral dress and twirled around her room. She was excited to join her friends in the Fireside Room for her bridal shower. She wasn't sure what to expect, as she had never been to one before. Helen had only told her that her aunt was coming, and there would be cake and gifts.

Ann entered the room and was welcomed with cheers and hugs. Peggy pinned a rose corsage to her dress and smiled. "You're the guest of honor tonight, Ann. Come, sit over here," she said, leading Ann toward a chair in front of the fireplace.

By the end of the evening, Ann had, indeed, been showered with gifts. Towels for her new bathroom, sheets, pots, and pans, and even a toaster oven were among the presents given to her. Ann looked around at the faces of the women she'd lived with for the past school year. She was grateful for each one of them. Not all of the women were coming back to the Sorrento in the fall—Ann , of course, being one of them. She wanted to remember this moment forever.

After the party was over, Aunt Rose helped Ann gather up all the presents. "Where am I going to put all this stuff?" Ann asked, half laughing, half-serious.

"Hmm ... you have a point. Do you want me to store it at my house until you need it?"

"Yes, thank you. It won't be for long. We're going house hunting next week!"

Twenty

The Seattle College class of 1939 commencement ceremony was about to begin. Upon the grassy lawn of the Union Green, chairs for friends and family were arranged in neat rows. President Corkery, Vice-President Halpin, and Dean McGoldrick sat on a platform behind the podium. The cloudless blue sky made it a beautiful day. The graduates made their way up the middle aisle toward the empty chairs in front while the school band played "Pomp and Circumstance."

Paul walked by in his cap and gown, and Ann's heart swelled with pride. She was seated between his mother and his grandmother, who were, no doubt, feeling the same way. The three women shared common ground in this.

People gave speeches, they sang, and finally, it was time to hand out the diplomas. One by one, the graduates walked up the steps of the platform. The president of the school called their names. Then they shook hands with the administrators and accepted their diplomas. Out of the class of fifty graduates, more than half were women. Pleased with that fact, Ann thought about the day when it would be her up there.

A happy group of graduates threw their caps into the air upon the conclusion of the ceremony, then exited back down the aisle toward the reception area.

Ann found Paul and his friend, Joe, in a conversation by the cake table, and she joined them, giving them both hugs and a big smile. "Congratulations, you two! How does it feel to be done?"

"As good as you might imagine!" Joe said. "I leave for basic training next week. I'm sorry that I'll miss seeing the two of you get married."

"That soon? Wow. Well, I wish you all the best," Ann meant it, even though she was going to miss her friend, and she was sad for Peggy, who would miss him even more.

"My grandmother has invited a few of her friends to her home this afternoon for a celebration. You're welcome to join us, Joe!" Paul said.

Just then, Paul's family came over to where they were talking. Introductions were made, and more congratulations were given. Paul's parents were perfectly polite and engaging. If one hadn't known otherwise, one might never suspect the tensions that lay hidden amongst the family.

After the reception at the college, the party moved to Elizabeth Lewis's home. There, Ann met many of Paul's relatives and family acquaintances. The feeling of being under a microscope prevailed throughout the afternoon. Ann pretended not to notice the surreptitious glances and whispered questions about who she was and where she came from.

Ann surmised that many of these people at the graduation party would be among the same group she would be meeting the following week at the engagement party. How well did any of them know Paul?

Mrs. Lewis knew how to host a beautiful party. There was no doubt about that. Fresh flower arrangements of white roses with lavender filled the rooms, scenting the air with their perfume. White-gloved waiters circulated through the crowd with silver trays, offering sumptuous buttery pastries and champagne.

The endless small talk was wearing Ann out. She looked around for an escape. Nobody was on the patio off the dining room, so Ann quietly took leave and went outside. Relaxing for the first time all day, she sipped her champagne while sitting on a porch swing. Peering out over the trees toward the lake, Ann noticed Joe and Paul walking back to the house from the dock. They didn't seem to see her, and she didn't want to interrupt their conversation, so she stayed where she was, waiting for them to get closer.

Paul had only just returned from Portland yesterday, and she didn't know yet how his trip had gone. That's why she paid close attention when she heard them talking about the newspaper job at *The Oregonian*.

"It's a good job, especially right now, when so many are having a hard time finding work," Paul said.

"Tell me about it," Joe said. "I must have applied to a hundred different companies before I decided my best option would be to join the navy."

"Ann doesn't want to move to Portland. She wants to go back to school in the fall. But this is just the way it is."

"Have you told her yet?" Joe asked.

Ann sat frozen. Should she make her presence known, or should she try to slip away? Her skin felt cold, and her heart was beating fast. They still hadn't noticed her. She got up from the swing and walked toward them as if she had just come from inside the house.

"Oh, hi, Ann." Paul offered her a smile. "I was coming to find you."

"Hey, Ann. I was about to leave. I guess this is goodbye, for now. I'll be in touch," Joe said.

"Hey ... actually, Joe, if you don't mind, if you're going back to campus, I was wondering if I could catch a ride with you. I don't want to take Paul away from the party, or his guests, but I'm getting tired— and I need to move out of the Sorrento tomorrow."

"Sure, no problem!" Joe said.

"Ah, thanks, Joe!" Paul shook his friend's hand. "Ann, I'll be by tomorrow morning to help you move your stuff over to the Delzer's. Ten o'clock?"

"Okay. Sounds good. I'll see you then," Ann said, betraying nothing of the anger she was feeling at the moment.

Ann said a quick goodbye to Paul's grandmother, then got in the car with Joe. She was sorry to say goodbye to him when he dropped her off at the Sorrento. He had been like a brother to her that year. She would miss him.

It would be her last night as a resident of the Sorrento. She had already said goodbye to Helen, who'd left the day before. There were too many goodbyes. Ann felt numb. She was still trying to process the conversation she'd overheard between Paul and Joe.

This is just the way it is. The words Paul had spoken upset her. They sounded callous. Ann ran different scenarios through her mind as she made her way up the stairs to her room. Talk to him first, before you get angry, she told herself. Maybe it wasn't as bad as it had sounded. It had been a long day. Ann decided to go to sleep and sort out her feelings in the morning.

***

Ann woke early on Sunday morning—Moving Day. It wouldn't be difficult, as she had few belongings. Everything she owned fit into one large suitcase, her small train case, and a hatbox. A massive box of books completed the load.

The Delzer children had made it clear that they were excited to have "Auntie Ann" come to stay in the guest room at their house. They'd been asking her every day when she was going to move in. Their enthusiasm and affection made it easier to say goodbye to her room at the

Sorrento. Ann would miss some of the luxuries she'd enjoyed over the past year, such as having someone else cook her meals, clean her room, and do her laundry— but living in the Delzer family home would have its perks too. It was a beautiful home, and Ann loved being there.

After dressing and putting the finishing touches on her packing, Ann went up to the dining room for breakfast with Nora, who was leaving today as well. There was a spread of bacon, scrambled eggs, toast, and strawberries arrayed on the buffet table. Ann filled her plate and took it to her favorite table by the window. Nora brought over some coffee and joined her. Pushing aside her thoughts on the hard conversation she knew she'd soon be having with Paul, Ann did her best to focus on the dear friend seated across from her at that moment.

"Are you excited to be going home today?" Ann asked.

"I am, but I'll miss being with the Sorrento Girls. I'm already looking forward to returning in August," Nora said, pouring cream into her coffee. "So, where's 'home' going to be for you and Paul? Have you found a place yet?"

"No, not yet." Ann paused. Should she say more? She debated back and forth—then told Nora everything.

"He should have talked to you first. Can't you say something? You're a strong woman. Giving up everything you want, for a man, doesn't seem much like you," Nora said.

"There's more to life than being a passenger ..." Ann said thoughtfully, quoting Amelia Earhart. "I don't know ... I need to talk to him first and let him explain."

Nora checked her wristwatch. "Time for me to go. I don't like goodbyes, and I don't want to cry. I will see you soon! Be strong, Ann. Amelia's right. You're not just a passenger. Take charge of your flight through life. Write to me. Let me know how it goes." Then she hugged her friend goodbye for the summer.

***

"Paul, before we take all my stuff over to the Delzer's, can we go for a walk first? We need to talk," Ann said. Paul had arrived to help Ann move, but there were other pressing things on her mind that she needed to clear up first.

Paul nodded. "Sure, are you ready to go now?"

When they were about a block away from Hotel Sorrento, Ann took a deep breath. She couldn't wait any longer to bring up her concerns. "I was outside last night, sitting on the porch swing, when I overheard you and Joe talking." She paused. "What's going on, Paul?"

Paul was quiet for a moment, as if searching for the right words, then he finally blurted out, "I took the job with *The Oregonian*. We'll need to move to Portland. I start in July. Maybe you can enroll in a college when we get there."

Ann felt her pulse quicken. "Shouldn't we have talked about this first, together?" Ann was stunned. Her voice was cold. "I feel like the issue is deeper than whether or not I can continue with school. This is my life too. Don't I have a say?"

Paul seemed surprised. Ann had never spoken to him like this before. "*The Post Intelligencer* wasn't hiring. We're getting married in a few weeks. I needed a job. What was I supposed to do?"

"Did you apply at any other Seattle paper other than the *Post*?

"No, I didn't. But you'll like Portland!"

Ann stopped walking. Then she turned around on her heel and headed back toward the Sorrento. Anger, both with Paul and with herself, washed over her. She didn't want this kind of marriage. This wasn't an equal partnership. They could have sorted this problem out together, finding a compromise they could both be happy with, but that opportunity had never been given to her. He was treating her like a child, making all the decisions on his own. She was angry with herself, too, because she had allowed it to happen. She had continuously pushed aside any feelings of discomfort, allowing herself to be satisfied with reassurances from Paul that all would be fine. It wasn't fine. So much for being her own "pilot." She'd handed the controls over to Paul.

Paul turned around when he noticed that Ann was no longer by his side. He called after her, "I'm sorry! I wasn't thinking!"

Ann paused and waited for the man she loved to catch up with her. She wanted to believe him. She took his outstretched hand. "This is our first fight. I don't like it."

"I don't either. I love you."

"I love you too," Ann said. Maybe they could find a way to both get what they wanted.

When they got back to Hotel Sorrento, Paul came upstairs with Ann to her room to help her carry her belongings out. It was the first time he had ever seen it. Ms. Patrick had been super strict about not allowing any men into the private rooms of the hotel. But now, she and most of the coeds were gone.

"Wow, this is a lot nicer than the room I had all year," Paul said, pulling her in for a kiss.

Ann stepped away. She appreciated the apology, but she still had some cooling off to do. Nothing had changed. The plan was still in place to move to Portland. She needed more time to think.

Twenty-One

Ann appraised the room that would be hers for the next month and smiled for the first time that day. Paul was in the backyard playing ball with Billy and David. Their voices rang out below through the open window. The boys loved it when Paul came for a visit. As soon as he'd arrived with Ann, carrying her suitcase over from the Sorrento, they'd pounced on the opportunity to invite Paul to join them in a game of catch.

Margaret and Sally had eagerly invited Ann upstairs to see the lovely guest room they had prepared for her. A pale green vanity table with a large mirror sat in the corner, and a large bed with a white matelassé cover, much like her bed at the Sorrento, filled most of the space. Only, this bed had a gray tabby sleeping on it. The

Delzer's cat, Bob, considered this his room. Ann was more than happy to share as she loved cats. Sunlight filtered through the white curtains making pretty shadows from the tree outside dance across the wood floor.

"I picked these for you!" Sally said, excitedly, as she pointed to a vase of dandelions on the vanity table.

"Thank you! They're beautiful, and this room is wonderful. You two sure know how to make a girl feel welcome," Ann said.

Mrs. Delzer came into the room just then. "We're happy to have you, Ann. You're part of the family."

"I hope I can make you all feel as loved and cared for as you have made me feel," Ann said.

It had been an emotional couple of days. Being here, right now, with this sweet family, gave Ann a feeling of stability and strength that felt like water to her parched soul. Ann took Sally's outstretched hand, and the little girl pulled her toward the hallway.

"C'mon! Let's go outside!" Sally said. "I want to go see Paul!"

Mrs. Delzer went back to the kitchen, and Ann, Sally, and Margaret joined the rest of the crew in the backyard.

The original plan had been to go house hunting with Paul on Sunday, but now, that was no longer necessary. Ann supposed they'd be taking a trip to Portland soon to find a house there. Their engagement party was in a week. The wedding, two weeks after that. How could they best use the time they had left to accomplish all that still needed to be done before their big day?

***

Ann and Mrs. Delzer had just finished putting finishing touches on the strawberry jam they'd been canning, the kids were playing with their neighbors, and it was time to sit down and rest. Ann sliced several pieces of fresh bread, still warm from the oven, and spread jam on them, placing the simple treat on two plates. Mrs. Delzer poured tea for both of them and carried the cups out to the table on the back porch. The two ladies watched the children playing and sipped their tea.

"We're looking forward to your engagement party this weekend, Ann." Mrs. Delzer paused. "Tell me, are you happy about moving to Portland?"

"No, I'm not, but I can adapt. I can learn to like it there, but to be honest with you, it's not the location that is bothering me the most ..."

"What is it, dear?"

"It's the fact that he decided without me. Is that really what marriage will be like?"

"Hmm ... sometimes, yes. But it doesn't have to be like that. Mr. Delzer and I make decisions together." She took a sip of tea. "Did you tell Paul how you feel?"

"Yes, I did, right before we got here today. He apologized, but I'm not sure if he understood the problem."

"You two are both so young." Mrs. Delzer took a deep breath. "You know, you're not locked into anything at this point, right? You can still change your mind," she said with compassion.

Not knowing how to respond, Ann just sat quietly. Many people had gone to much trouble for her. The party, the presents ... how could she back out now?

***

On Saturday afternoon, Ann was feeling much better about the whole state of her current situation. She stood in front of the dressing mirror and assessed her appearance. Ann was wearing her favorite emerald-colored silk dress, the one Aunt Rose had bought for her. It was the same one she had been wearing when she first met Paul. Ann felt confident and beautiful, knowing Paul loved this dress. After applying a swipe of red lipstick, she was ready. Paul was already downstairs, talking to Mr. and Mrs. Delzer while waiting to drive her to their party.

When Ann came downstairs, she smiled at her handsome fiancé and said hello. "Wow, you look fantastic!" Paul said.

"Yes, you're beautiful, Ann," Mrs. Delzer said. "I've just got to finish getting the children ready. We'll see you in a little while."

Paul led Ann to his car and opened the door for her. They were quiet on the ride to his grandmother's house. Driving through the arboretum, Paul pointed out the place they'd had their picnic for Ann's birthday. "We should have another picnic there before we move," he said.

Ann still didn't want to think about moving. She kept hoping that something would change. Maybe one of the Seattle newspaper companies would contact Paul in the next few days and offer him a job. To Paul, she merely said, "Yes, how about dinner here sometime this week? I can make us some sandwiches. I'd love to take a boat out on the pond again. That was fun."

When they reached the house, a valet opened the door for Ann. Paul's grandmother had gone all out. A crowd of people had already gathered inside, most of whom Ann didn't know. She searched to see if Aunt Rose and Uncle Gary were there yet. Ann didn't see them, but she did see Mr. Ferguson standing by the fireplace in the sitting room. He spotted her at the same moment and waved to her. "Mr. Ferguson! Thank you for coming! I'm so glad you could come today!"

"I'm happy to be here. How are you doing, Ann?"

"I'm good, thank you. I've missed my last few Saturdays at the soup kitchen, and I'm afraid I might be done. Paul starts a job in Portland in July. I'm hoping he'll find something here in Seattle before then, but we'll probably be moving."

"Ah. Well, I'll miss seeing you around! I wish you all the best. Are you going to continue your teacher training in Portland? You're a gifted teacher, you know."

Just then, Paul's grandmother, Mrs. Lewis, joined them. "Mr. Ferguson, it's so nice to see you again," she said.

Ann spent the next hour meeting people and making small talk. Finally, Pepper, the butler, called everyone into the dining room for dinner. The long table was glittering with candlelight, silver, and crystal. White roses filled the centerpiece arrangements. Ann found her place card and was pleased to see that she was seated near

Aunt Rose. She wished her father could be there, but he had not been able to take two weekends off for travel in June, so naturally, he had chosen to be at the wedding in two weeks.

After dinner, a chocolate tiered cake was brought out on a cart. The waitstaff poured champagne for all the guests. Mrs. Lewis tapped her fork against her crystal flute, bringing everyone to attention. "Thank you, dear friends and family, for coming today to celebrate the upcoming marriage of my grandson, Paul, and his fiancé, Ann Brooks. They will have a small private ceremony in two weeks, and the reception will be in August, but this gathering here today is a way for us to wish the happy couple all our best in the upcoming days. I want to welcome Ann into our family, and I want to say just how happy I am that Paul has found such a wonderful wife. Cheers!"

Ann smiled and nodded in grateful acceptance of the kind words. Paul looked at her, smiled, and squeezed her hand. The toasts continued for several more minutes. Ann was uncomfortable with being the center of attention. She felt loved, nevertheless. By the end of the evening, she was tired but happy.

When Paul drove Ann back to the Delzer's house, they made plans to go to Portland the following weekend to search for a rental home.

"Can we check out some houses here too—in case we're able to stay after all?" Ann asked.

Paul was quiet for a moment. "I already accepted the job in Portland ..."

"I know, but I'm still hoping ..." Ann said. It was late. Paul had arrived at the Delzer's house, but they were still talking, so Ann and Paul sat in the dark car, continuing their conversation in privacy.

"I'm not backing out now," Paul's voice was gentle but firm.

Tears pricked at the corners of Ann's eyes, as they had so many other times throughout the week. Did all brides feel this way right before their weddings?

"I'll go to Portland, and I'll look at houses with you, but I think it would only be fair if you kept an open mind about finding something here. I don't think Portland is our only option," Ann said with conviction.

Paul nodded but didn't say anything. He opened his car door and walked around the front to open Ann's door and escort her to the porch. After a quick kiss, the two said goodbye, and Ann went inside.

***

On Sunday, Ann offered to make breakfast for everyone while Mrs. Delzer ran around, getting the children ready for Mass. She scrambled eggs, fried bacon, and toasted bread, setting it out for the family. After that, she made a pot of coffee and poured some milk for the children. They would all walk to St. James together this morning.

Mr. Delzer made it to the table first and started eating. He opened his newspaper and read, seemingly oblivious to the chaos that could be heard coming from upstairs. He was a nice man —but not very helpful.

Margaret and Billy came to the table next. The meal would need to be eaten in shifts, based on whoever was ready to go. Ann sat down with the older two kids and Mr. Delzer to eat her breakfast. They could hear Billy shouting something about not being able to find his shoes, followed by Mrs. Delzer's instructions to search under his bed.

Sally arrived in the kitchen wearing pigtails and a navy smocked dress. She looked adorable as she sat down to eat with a big smile. "Bacon is my favorite!"

At 8:45 a.m., everyone in the Delzer household was dressed, fed, and ready for Mass. David claimed Ann's hand as they walked to St. James together. It had been a busy morning already. Knowing that Mrs. Delzer didn't usually have her help, Ann marveled at how the woman managed to get her family to Mass on time each Sunday.

The short walk to the cathedral was enjoyable. Ann loved this neighborhood. It was different, though, without all the college students around.

As soon as they arrived at their destination, the children scattered. They had Sunday school classes to attend. Ann saw Paul in their usual spot, where he had saved her a seat. She excused herself from Mr. and Mrs. Delzer's company and joined him there.

The homily that day was on asking God for guidance and wisdom when making decisions. What if she prayed about her questions? Could she still trust God if his answers were different from what she wanted?

Twenty-Two

People were crowded tight on the streetcar that morning. Ann stood near the front, holding onto a strap to keep from falling as the car made its way up the steep grade of Queen Ann Hill. The city scenery unfolded like a movie before her. Seattle was a place that had first grabbed hold of her heart when Ann had come to visit her aunt as a fourteen-year-old girl. Even after nearly a year of living here, she still found it exciting, colorful, and full of beauty. The tall buildings, the hustle, and all the people were a big part of its appeal for her.

Now, Ann was on her way to meet Aunt Rose at her home for lunch.

Mrs. Delzer had encouraged Ann to take the day off at breakfast that Tuesday morning. "Go, enjoy yourself. See your aunt while you have the chance. You'll be gone soon, and I know you'll miss her," she said.

Ann had gratefully accepted the offer. She carried a box of chocolates in her handbag for her aunt, a small contribution toward what was sure to be a pleasant afternoon. She always enjoyed her time with Rose.

After getting off the trolley, Ann walked up the block toward Rose's house, and she noticed that many of the people in the neighborhood had planted vegetable gardens in their front yards. It seemed as if everyone had a garden these days. Even in the more well-to-do areas, people were finding it necessary to grow their food and stretch their pennies as far as possible.

Rose came to the front door wearing her curly hair pulled into a messy knot on the top of her head, a white button-up shirt that belonged to her husband, and a pair of baggy brown trousers. She'd tucked a pencil behind her ear. "Ann! Come on in! I'm so glad we get to spend some time together today. Oh! Chocolates! Yum … thank you. Please, excuse my appearance. I've been writing all morning, and I haven't had a chance to pull myself together yet," Rose said, laughing.

"You look beautiful, as always! How's the writing going?"

"Ah, thank you. It's going well. I need to get this manuscript off to my publisher by Friday, so I'm just working on wrapping it up. But I'm glad you could come today. I needed a break!" Rose said, leading Ann toward the back of the house. "I made us a green salad, and I thought I'd make some sandwiches to go with it. How does that sound?"

"It sounds great! What can I do to help?" Ann asked. Just then, Rose's poodle, Mimi, came inside from the backyard. The dog was excited to see Ann. Mimi came and sat down next to her, nudging Ann's hand so she would pet her.

"Nothing. Just sit down, relax, and chat with me."

"Paul and I are driving to Portland on Saturday to find a house to rent. Have you ever been to Portland?" Ann sat down at the kitchen table.

"I have. It's like Seattle in some ways. How do you feel about everything—the wedding and moving?"

"I don't know. Excited. Nervous. Conflicted. I'm checking into Albany College as a possibility in Portland, but I haven't withdrawn from Seattle College yet. I keep hoping ..."

"Albany College is a good school. You have a lot of changes happening right now. You're hoping you can stay at Seattle College?"

"Yes." Ann scratched Mimi's head. "How's married life going for you?" Ann was skirting around the questions she wanted to ask.

Rose knew her niece well. "If you're wondering if I'm still angry about being fired for marrying a faculty member ... yes, I am. It wasn't right what happened. Gary didn't know about the school's new policy, though—not until after we were married. We were all surprised. He's still fighting against it, not just for me, but for the other women. He wanted to resign in protest after it happened. I pleaded with him not to. There was no point in both of us being out of work. He's a good man, and I'm a lucky woman."

"Do you think you'll continue writing if you have kids?" Ann was curious.

"I don't know. I don't even know if we can have children. I'm not so young anymore." Rose sighed.

Ann reached over and took her aunt's hand. "I'm sorry."

Rose smiled at her niece. Then she stood up from the table and walked over to where the bread box was on the kitchen counter. "We have some leftover roast chicken from last night. Would you like a chicken salad sandwich?"

"Yes, please. That sounds good." Ann paused, choosing her next words carefully. "I'm angry—I think—at Paul. But I love him so much. What if I'm making a mistake?"

"A mistake in getting married?" Rose studied Ann's face carefully. "You're not married yet. You can still change your mind."

That's what Mrs. Delzer had said. Ann felt guilty all of a sudden, as if she had betrayed Paul, somehow. "I want to marry Paul. I don't even know why I said that. Silly. I'm silly, that's all."

Rose set a plate with a half sandwich and some green salad in front of Ann. "You're not silly. I'm glad you're thinking carefully before deciding this. I'd be worried if you weren't!"

After they finished with lunch, Rose suggested they take Mimi for a walk. It was a sunny day. The two of them made their way toward Kerry Park.

"I can't believe I forgot to tell you! Paul and I visited First Presbyterian a couple of months ago. I met your old Sunday school teacher, Mrs. Carson. She asked if I was a Fairbanks girl. She said I resemble my mother. It was nice talking to her," Ann said.

"You do look like your mother. Wow! I remember Ms. Edith! How is she?"

"She was friendly and seemed to be in great spirits. She told me to say 'hello' to you."

They were at Kerry Park now. From where Ann stood, she could see the sparkling blue water of Elliot Bay dotted with white sails, majestic Mt. Rainier off in the distance, the city skyline, and Bainbridge Island. The view was spectacular.

"Gary and I should go back and visit First Presbyterian sometime. That would be good. I stopped going after my parents—your grandparents—passed away. I don't know why, really," Rose said.

Two young boys were playing on the swings in the lower part of the park, down an embankment. Skronk, skree-skonk, went the metal chains on the swings. The familiar sound brought Ann's memories back to her happy childhood. There was undoubtedly sadness, and the feeling of missing her mother was always a part of it, but there were also a lot of good times. What was her father doing at that moment? She wanted to go home one more time before she was married but wasn't sure if she'd be able to.

"Will you come to see me in Portland?" Ann asked her aunt.

"Of course!" Ann nodded, smiled, and continued to watch the little boys as they played. She could picture herself living in this neighborhood with Paul. Brick, Queen Ann-style homes with pretty lawns and flower-pot-filled front porches populated the tree-lined streets around them. Gary and Rose lived here.

"Will you show me the house that you and my mother grew up in, sometime? Is it nearby?" Ann asked.

"It's about a ten-minute walk from here. We could go now if you like ..."

"Yes, please!" Ann and Rose walked down Highland Drive, then turned up Sixth Avenue. It was hot outside, and Ann's feet were starting to hurt, but she was curious.

"Here it is!" Rose gestured toward a large white Victorian mansion with two turrets and a wraparound porch.

Ann gasped. It was a magnificent house. "It's beautiful!"

The two ladies stood still on the sidewalk gazing up at the home, one remembering, and the other, imagining.

"What was it like growing up there?" Ann asked.

"It was lovely—most of the time. Your mother and I were best friends, and I loved having her as a sister. Our mother was very stern, and we didn't spend a lot of time with her. But our nanny's name was Miss Patty. She was the one we went to for everything. We had a lot of servants. It was necessary for a house of this size. Though it was hard to sell the house, I thought it was the right thing to do. It was too much for me to take on by myself."

"I completely understand," Ann said. "Thank you for showing me."

Ann thought about her own little Wenatchee house where she had grown up. By the time she was ten, she was taking care of a good part of the cooking and cleaning for her father and herself, all while going to school. It had been a lot. She could understand why her aunt had decided to sell the family home. She wished she could see inside. It didn't seem like anyone was home. "Do you know who lives there now?"

"I don't. The people who bought it from me lost their fortune in 1929, and I'm not sure who owns it now," Rose said. An old gardener at the house across the street was weeding a flower bed, and he waved at Ann and Rose. They both waved back. "Mr. Gerald? Hello! It's me, Rose! I used to live there," she said, pointing to the mansion.

"Rose! Isn't that something. You're all grown up! It's good to see you," the man said. Then he looked at Ann. "Hello. That's a beautiful dog you have there."

"This is Mimi," she said, pointing toward the dog. "I'm Ann, Rose's niece."

Mimi wagged her tail. She seemed to like being told she was beautiful. The three of them talked for a few more minutes. Mr. Gerald, Ann soon learned, had been the gardener at the Fairbank's house many years ago.

"Your old house is vacant right now. It has been for about a year. I'm not sure what's going on. Someone comes and takes care of the grounds, but that's all I know," Mr. Gerald said.

Ann and Rose were quiet on the walk back. They were both deep in thought.

"What if your old house was put up for sale? Would you want it back?" Ann asked.

"No, I don't think so. Gary and I are both happy where we are. We couldn't afford to live there anyhow."

If only Paul wasn't set on moving to Portland. If they stayed in Seattle, would they have even the smallest chance of someday purchasing this lovely home? How wonderful it would be to keep the house in the family—a place where they could raise their own children.

***

On Wednesday, Ann offered to take the Delzer children to the city pool. "You gave me a day of rest yesterday. Now it's your turn! I can manage the children on my own," Ann said.

Mrs. Delzer was happy to take Ann up on that offer. "Thank you! I want nothing more than to relax with a good book today. I'll pack everyone lunch."

On Thursday, the children wanted to go back to the pool again. This time, Mrs. Delzer came along too. The women relaxed in lounge chairs, chatting, while the children swam. "It's been wonderful having you stay with us these past few weeks, Ann. I'm going to miss you when you're gone," Mrs. Delzer said, shielding her eyes from the bright sun.

Ann sipped the refreshing lemonade she'd purchased at a poolside stand. "The feeling is mutual. You've made me feel like part of the family."

"In that case, you should be calling me Barbara, not Mrs. Delzer!" Barbara rummaged around in her pool bag, searching for something. "Have you seen my sunglasses?"

"Okay—Barbara. I can do that. Oh, here's your sunglasses," Ann said. The sunglasses had somehow ended up in one of Sally's shoes.

Tomorrow would be Ann's last day working for the Delzer family. After that, on Saturday, she'd be going to Portland with Paul to find a house, and she was going back to Wenatchee on Sunday to see her father and bring back her wedding dress. He would be coming back on the train with her. Her wedding day was barely more than a week away. Why did she feel like she wanted time to slow down?

Twenty-Three

Paul's red Plymouth was out front. Ann watched from the upstairs window as he got out of the car and walked to the front door. The sun was just rising, and everyone else in the house was still sleeping. Ann grabbed her hat, purse, and shoes and tiptoed down the stairs as quietly as she could.

"Good morning," she whispered to Paul when she opened the front door.

"Hello, beautiful. Are you ready?"

Ann nodded. Closing the door behind her, she sat on the front step to put on her shoes.

"I've got some coffee for you in the car," Paul said.

Not only did he have coffee, but there was also a bag of donuts on the front seat. Ann smiled and kissed Paul. They had a long day of driving ahead. The plan was to go to Portland, check out a few rental houses that Paul had found in classifieds, put down a deposit, and push back to Seattle. They wouldn't return until late that night, but Ann was looking forward to spending the day with Paul. They'd have lots of time to talk.

Paul drove along Madison and past the Sorrento—so lovely in the early morning light. Soon they were outside of the city, headed south on US Route 99. The dense forest surrounded both sides of the road.

"I'm curious," Ann said. "What was your connection to *The Oregonian* newspaper? What made you decide on Portland?"

"My friend, Sam, is on staff there. He was the editor of the school newspaper when I first came to Seattle College, and he taught me a lot. He helped me get an interview," Paul said.

"Ah. That was nice." Ann was determined to turn her feelings about moving to Portland around and make the best of the situation. Paul was, after all, doing his best, and that's all anyone could do.

An hour later, they drove through Olympia. Ann was thrilled that she could see the dome of the Legislative Building from the road. She had only seen it in pictures. It was much more impressive in real life.

"I saw the house where my mother and my aunt grew up this week. It's near Queen Ann Hill," she said, trying to make conversation. "It's vacant, I think. Sad. It's a beautiful old mansion."

"Oh? Well, we won't be looking at any mansions today, but hopefully, we'll find something comfortable. Whatever we find today will be temporary," Paul said.

After a couple more hours of driving, they made it to Portland. A sign said, "Welcome to Portland, The Rose City." They had made good time as it wasn't even lunchtime yet.

Ann gazed out the window. A large mountain served as a backdrop over the city skyline. "Is that Mt. Hood in the distance?"

"Yes, and that's Jantzen Beach right there," Paul said, as he pointed toward the biggest wooden roller coaster Ann had ever seen. "There's a huge pool there too—and picnic grounds, more rides, and a dance pavilion. We could go there to celebrate the Fourth of July!"

Ann smiled. That sounded like fun.

They crossed a bridge over the Columbia River and drove into the downtown area. The city wasn't as big as Seattle, but it was still larger than Wenatchee. Portland was a charming place, and there were, in fact, roses everywhere.

Paul pulled over to the side of the road and parked. Pulling out a map and a piece of paper with some addresses scrawled on it, he turned to Ann. "How are you at navigating? Do you think you can help me find this first address? This one is an apartment."

Ann took the map and studied it. "I'll do my best." According to the map, the building was right around the corner. The Admiral apartment building was a five-story Tudor-style brick structure on Park Avenue. Paul and Ann walked together, holding hands, into the lobby. A grand curved marble staircase with a dark mahogany banister led to the upper floors. Paul checked his paper for the manager's apartment number, discovering it was on the first floor. Finding the place, he knocked. An older woman of petite stature opened the door, peering at them expectantly.

"Hello, I'm Paul Lewis. I'm here to see about renting an apartment. Are you Mrs. Nelson?"

"Yes, I am. Good to meet you. Here, let me grab a key, and I'll take you upstairs. I have one two-bedroom unit available. I'll show you," the woman said.

After they climbed three flights of stairs, they walked down a long hallway. The building had a faded, shabby sort of beauty, as if it had seen better days. Mrs. Nelson opened the door to Apartment 404 and let Paul and Ann inside. The rooms were surprisingly lovely. High ceilings and a large bay window made the small space feel more substantial. The walls were a little dingy, but that was nothing a little soap and water couldn't fix. The empty space reminded Ann that they possessed no furniture. Would they be sleeping on the floor their first night there?

"What do you think?" Paul asked.

"It's lovely," Ann said.

"Twenty-five dollars a month, first and last. I'll waive the deposit for you two," Mrs. Nelson said.

"Can we let you know by the end of the day?" Paul asked.

"Sure, no problem. But I can't hold it any longer than that," the woman said.

Outside again, on the front steps, Paul raised his eyebrows and smiled at Ann. "I don't know ... how about we get some lunch and check out a couple more?"

They found a cozy diner farther down the block and settled into a booth. After studying the menu, Ann decided on the soup with a turkey sandwich.

"I liked the apartment, but it's very far from Albany College. How would I get to school?" Ann asked.

Paul put down his menu and focused on Ann. "Oh. I didn't think of that. Did you want to start school this fall?"

A waitress came over to the table just then. Ann used the time it took to place their orders to compose herself. She had told Paul many times how important it was for her to continue with school. She was irritated by his question. "Maybe I could learn to drive, and you could walk to work? Is your office close by?"

"Hmm. That's an idea." He frowned. "But I'll probably need my car to go out on assignments."

"Well, let's see if we can find something closer to the school then." Ann felt her anger rising, and it made her uncomfortable, so she changed the subject, bringing up another topic that had been on her mind. "What can we afford? Are we going to have enough money to get some furniture?"

"Don't you worry about that. I've got it handled." Paul took a sip of his coffee. "I thought you'd want to take some time off, get settled first, and maybe *then* go back to school."

The waitress brought their food. Ann had been quite hungry a few minutes ago, but now, her appetite was gone. Were her expectations wrong in wanting to be a part of the decisions made in their marriage? She didn't wish to have "everything handled" for her.

"I'm not worried," she said. "I want to know these things. I want to be a part of the decisions. And I don't want to take any time off from school. The summer months are enough."

"Fine, fine" Paul said, raising his hands as if he was surrendering. "I don't want to argue." He leaned back in his seat and scowled, as though frustrated. "Don't you trust me? I'll show you the numbers sometime," he said, brusquely.

"Of course, I trust you," Ann said.

They ate the rest of the meal in silence. Ann was glad to leave the diner after Paul took care of the check. They went back to the car, and Paul pulled out the map once more.

"This next house is only a couple of blocks away. Maybe we should walk?"

By three o'clock, they had looked at two apartments and one house, all in the downtown area. None were close to Albany College. Ann was tired. The first apartment they'd seen was still the best one on the list.

"Shall we go put a deposit on the one in the Admiral building?" Paul asked.

"Okay, let's do it," Ann said.

Mrs. Nelson seemed pleased to see the couple again when Paul knocked on her door. When they left, Paul had the key to Apartment 404 in his pocket. They'd done it. They had their first home. Now all they had to do was furnish it.

Ann tried to stay awake to keep Paul company on the drive back to Seattle, but eventually, the vibration of the tires on the road lulled her to sleep. Her head dropped and finally rested on Paul's shoulder. He smelled so good—clean, like soap.

When she woke up, they were driving through Tacoma. Dusk was beginning to settle in. "Hey, did you have a nice rest?" Paul asked. "I need to stop and put some more gas in the car. Are you hungry? I think there are a couple of donuts left in that bag on the back seat from this morning."

"Oh! I slept for a long time. Sorry about that. And yes, I'm starving," Ann said as she reached for the donuts.

"You'll be up early in the morning, catching the train to Wenatchee. You need the rest.

Here's a gas station. I hope it's still open ..." The gas station was closed, so Paul kept going. "Hmm ... there's still a little in the tank. Maybe we can make it. Keep your eyes open for a gas station. I'll keep going toward Seattle."

The thought of running out of gas before they reached Seattle filled Ann with anxiety. She didn't want to be stuck on the side of the road at this time of night. They passed a few more roadside stations, but each one was closed.

The car was still moving along okay when they reached the outskirts of Seattle. Ann thought about what Paul had asked her earlier in the diner. *Do you trust me?* He was her sweetheart. He was charming, handsome, and funny. Paul was amazing. He treated her with such kindness. But did she trust him?

The car could run out of gas at any minute because they hadn't planned very well when they left. The immediate fear of running out of gas mingled with the broader concerns that she had been pushing down throughout their whole engagement. Were they ready to get married? Was Paul the kind of man who would treat her as an equal partner in their marriage?

Ann felt relieved when they finally reached the Delzer's home. She didn't say anything about what she had been thinking, and she was tired, so she didn't trust her thoughts. She couldn't wait to go home and see her father in the morning.

"I'll see you in a few days. I'm glad we made it back okay. Good night. I love you," Ann leaned over and gave Paul a quick kiss on the cheek.

"I love you too. I hope you have a good trip. I'll miss you." Paul turned off the car and walked around to open the door for Ann. He walked her up the front steps to the house.

Billy opened the front door. "Hi, Ann. Hi, Paul! Did you find a good house today?"

Paul grinned. "Hey, Billy! Yes, we found a house. What did you do today?"

"Played baseball with my friends."

"Ah, well, that sounds fun. I'll see you around!" Paul gave a quick wave, then headed back to his vehicle.

Ann waved goodbye and went into the house. She was sad that it would be her last night with the Delzer family. She was going to miss them.

Twenty-Four

The red Plymouth was still parked outside the Delzer's home the next morning when Ann opened the front door, suitcase in hand. Mr. Delzer had offered to take Ann to the station. David and Billy were coming along, too, to say goodbye to their favorite auntie.

"Isn't that Paul's car?" Mr. Delzer asked.

"Yes, it is ... we almost ran out of gas on the way back from Portland. I wonder if he couldn't get it started again after he dropped me off?" There was no sign of Paul. He must have called a cab. Why hadn't he just knocked on the door and asked for help?

"I would have been happy to have given him a ride home," Mr. Delzer said.

Not wanting to ask for help seemed to be a characteristic of Paul, something Ann was noticing more often.

"What's Wenatchee like?" David asked.

"There are lots of orchards there, and it's a small town. It's the kind of place where you know almost everyone. It's pretty—nestled in the foothills of the Cascades, with the Columbia River running alongside it," Ann said.

"Are you going to come back and visit us?" Billy asked.

"Definitely! I will."

They had reached King Street Station. Mr. Delzer parked the car and got Ann's suitcase from the trunk, then Ann kissed both little boys on the tops of their heads and said goodbye. She hugged Mr. Delzer. "Thank you for everything. I'll keep in touch. Goodbye." Ann waved as the car pulled away from the curb, then she turned toward the giant clock tower and noted that it was almost 7:00 a.m. Her train would be leaving soon. Ann hurried through the lobby area and out toward the platforms, finding hers quickly.

The train pulled away from the station, and Ann settled comfortably into her seat by the window. She relaxed, knowing she would soon be home. She couldn't wait to see her father.

Feeling reflective, Ann thought about everything that had happened over the past year. She was grateful for her year at Seattle College, for the friends she had met, and for the confidence gained as she learned to navigate life on her own. And now, she was getting married.

The diamond ring on her finger sparkled in the sunlight streaming through the window. It was an extravagant ring, a reminder that her new life with Paul would be very different from what she'd known for most of her life. She hadn't intended to fall in love. Finding a man to marry at college wasn't the reason she'd gone, but now, Ann had to admit that there wasn't much difference between herself and those girls she'd scoffed at when she'd first arrived in Seattle.

The lush landscape of the west side of the state was gradually changing from the tall, jagged, forested peaks of the Cascades to the softer grass-covered foothills of Central Washington as the train reached closer to home. Outside, Ann watched as the train chugged on the tracks through Cashmere. The raging rapids of the Wenatchee River ran beside the tracks. Well-tended orchards stretched out from the banks of the river and up into the hills.

The whoosh of the brakes and the screech of the train's whistle announced the train's arrival in Wenatchee. Ann could see her father outside on the platform waiting for her. He was alone. When she exited her car, his face lit up with a bright smile. Ann ran to him and gave him a big hug.

"Hey, bug!" he said. He hadn't called her that in years. She liked it. "Did you have a good trip?"

"Yes, I did. The dining car was full the whole time, though. Let's get something to eat. I'm hungry!" She hadn't had anything more than a cup of coffee yet that day. Her father pulled an apple out of his pocket and handed it to Ann, just like old times. The old Model T her father drove was the only car in the lot. When Ann saw it, she thought of something.

"Hey, Father, do you think you could teach me how to drive while I'm here this week?"

"Of course! It would be a pleasure," her father said as he opened the door for his daughter.

Ann was surprised to see that her father had painted the little house on Hawthorne Street since she'd last seen it. Instead of being white, as it had always been, it was now blue. "The house looks great!" Ann said. "Did you paint all of it by yourself?"

"Thank you. I did. Just trying to keep busy, you know."

Ann was used to everything in Wenatchee staying the same. The new color was nice, but she wasn't sure if she liked the change. It was unsettling. As soon as Ann opened the front door, Noel showed up with her tail wagging, eager to greet the arrivals. The dog excitedly sniffed the suitcase Ann held.

"Noel! Hey, sweet doggy." Ann had missed the old dog, but she was glad that Noel and her father had each other to keep company with these days.

Her dad took Ann's suitcase back to her childhood room and placed it on the bed. Her room was just as she'd left it. A pink floral quilt covered the comfortable bed in the center of the room.

A sturdy wood desk stood with a stack of books and a gooseneck lamp under a lace curtain framed window, and in the corner, sat a rattan rocking chair. Ann plopped onto the bed next to the suitcase and sighed with happiness. The familiarity of it all was a comfort.

"I'll go fry up some bacon and eggs. Is it too late for breakfast?" her father asked.

"That sounds perfect. Thank you! Do you mind if I make another pot of coffee to go with them?"

After they prepared the meal, and father and daughter sat at the kitchen table with breakfast in front of them, Ann told him about the apartment in Portland.

"It's a cute little place on the fourth floor, overlooking downtown," Ann said.

"Oh? That's great. I hope you'll be very happy there."

"How are you doing, Father? You're not just working all the time, are you?" Ann had spotted a box of heart-shaped cookies in the kitchen. On the outside of the box, someone had signed, *Love, Sophia.* Ann was smiling. She didn't like the thought of her father being alone, and now, she wanted to know more about the mysterious cookie maker. But her father, close-lipped as always, didn't take the bait.

"I'm doing fine," he said, smothering a piece of toast with strawberry jam. "Just hired some new guys to help with spraying the orchards."

There was no point in beating around the bush with this guy. Ann would have to come out with it and ask. "So, who's Sophia?" .

He couldn't hide the tiny smile that flickered for a moment at that question. "Sophia? Oh.

She's a friend. Just moved in next door. A widow. From Chelan."

"May I meet her?"

"Sure. But I don't think Sophia is home right now. I haven't seen her in a couple of days. Must be out of town. I'll introduce you if we see her."

"I want to know more. Why is she making you heart-shaped cookies? What's she like?" Ann pressed on, enjoying the moment. She knew her father well enough to understand, without words, that whoever this Sophia lady was, she was making her father happy. That was enough. But she couldn't help giving him a little bit of a hard time.

"What's to know? She likes to bake."

***

The next morning was Monday. Five more days until the wedding. Ann woke up in her childhood room and lay there a while, thinking. Being home was good. From her bed, Ann could see through the window into the backyard. The rose garden her mother had planted, before Ann was even born, was in its full glory. Ann made a plan to get up early and pick a bouquet before she headed back to Seattle on Friday morning. It would be the perfect way to have a little part of her mother with her on her wedding day. With that thought, Ann got out of bed and opened her closet door.

Inside the closet hung the wedding dress. Ann touched the lace to her face. She decided to try it on since it had been several months. Hopefully, it still fit.

Ann stared into the dressing mirror and pulled up her hair. How should she wear it on her wedding day? She couldn't button up the back on her own, but it seemed as if the dress would fit perfectly. The pearl earrings from Paul would pair nicely. She sighed. Just then, she heard a knock. "Come in."

Her father opened the door to her room. "I need to go into work for a few hours this morning, but ..." He paused, then smiled when he saw his daughter in the dress. "Wow, you look beautiful ..."

"Thank you. I just wanted to make sure everything's ready. Is there anything you need me to do around the house today while you're gone?"

"No. Relax. Enjoy your day. I left some money on the counter. If you want, you can take it to the market and pick up something for dinner."

***

That night they had a chicken pot pie for dinner. Ann knew it was her father's favorite meal.

She'd spent most of the day reading in the quiet house, alone. By three in the afternoon, Ann was ready for some company. The short walk to the market provided just that. Along the way, she ran into one of her former classmates, Mary Collins—no, Smith, now. Mary had gotten married a few months ago. Of course, Mary had noticed the sparkling diamond on Ann's ring finger and had asked about it. Ann was sure the whole town knew of her engagement within five minutes of that conversation.

Back at home, Ann had kept an eye out for the new neighbor, but so far, it seemed like nobody was home. She had just finished setting the table when her father walked in.

"Oh, wow ... I could smell that pie before I even got in the door!" Her father's grin almost reached both ears. "It's sure good to have you back!"

Ann smiled, pleased she'd made an effort. It had been a long time since she'd made the recipe. She'd almost forgotten how. Would Paul appreciate her pie as much as her father did?

***

On Thursday night, her father suggested having dinner at The Windmill, Ann's favorite place to get a steak. They were leaving early the next morning. This time, Ann and her father would be taking the Model T across the mountains on the return trip to Seattle. They had gone out driving each night that week after dinner. Her dad seemed pleased to have the opportunity to pass along one more skill to his daughter before she left to get married. Now, Ann was feeling more confident in her driving abilities. She planned to get her license as soon as she moved to Portland.

On Friday morning, she carefully wrapped the wedding dress and placed it on the backseat, along with a generous bouquet of roses from the backyard. Ann's luggage was squeezed into the trunk. Noel, who loved car rides, hopped into the front. Noel would be dropped off with one of her father's employees along the way. Though, Ann would have liked it if the dog could have come along too. The car was full. By 7:00 a.m., they were pulling out of the drive.

Ann glanced back at the little house one more time and quickly wiped away a tear, trying not to let her father see. She felt like she was saying goodbye to her childhood.

Twenty-Five

Rose carefully buttoned up the long row of tiny silk-covered buttons running along the back of Ann's dress. She'd done the same for her sister, nearly twenty-two years ago. Neither woman spoke. Ann felt surprisingly somber for the occasion.

Ann looked at her reflection in the mirror as her aunt helped her get ready for her wedding. Her dark glossy hair was worn down in waves. She wore the pearl necklace that Paul's grandmother had given to her only yesterday. The two of them were alone in Aunt Rose's guest room. Down the hall, her father and Uncle Gary were having coffee together, waiting. In a few minutes, they would all leave together and drive to

St. James, where Paul and his family would meet them.

After the simple church ceremony, the plan was to attend a luncheon at the elder Mrs. Lewis's home with the families, then Paul and Ann would leave for their honeymoon. Ann still didn't know where they were going. Paul had wanted it to be a surprise.

"Ann, you are a picture of elegance and beauty," Rose said. "Is everything all right?"

Ann hesitated before answering with a question of her own. "What if we're not ready?"

"Oh, dear. Being nervous is perfectly normal …"

"Were you nervous when you got married?"

"With Gary and me, it all happened so quickly! I didn't even have time to think about what I was doing," Rose said.

"I'm probably just overthinking. I do that." Ann had a wonderful man who loved her waiting at the church. A beautiful life lay ahead of her. *I'd be a fool to throw it all away, right?*

"I'm here for you. I'm on your side, Ann."

Ann turned around and hugged her aunt. It was good knowing that she had such unconditional support and love.

"What do you think of the bouquet? My mother planted those roses," Ann said, gesturing toward the flowers she'd arranged the night before, now sitting on a shelf.

"They smell divine," Rose said. "So, I think it's time to go! Are you ready?"

Ann straightened her shoulders, picked up the bouquet, and followed her aunt out the door.

***

The most effective way to do it—is to do it. Ann thought of the phrase, made famous by her childhood hero, Amelia Earhart, and repeated it in her mind, like a mantra. Standing in the atrium, she could hear the strains of the organ playing, "Fur Elise." Looking at her father, standing beside her, Ann felt bolstered in courage.

"I need to talk to Paul. Do you think you could get him?"

"Now?" Her father's surprise quickly changed to understanding. "Yes, sweetheart. I can do that."

Waiting alone, knowing this was the right thing to do, no matter how difficult or poorly timed, Ann took a deep breath and resolved herself for what was next. Paul walked into the atrium. Ann's father stepped outside to wait, giving them privacy.

"Paul, I can't. I'm so sorry. I didn't want to hurt you. I thought I could do this. I love you, but this isn't right," Ann's voice shook with emotion. Her knees felt like they were going to buckle. The room suddenly felt like it was a hundred degrees.

The color left Paul's face. He squeezed his eyes shut, rubbed his temples, and shook his head as if trying to shake himself from a nightmare. "Why?" He croaked. When he looked at Ann again, his eyes flashed with anger. "No... never mind." Then, without saying anything, he walked out the front doors, past Ann's father, got in his car, and left.

Ann could hardly blame him. She wanted to disappear. Her father came back at that moment. He said nothing, just wrapped his arms around his daughter and waited for her to speak.

"I can't go in there. Can you let them know?"

"Yes."

"Wait! Here ..." Ann took the pearl necklace off and held it out to her father. Then she took off her ring. "Can you please give these to Mrs. Lewis?"

***

Back at Uncle Gary and Aunt Rose's house, Ann asked to be left alone and went to the guest room. The car ride back had been quiet. Ann's family had kept to a respectful silence the whole way home from the church, knowing she'd talk when she was ready.

What have I done?

Ann couldn't stop the question from circling in her mind in an endless orbit. Oddly, she felt more at peace than she had in a long time. Still wearing her mother's wedding dress, Ann lay on the bed, staring at the ceiling. She needed help, as she couldn't get out of the dress on her own. It had too many buttons. It would feel good to take it off and put on something more comfortable.

The gentle knock on the door was welcome. "Ann? May I come in?" Rose asked.

"Yes. I need help unbuttoning this dress ..."

"Of course. Listen. You're going to be alright. Paul will be too," Rose said, turning Ann around so she could reach the buttons. "What you did wasn't easy. I know that. You're a brave woman, and I'm proud of you."

"Thank you, Aunt Rose. I couldn't go through with it. I love Paul. But I'm not interested in a marriage where my voice doesn't count. When he decided to move to Portland, without talking to me first, I tried to brush it off. I tried." She brushed away a tear. "I kept thinking it was too late to call off the wedding until it very nearly was. I'm so sorry! I know you went to great effort to make this a beautiful day. A lot of people did. I have so many people to apologize to!"

"A wedding is just a day. Marriage is for a lifetime. It was better to speak up now. No apology is necessary," Rose said, giving Ann a hug. "How about I make us some dinner?"

Ann stepped out of the wedding dress, then hung the beautiful garment in her closet. Then she slipped into a pair of slacks and a gray cotton blouse. She would deal with everything that needed to be dealt with tomorrow. Tonight, she was going to take it easy with her family. She'd been surprised by their understanding. But what about everyone else? Had she just made herself the most hated woman around? And could she blame them?

Twenty-Six

"Gary and I are leaving for our vacation in Montana next week. We'll be away for three weeks. It sure would be nice to have someone keeping an eye on the house while we're gone. Does that sound like something you might be interested in, Ann?" Rose asked as she handed her niece a hot mug.

Ann took a sip of coffee and thought for a moment. It was the day after the day that everything changed. Staying here, at Rose's house, sounded like an excellent way to pull her thoughts together and make a new plan. "Yes, I would be happy to do that. Thank you!"

Her father joined the two ladies at the breakfast table. He took a couple of pancakes from the platter in the middle and poured a generous helping of syrup on them. Then he looked at his daughter. "Take your time figuring out what you want to do next. I need to get back to Wenatchee today. You're always welcome to come home, for as long as you wish, but it sounds like a good plan to stay here at Rose's."

"Thank you, I never registered for classes in Portland," Ann said. "I just kept putting it off."

Her father poured a cup of coffee for himself. "Do you think you'd like to go back to Seattle College in the fall?"

"Yes. But I'm embarrassed. What will I say to people?"

Rose, who was standing at the stove frying eggs, turned and pointed her spatula at Ann. "Never mind what people think. It's your life. You don't owe anyone an explanation."

"I think I probably owe Mrs. Lewis one." Ann was too afraid to ask about the reaction when her father had gone to tell everyone that the wedding was off. Ann hadn't stayed around to find out. She'd gone straight to the car, where she'd waited for Aunt Rose, Uncle Gary, and her father to return.

"You do what you think is right," her father took a bite of his pancake. After a few more minutes, he checked his watch. "I've got to hit the road. Rose, thank you for your hospitality."

Ann walked outside with her father as he prepared to leave. "Say hello to Sophia for me," Ann said with a teasing smile.

"Sophia?" her father asked. As if he didn't know to whom Ann was referring. Then, changing the subject, he said, "You're ready to take your driving test. You should do that soon, while it's still fresh. Maybe Gary would let you use his car ..." And then he was gone.

Ann felt older than she'd ever felt before—and *not* in an unpleasant way.

Yes, she'd gained confidence—matured. But she still needed to decide what would come next. What would her future look like now?

***

A week later, Ann waved goodbye to Rose and Gary as they left for Montana. She'd hidden away in the garden for the past week. Ann had to admit that it was time to get on with her life.

Rose's vegetable garden was looking neat and tidy. Ann, however, was a bit more unkempt. She hadn't washed her hair all week. Ann tucked her disheveled locks under a scarf for the moment. Her hands and fingernails were a mess, as she hadn't worn gloves while working in the dirt.

It was time for a trip to the salon. Ann put on a plaid A-line skirt and paired it with a white cotton blouse. It was the first time in a week she'd worn anything but an old pair of Uncle Gary's overalls. She replaced the scarf on her head with a hat and added some color to her lips with a swipe of Max Factor Rose Red. It would have to do for now.

Unsure of where else to go, Ann decided to return to Alice's Beauty Shop near the Sorrento, the one Helen had introduced her to a few months prior. As she rode the streetcar, Ann nervously glanced around. She didn't want to run into anyone she knew.

Alice, however, was a welcome sight. The hairdresser took one look at Ann when she came through the door and swooshed up to the front of the shop with the air of a fairy godmother about to transform the poor bedraggled girl. "I remember you! Ann, isn't it? How can I help you today?"

"Yes, I'm Ann. You have a good memory! I need a wash n' set and a manicure, please."

Alice directed Ann to a chair by the sink, wrapped a cape around her neck, and tipped her back to begin washing her hair. It felt wonderful. While she worked, Alice kept up a steady stream of chatter. Ann relaxed, knowing that not only would she leave this salon a new woman, but she wouldn't have to answer any questions either.

Ann glanced at her watch when she stepped out of the salon onto the sunny street. It was strange, not having anywhere to be or anyone wondering where she was. It was only two o'clock. She could walk over to the college campus and see if anyone was in the admissions office today. Maybe it wasn't too late to see if she could register for fall classes.

Inside, the building was quiet. It was a stark change from the usual bustle and activity when school was in session. Ann walked down the long hallway until she reached the door that said, Mrs. Prouty, Dean of Women. Should she knock or just go in? Suddenly, Ann's nerves rattled her. Her spur of the moment decision meant that she was going to have to explain what happened.

While she was standing there deciding what to do, Ms. Danson, her math teacher, came out of the dean's office. "Hello, Ann. How are you?"

"Hello, Ms. Danson, I'm well, thank you. Is Mrs. Prouty in today?"

"She is. Go on in. Will we be seeing you again this fall?"

"That's what I'm here to find out."

"Ah. Well, I hope to see you in my classroom again. Have a nice day!"

Mrs. Prouty, having heard overheard the conversation, met Ann at the door. "Ann! What can I do for you?"

"I didn't register for fall because I thought I was moving to Portland, but plans have changed. Would it be too late for me to register at this point?"

"We've had a surge in registrations this year, and our core classes are full, but since you'll be taking upper-level classes, I think we can make it work."

Ann smiled gratefully. Would it really be this easy? Mrs. Prouty didn't even ask about the reason behind her change of plans. No doubt, she'd figured it out. Mrs. Prouty knew about everything that went on with the women at Seattle College.

When Ann walked out of the Admin building, she was, once again, a student at Seattle College.

***

The pile of presents from the wedding shower the Sorrento Girls had given her were in the corner of the guest room at Aunt Rose's house. She would have to deal with them. Their presence was a constant reminder of what she had done. She couldn't keep them. Ann supposed the thing to do would be to package them up and send them back. It would be an enormous task.

I'll start first thing tomorrow morning, but what will I say?

Ann still hadn't heard anything from Paul. She missed him and figured he was probably in Portland by now, as he would be starting his new job soon. She thought about writing him a letter but didn't even know where to begin.

At first, Ann had enjoyed having the house all to herself, but tomorrow would be Independence Day, and for the first time in her life, she'd be spending it alone. It was a depressing thought. *Would it be weird to go to the parade by myself?*

It was almost dinnertime. There wasn't much food left in the house. The garden was looking great, but so far, all that it was producing was lettuce and peas. That wouldn't be enough to eat. The market would be closing soon, so she'd have to hurry.

Questions and plans swirled about her mind as Ann left the house and made her way up the Counterbalance toward the market in the late afternoon heat. She liked her aunt's neighborhood. It had a friendly feel to it. Farther up the hill was Nelson's Quality Grocery. Thankfully, it was still open. Ann picked out some cheese, bread, peaches, coffee, salami, and a copy of *McCall's* magazine.

"We'll be closed tomorrow for the holiday," the matronly woman behind the counter said. "You going to the parade?"

Ann smiled. "I think I might."

"Are you new around here? I haven't seen you before."

"Rose Francis is my aunt. I'm staying with her for a few weeks."

"Ah, yes! Welcome! Rose is a good customer. Here, I baked some carrot cake. Let me wrap up a piece and send it with you—on the house."

There was a phone booth outside the market. A quick call home to her father would be good. Ann was happy to hear her father's voice on the other end of the line. "Hello, Father. I just wanted to wish you a happy Fourth and check in with you. How are you?"

"Hi, Ann! Everything is good here."

"Are you doing anything special tomorrow?"

"I'm taking Sophia for a picnic."

"That's great. You should pick some roses from the backyard and give them to her."

After talking to her father, Ann was glad she'd stayed in Seattle instead of going back to Wenatchee. It wasn't that she didn't miss him, but if she were there, her father would probably spend the holiday with her instead of Sophia. Ann was happy that he was finally dating. He deserved happiness.

She decided to take a different route back after she hung up and left to head back down the hill to her aunt's. Ann wanted to walk by her family's old house and see if it was still vacant.

The old Victorian looked as stately as ever. It sat back from the street with a series of stone steps leading up to the entrance. The green lawn was still neatly clipped. This time, however, there was a red sign in the front yard that announced the house was for sale. Ann wanted to see inside. Maybe there would be an open house soon. One could hope.

Back at Rose and Gary's house, Ann made herself a simple dinner with what she had brought home from the market and sat down at the kitchen table with her plate and her new magazine to keep her company. She didn't like eating by herself.

Today, she'd surprised herself, and she was proud. Had she known that a trip to the salon would have led to her meeting with the Dean of Women at Seattle College and to getting back on track with school, she might have avoided the trip out of embarrassment and fear, but she hadn't allowed herself to back out after making up her mind.

I'm stronger than I knew.

Twenty-Seven

Dear Paul,

I hope this letter finds you well, and I pray that you are enjoying great success with your new job in Portland. There are no adequate words to convey how much I am sorry for the way I ended things. I won't blame you if you choose to never speak to me again. It was wrong of me to wait so long to tell you how I was feeling. I did not want to embarrass you or hurt you. The truth is that I love you. I knew it the day we took that boat ride to Kirkland.

That day when I was standing in the atrium at St. James, waiting to walk down the aisle and become your wife, I knew that it wouldn't be fair to either of us if I continued to pretend that it didn't matter how I was feeling. I don't want to be married unless that marriage is an equal partnership.

To me, that means making big decisions as a team on things like where to live. I don't think I communicated effectively, and for that, I ask for your forgiveness. As much as I love you, I can't be the kind of wife that I believe you want. It isn't any fault of your own. I know my views fall outside what is traditional. I wish I could be that kind of woman for you, but in the end, I knew it would be wrong to spend a lifetime pretending.

I will always remember you with love,
Ann

***

The last of the wedding gifts from the Sorrento Girls were finally in the mail. Ann had saved the most difficult ones until last—those from Peggy, Helen, and Nora. She wished she could have told them all face-to-face. She missed her friends. Ann had been taking an armload of packages to the post office each day until finally, she'd finished. It had been quite a task to track down all the addresses she needed. Some replies were already starting to trickle in, mostly expressing surprise, with a few questioning if she'd be back at Seattle College in the fall. Not wanting to ring up an expensive phone bill for her aunt, Ann had mostly stuck to communicating the old-fashioned way, through the mail. The benefit was that she could choose her words carefully.

Ann hadn't heard back from Paul, and she didn't dare to hope that she would. She was mindful, when people asked, to place the responsibility for the breakup solely upon herself. Paul had been kind to her.

The phone rang while Ann was dusting the front room. "Hello, Ann?" asked a familiar voice. "It's Barbara Delzer."

"Yes, this is Ann. Barbara, how nice to hear from you."

"I wanted to check on you and make sure you were okay. You expressed some doubts to me about the marriage earlier, so I wasn't surprised to hear that you had changed your mind about the wedding. I know it took a great deal of strength to follow through on what you knew was the right thing to do."

How kind of Barbara to call and offer understanding and encouragement. "Thank you. I'm doing okay. I miss Paul. Maybe we should have just had a longer engagement. I don't know. I keep thinking, if I had just talked to him earlier, we might have been able to work out our problems ..."

"Honey, I don't know either. These things are difficult." Barbara paused. "How about we meet for lunch sometime this week? Tuesday, at noon? My treat. How about Top O' the Town at the Sorrento? We can talk more then."

"Yes! That would be wonderful. I've missed you. How are the children?"

"They miss you! We all do. I'll see you on Tuesday. Got to go now. Sally is asking for something."

Could she dare to hope that she might get her old job back?

***

Dear Ann,

Thank you for your letter. Being a reporter for The Oregonian has kept me busy, and the job is satisfying but not nearly as much as I had anticipated. I miss you. I was angry at first, but I have had a lot of time to think. You have my forgiveness, though I think it is I who owes you an apology. I ask for your forgiveness for not considering your feelings more. I see now, how presumptuous my actions were. I messed up. You tried to tell me how you felt, and I didn't listen. I did not work hard enough to find a job in Seattle, and I was selfish. How I wish I could go back and do it all differently.

I will always love you. Though it was a painful experience to be left at the altar, I have nothing but respect for you.

Based on the return address of your last letter, I assume you are still living in Seattle. Are you returning to Seattle College this fall? I hope so. You will be an excellent teacher one day.
With love,
Paul

***

The letter dropped to the floor. Ann grabbed a handkerchief. She wasn't one to cry often, but his words and his kindness were a balm to her broken heart, and she was suddenly very emotional. What now? He had asked her about school. Did that mean he wanted her to write back? Would that be wise? Wasn't a clean break healthier for both of them? She didn't know. Ann tucked the letter away in her hatbox. She would wait to decide what to do.

Today was Tuesday. With a quick glance in the mirror, Ann applied a touch of powder to her nose and smoothed her hair. She needed to leave soon if she wanted to make it on time to meet Mrs. Delzer at the restaurant. Ann was excited to be returning to the hotel, if only for lunch, and she was even more happy to be meeting with a friend. Living alone for the past three weeks had been lonely. She was ready for some company.

Andy, the doorman, gave Ann a big smile when she came through the front door of the

Sorrento. "Miss Brooks! Welcome back. Are you checking in?"

"I'm just meeting a friend upstairs today. It's good to see you, Andy. I've missed this place. What's new?"

"Well, it has been pretty quiet around here without the students around."

"Enjoy the peace while you can. We'll be back before you know it!" Ann was sitting in her favorite spot by the fireplace, feeling like she was at home again, when Mrs. Delzer came through the front door and spotted her. "I have so much to tell you," Ann said when she saw her friend.

"You sure do. I want to hear everything," Barbara said with a sympathetic nod.

While they dined on Waldorf salad, Ann did her best to recount the events of the past month. She even told Barbara about the letter she'd received from Paul, just that morning. "What do you think I should do?" she asked.

"Hmm ... I guess, maybe a quick, cordial response wouldn't hurt. But be careful. You've both been through so much heartache. You need time to heal."

Ann appreciated the advice, but she was starting to feel uncomfortable with the conversation centering on her, so she switched topics. "You know, I saw a place in Portland called

Jantzen Beach that looked like fun. There's a huge roller coaster. Have you ever been there with the children?"

"No, but I've heard of it. It's a place I'd like to take them. I'm afraid we probably won't be able to take our usual vacation this August. Mr. Delzer has a new project at work that's keeping him busy. They're down to a bare-bones staff at his company right now, trying to cut expenses. I'm just thankful he's still got a job."

There wasn't a person who'd not been touched by the economic fiascos of the past ten years. Ann learned while they chatted that Mrs. Delzer had not hired another mother's helper after her departure. Her friend was probably cutting back on her staff and expenses as well. Ann didn't ask about coming back, either, knowing that to do so might cause embarrassment.

"I hope you know that I would be happy to watch the children every once in a while, when you need a break, strictly on a volunteer basis—as a friend. You know I miss them, and it would be a pleasure."

"You're a dear, Ann." Barbara smiled gratefully. "I hope you know that you're welcome in our home anytime."

While riding the streetcar back to her aunt's house, Ann thought about the people in her life that she'd come to know over the past year. Some, like Mrs. Delzer, had been like angels sent from heaven. God was watching out for her.

***

Dear Paul,

I am overwhelmed with gratitude for the kindness and understanding you communicated in your last letter. Thank you. In answer to your questions—yes, I'm still in Seattle. I have been house-sitting for my aunt over the past few weeks. I have had a lot of time to read and work in the garden. I will be returning to Seattle College in the fall after a short visit back to Wenatchee.

I went to the library yesterday, and I saw the article you wrote in The Oregonian about the riots. It was very well written. Portland is lucky to have you.
Sincerely,
Ann

***

Dear Ann,

My sweet, dear friend! You did not need to send back the mixing bowls. My goodness, I was surprised when I received your letter. You have my full sympathy and support for what I know must have been a tough decision to make. That must have created quite some drama! I want to hear all about it. But seriously, it was better to call it off when you did then to get married, knowing it was wrong. Selfishly, I'm rather glad to find out you'll be sticking around.

I'm excited to see you when school starts! You are coming back to school. Right?
Your friend,
Helen
p.s. Do you have a roommate yet?

Twenty-Eight

The fall of 1939 started much like the previous one. Helen and Ann were roommates, once again, as were Nora and Peggy. They'd quickly resumed their comfortable routine of gathering in each other's rooms to gossip, listen to the radio, and get ready together before going out on the weekends. It was Friday night. They were all going to a dance held at the school.

Ann was arranging Nora's hair for her when the music they were listening to suddenly stopped, interrupted by a news bulletin. The German army had attacked Poland. The announcer talked about the possibility of a large-scale conflict throughout Europe.

"That's awful!" Helen said as she walked over to the radio and moved the dial. "But I don't want to hear about that tonight. What else is on?"

"Let's put on a record instead. I have a new Billie Holiday one that I haven't played for you yet. I'll go get it from my room," Nora said.

Ann put the last of the pins she was using into Nora's hair. "Done! You're ready for a night of dancing." She twirled Nora around so she could see the mirror.

"I love it! Thank you!" Nora said, admiring her reflection. "Hold on, ladies. I'll be right back."

"Ann, let me do your hair for you tonight." Peggy gestured toward the chair. "Here, sit down. My Marcel Waver is hot. I'll give you some waves."

"Do you think there will be another war in Europe?" Ann asked as she sat down. She was still thinking about the news bulletin.

Peggy shrugged. "I don't know. I hope not. I don't think we'll get involved though, even if there is." Peggy leaned against the front of the dressing table. "By the way, I got a letter from Joe today. They're sending him to Hawaii. It sounds like a vacation to me."

"Oh, yeah? Are you two still staying in touch?" Ann asked.

"We are." Peggy smiled. "He writes such sweet letters."

Ann thought about Paul. Would she ever hear from him again?

***

The next day, Saturday, Ann woke up early. She was ready to get back to her volunteer work at the soup kitchen. They weren't expecting her, but hopefully they'd welcome her help and have a place for her. Did Mr. Ferguson already know about her broken engagement? He was, after all, friends with Mrs. Lewis.

At school, she hadn't needed to do nearly as much explaining as she'd dreaded. Word traveled fast. Most people didn't say anything directly to her, but she knew they were talking, and she could feel their stares when she passed by. She was no longer writing for *The Spectator*. It was too uncomfortable.

Ann walked down Fourth Avenue, past the University Bookstore. It was still closed at this early hour, but she paused to peek in the window. Her aunt's book was due to be released any day now, and Ann had been keeping an eye on the store, excited to see it in print for the first time. Quickly scanning the display, Ann nearly moved on, but then she saw it—*A History of Cathedrals in Great Britain* by Rose Fairbanks

Francis. There it was! Ann was so proud of her aunt. She couldn't wait to get her hands on that book and to congratulate Rose.

Just then, Mr. Ferguson approached. "Hello, Ann! What a pleasant surprise to see you here."

"Hello, Mr. Ferguson. That's my aunt Rose's book!" Ann couldn't contain her excitement.

"Look at that! How wonderful. You must be so proud of her," he said with a smile. "I'm headed to the soup kitchen."

Ann smiled. "So am I." The two walked on, together, the rest of the way. Ann was grateful for the opportunity to explain her unexpected presence to Mr. Ferguson in private before they reached the soup kitchen. He was kind and supportive, just as she knew he'd be.

"I'm sorry," he said.

"So am I," Ann said, unable to completely hide the sadness in her tone. "But life goes on."

"Yes, it does, and I know your help will be welcome at the soup kitchen. Everyone will be happy to see you."

The rest of the morning, Ann stayed busy making coffee and cleaning tables. It was good to feel useful.

On the way home, she stopped by the bookshop and bought a copy of Rose's book. She made sure to tell the sales clerk that the author was her aunt.

***

"Pete Haskins asked me if I could introduce him to you today," Helen said on Monday night.

Ann, who was putting her clothes away in the closet, stopped and laughed. "Oh? I'm not interested in dating right now if that's what he means."

"He's a nice guy, Ann, and cute too! You're not engaged anymore. It's time to get out there and have some fun!"

"I don't want any distractions. I'm trying to finish school a year early, so I've got an extra full load of classes." She was doing it to save money.

"Okay. Fine. But will you still let me introduce you if I make it clear that you're just interested in being friends?"

Ann studied her friend, knowing Helen was going to keep asking until she relented. "All right. When?"

"Tomorrow. Meet us for ice cream at Jack Frost after school. Four o'clock."

"Helen, I don't know ..." Ann sighed, not wanting to say yes, but not wanting to seem like a stick in the mud either. "Okay."

"Great! I didn't want it to be awkward. I'm meeting Pete's friend, Andrew, there. I think I like him, but I don't know ..."

"Ha! I get it. Listen. I'll be your chaperone, but not Peter's date!"

"You're the best, Ann!"

Ann just rolled her eyes and sat down at the desk. "I've got some studying to do."

***

September must be the most beautiful month of all in Seattle. Ann took off the cardigan she was wearing and put it over her shoulders. It felt like a perfect late summer day. As she walked from her science class toward the Sorrento, she remembered her promise to meet Helen at Jack Frost that day.

The ice cream shop was crowded, as usual, when Ann arrived. It was a favorite hangout for the students at Seattle College. Every one of the red vinyl booths was full. She spotted Helen toward the back.

Her friend looked up and waved. "Hi, Ann! Andrew, Pete, hello!"

Ann turned around to see the two students—Andrew and Pete—who had just arrived behind her. Andrew wore a Chieftain letterman jacket and an adorable, friendly smile. Probably a basketball player, judging from his height. Pete had red hair, freckles, and glasses. His shy smile was endearing.

Introductions were made, and they all squeezed into the booth. Ann ordered a cherry lemon sour and relaxed. Helen was enjoying herself. Both Pete and Andrew were charming company, and it seemed both men were vying for Helen's attention alone. Ann didn't need to worry.

Several booths away, a couple of guys that Ann used to work with on *The Spectator* were watching her. They were Paul's friends. It probably appeared like she was on a date. What did it matter? But still, she hoped they wouldn't say anything.

After an hour, it was time to say goodbye. Ann couldn't help but tease Helen a little on the walk home. "Pete wanted to meet me, huh? I don't think he took his eyes off you the entire time. I'd be jealous if it weren't for the fact that I've decided to swear off all dating for a year."

Helen gasped. "A year! Oh, honey, no. Why? Are you still in love with Paul?"

"I'll always love him, but I did the right thing. I know I did. Still, it will take me awhile to get over the loss."

"I get that. But promise me you'll let yourself have some fun this year too."

Ann laughed. "I promise!"

"So, what did you think of Andrew? Cute?"

"Definitely. I think you should give him a chance."

It was time to get ready for dinner when the women got back to the Sorrento. Ann stopped by the front desk and picked up her mail. Glancing through it, she saw there was a letter from Paul. She could feel her heart racing as she took a deep breath and tucked the envelope into her handbag. It would have to wait. She wanted to be alone when she read it.

Twenty-Nine

Dear Ann,

Thank you for your kind words about my article. Are you still writing for the school newspaper? I miss those days of working together on The Spectator. I miss our friendship. I miss you.

My time at The Oregonian was short-lived, as my last day on the job will be tomorrow. I never even got around to furnishing the apartment. I used a sleeping bag on the floor the whole time I was there. I've accepted a position as a reporter with the Associated Press. I will be working out of the New York office. My current boss is the person I have to thank for setting it all up. He recommended me, nice guy. He said the experience would do me some good and that I'd be welcome back anytime. The new job will involve a lot of travel, which has always been something I've wanted to do —see the world. With the war in Europe, there will be a lot of stories to tell.

I will send you an address where you can reach me, as soon as I know what it is. I hope you'll write.
Love,
Paul

***

Ann sat on the edge of her bed in stunned silence after reading the letter. He was moving on. She knew she should be happy for him. It was, no doubt, a dream job for Paul, and she was happy, sort of—but it also sounded dangerous. Then there was the final sentence. *I hope you'll write.*

Yes, I'll write back. And she would pray for his safety. Every day.

When Helen returned to the room later that night, Ann kept the news to herself. She knew her friend would have questions. Ann had her own. Was it normal to be corresponding with an ex-fiancé? Was their relationship being rekindled? Was it wrong to want something like that? She didn't know the answers. Ann only knew that she felt a tender happiness and a growing sense of hope.

***

Mrs. Lewis was at Mass on Sunday, settled in near the front. Ann was sitting with her friends in the back when she noticed her. It was right after the "Kyrie Eleison." Elegant, as always, Elizabeth Lewis was unmistakable, even from behind. There she was, her white hair perfectly coiffed under a small purple hat.

Ann's pulse quickened, and a dizzy feeling came over her. She'd only seen Paul's grandmother at St. James on one other occasion in all the time she'd been attending, and never, since the day she'd walked away from her wedding. Of course, this had always been a possibility, one that had nearly prompted Ann to return to First Presbyterian, for good. In the end, Ann had decided to stick with her commitment as a Catechumen. She wanted to continue what she had started.

Not sure if Mrs. Lewis had seen her, Ann's thoughts raced through various scenarios of how it might go when, or if, she came face to face with the woman who would have been her grandmother-in-law. Ann nudged Helen and wordlessly used her eyes to communicate her current predicament, nodding toward the place where Mrs. Lewis was seated.

Helen's eyes widened with shock when she realized what Ann was showing her. "What are you going to do?" Helen whispered.

"I guess, I'll just say hello."

"You could sneak out …"

"There's more chance of her seeing me if I do that—and then she'll know, for sure, that I'm purposely avoiding her."

"You didn't do anything wrong. People call off weddings every day."

Ann appreciated her friend's attempt at making her feel better. She gave Helen a wry smile, which soon turned into a stifled laugh. No, Ann didn't do anything wrong, but the absurdity of the latter part of that statement was too funny. Yes, maybe people called off weddings, every once in a while—but she certainly didn't know anyone else who had run away, like she had, right before they were set to walk down the aisle.

Helen looked at Ann, and recognizing the humor of it, covered her mouth to keep from giggling herself. "I'm glad you can smile about it now!"

It felt good to laugh about it. Ann squeezed Helen's hand. *I can handle this situation with grace.* Mrs. Lewis was a lady of dignity and good manners. There was no need to worry about her saying anything ugly, even if the woman did have resentment toward her, and Ann wouldn't blame her if she did.

Ann had never wanted to hurt her grandson. Yet, she had. But Mrs. Lewis wasn't the type to air her grievances in public. The thing was, Ann didn't want Mrs. Lewis to think badly of her. She respected the woman too much. If there were any ill feelings against her, Ann would try to make it right.

When the service was over, Ann didn't hurry away from the church to avoid Paul's grandmother. Instead, she lingered near the door. When Mrs. Lewis walked out into the sunshine of that September morning, Ann nervously nodded and smiled at the woman. "Hello, Mrs. Lewis. It's lovely to see you."

"Ann! How wonderful to see you, dear. How are you?" Elizabeth Lewis offered nothing but warmth as she reached out and took Ann's hand.

"Very well, thank you, and you?" It wasn't the time or place to go beyond basic pleasantries.

"Excellent," Mrs. Lewis said with a nod and a smile. "I must go. My driver is waiting, but I'm pleased to see you. You look well. Have a wonderful day." And with that, she continued walking down the front steps toward her car. The potentially awkward encounter was over, and all was well.

Ann breathed a deep sigh of relief.

***

It was October before Ann heard from Paul again. He'd barely landed in New York before being sent on assignment to London. England had declared war on Germany, but so far, much to Ann's relief, there had been no military action. Paul's latest letter was short and newsy, but he signed it, *love*. She wasn't sure what to make of the unanswered questions of where this relationship stood, which suited her just fine. Paul was busy, enjoying his new job, and Ann was also working hard—with an extra full load of classes. She was content with focusing on school and corresponding with Paul through the mail.

Ann was on her way to the science building—her thoughts on Paul—on a Friday morning when she happened upon Pete, the basketball player from the ice cream shop that Helen had tried to set her up with.

He grinned, waved, and pushed up his glasses when he saw her. "Hey, Ann! How are you?" he said, falling into step beside her.

"Pete! Hello. Are you coming to game night at the Sorrento tonight? We need a Scrabble rematch."

"Oh? Sure. What time is it?" Pete was the only person who had ever beat Ann at the game, and she was determined to win back her bragging rights as the champion Scrabble player among the friends who'd been meeting in the Fireside Room on Friday nights.

"Seven o'clock."

"I'll be there. Then you'll know my win wasn't just a fluke," Pete teased. "Do you have a class in this building?"

Ann laughed. "We'll see about that. And yes, I do. Biology."

"That's my major! If you ever want any help, just let me know."

"Thanks! I'll probably take you up on that. This is my room," Ann said, gesturing to the nearest door. "I'll see you later."

***

After dinner, the Fireside Room began to fill up with students. Small groups started to organize around tables, starting board games such as Monopoly, Scrabble, chess, and Sorry. The Fireside Room at the Sorrento had become a favorite place for students to meet. It was usually crowded, and tonight was no exception.

Coming down from the dining room with her friends, Ann glanced about and decided she probably had time to run upstairs and write a quick letter to Paul. "Nora, can you please save me a seat at the Scrabble table? And maybe one for my friend Pete too? I'll be right back. I have to get something in the mail before the morning pickup."

It was nearly eight before Ann came back downstairs. She'd lost track of time. Walking into the lobby to drop her letter off at the front desk, Ann saw Andrew and Pete come in through the front door together. Pete waited for Ann while she exchanged the outgoing message for her incoming mail. There was just one letter. The return address on the small crisp envelope indicated it was from Elizabeth Lewis. Ann opened it quickly, curious as to its contents. It was an invitation to tea next Saturday at three.

"That's curious," Ann said, to no one in particular.

"Oh? Tell me!" Pete said, before turning red and apologizing. "Sorry. I'm nosy. Never mind."

Ann looked at Pete, considering. She wanted to tell someone. She'd remained secretive around her girlfriends about the correspondence with Paul, embarrassed at the thought of them thinking of her as fickle. Pete was a neutral friend in all of this. He didn't even know Paul.

"It's an invitation to tea with my ex-fiancé's grandmother."

"Wow, this sounds like a story I need to hear," Pete said, raising an eyebrow.

Ann tucked the letter into her skirt pocket and laughed. "I'll tell you. But first, let's see if we can still get a place at the table for Scrabble." Her friends had probably started without them after all this time.

The tables were full, so Ann and Pete found a spot near the fireplace and waited for the next round. Pete turned to Ann. "Okay, now tell me everything. You have an ex-fiancé? And why is his grandmother summoning you to tea?"

Pete was a good listener. Ann told him everything. They forgot about playing Scrabble, and instead, talked for hours. People noticed, and she could surmise what they were thinking, but Ann didn't care.

***

Tea was served in the library at Mrs. Lewis's home on Saturday. Ann sat nervously on the edge of her chair, ankles crossed, hands in her lap, feeling like a child summoned to the principal's office. Ordinarily, Ann thought she was good at reading people, but Elizabeth Lewis had always been the exception to that rule. She had no idea what was about to transpire.

The fireplace held a warm crackling fire that gave the grand room a hint of coziness, in spite of the grand scale of the vaulted ceiling and the imposing stone gargoyles that flanked each side of the French doors. Paul's grandmother sat across from Ann. She took a sip of tea from a delicate china cup and watched as Pepper, her butler, opened the curtains. The action did very little to lighten the darkness. Outside, the rain poured down in sheets from a steel-gray sky.

When Pepper left, Elizabeth set down her teacup and nodded at Ann, her eyes serious. "Ann, dear, I invited you here today because I wanted to clear the air. I want you to know that as far as I'm concerned, there are no hard feelings. I want the best for both you and Paul."

Ann felt every part of her relax at that moment. She realized then that she could trust, from then on, that Paul's grandmother was one of the kindest, most forgiving, and open-hearted individuals she knew. She was happy for Paul that he had someone like Mrs. Lewis on his side.

Thirty

The gymnasium was hot, crowded, and noisy. The tension was thick. The Seattle Chieftains were tied with the Italian Athletic Club 15-15 in the last two minutes of the game. Ann and Nora had both become basketball fans that season. They were at every home game. Ann started going because Pete had asked her to, and as his friend, she thought it was a supportive gesture. He was the team's power forward. A talented and upcoming star, he had plenty of fans to cheer him on at the games, but Ann knew her presence meant something to him.

They'd developed a close friendship over the past few months, linked by a shared sense of humor and an easy rapport, along with some commonalities in their backgrounds. Pete, like

Ann, came from Eastern Washington, and he'd also been raised around the orchards. Most people at the school thought they were dating, but it wasn't like that. Pete was more like a brother, and he saw her in a similar light. It was nice to have an escort to the dances without the pressure of dating. She was receiving letters from Paul and writing back—and she'd finally let Peggy, Nora, and Helen in on the secret.

Pete had the ball. The clock was running out. He reached up and took his shot. Swoosh. Into the net. The crowd went wild. The buzzer went off, and the tension was gone. The Chieftains had won!

After the game, Pete and a couple of his friends were coming by the Sorrento to hang out. There would be a jazz band playing that night in the Fireside Room. Ann and Nora decided to wait around and walk back with Pete and his friends rather than alone. The streets were dark and icy, and the girls were both wearing entirely inappropriate footwear for the weather.

Exuberant from the recent win, the group came into the lobby of the hotel laughing and pink-cheeked from the cold air. Ann was still clutching Pete's arm as she had been doing on the walk back. He'd managed to keep her from falling, in spite of the flimsy saddle shoes she'd been wearing. Sitting in a chair by the elevator, much to Ann's surprise, sat Paul. Handsome as ever. Ann's heart skipped a beat when she saw him. He'd been waiting for her. The expression on his face when he saw her with Pete was unmistakable. He'd misunderstood everything.

Ann stopped in her tracks. "Excuse me, everyone. I'll meet up with you later."

Paul stood and greeted Ann stiffly. "Hello. Sorry to interrupt. I was hoping to talk to you for a moment."

"I'm so happy to see you! I didn't know you were back in Seattle. When did you return?" It was then that Ann noticed how sad and tired Paul appeared. He had dark circles under his eyes, and his skin was pale.

"It's my grandmother. She passed away last week. Peacefully. In her sleep. There will be a memorial service on Monday. I thought you might like to know."

Ann gasped. "I'm so sorry, Paul. I'll be there." She reached out to hug him, but Paul stepped back.

"Thank you. I know she cared about you." Paul gave a weak smile. "I need to go now. Have a good evening." Then he walked out the front door.

Ann had thought often over the past months about what it would be like to see Paul again. She'd missed him. This situation was not how she'd imagined it.

***

Elizabeth Lewis's memorial service was on Monday, January 15, 1940, at St. James Cathedral. She had lived a full and productive life until the age of ninety-five. A widow for the last twenty-five years, she remained, until her final days, a powerful scion of Seattle society. She had marched with the Suffragettes, and much to Ann's surprise and delight, had been one of the organizers behind Amelia Earhart's 1933 visit to Seattle—the very one that had also first brought Ann to Seattle as a wide-eyed fourteen-year-old.

Ann credited that experience as one that had set a course for where she was today. It had inspired her. Ann read about Paul's grandmother in the program she had been given as she'd entered the sanctuary. She realized that the woman hadn't talked about herself much. Ann wished that she could have had more time to get to know her better. On the back of the program was a quote that Ann thought was quite fitting in the way it described Elizabeth Lewis.

"A single act of kindness throws out roots in all directions, and the roots spring up and make new trees. The greatest work that kindness does to others is that it makes them kind themselves."
~ Amelia Earhart

Ann sat by herself toward the back. She planned on blending in with the large crowd of mourners who had come to pay their last respects to Mrs. Lewis. Paul was sitting in the front with his family, and she'd give him his space today. They could talk later. Hopefully, Ann would be able to clear up any misunderstanding. She hadn't stopped thinking about the look on his face when he'd seen her with Pete. It played out like a bad record stuck on repeat.

The service was lovely but sad. Ann knew this loss had deeply hurt Paul. She could see him sitting next to his parents. The two of them had disconnected from him long ago, so caught up in their problems that they'd been oblivious to the fact that they had a son, a son who still loved them but had ceased expecting anything in return. As far as his family was concerned, Paul seemed very much alone now. His grandmother had been a steady rock in his life. Even Ann had let him down.

***

It wasn't until Monday afternoon that Ann saw Paul again. He'd left a message for her at the Sorrento, inviting her to meet him for coffee at a diner on Madison street. Ann arrived first. She sat in a booth near the window and watched as people passed by clutching umbrellas, stepping over puddles, and tucking books underneath coats, trying to avoid the downpour that had been consistent for the past week.

Arriving ten minutes late, Paul apologized as he slid into the booth across from Ann. He took off his hat and set it next to him on the seat, smiling at the waitress at the same time as she walked over to take their order. That smile could make any girl melt. It had certainly worked on Ann, and now she wanted that warmth directed at her again.

"Two coffees, please, black. Thank you," Paul said.

He knew the way she liked her coffee, her favorite flowers—pink roses—and the meaning of countless little things, like the way she straightened up to her full height and raised her left eyebrow when she was holding back on something she wanted to say.

And she knew him. He was, above all, a gentleman, and he would never be anything but cordial with her, even if he were upset. But when he spoke in staccato sentences and bit the bottom corner of his lip like he was doing now, something was wrong. They shared some of the same reserved Nordic character traits common among those in the Pacific Northwest.

Ann was sitting as if an invisible string was pulling her toward the ceiling.

After the waitress poured some coffee and left, Ann took a deep breath. She'd be honest, speak her mind, and explain the best she could. "I'm not sure where we stand right now, but I know when I open a letter from you and read your words, it's the best part of my day. I know we've both moved on from the hurt of our failed engagement and that something new seemed to be happening with us. I want you to know that I don't have feelings for anyone else but you. Pete —the guy you saw me with—is just a friend."

"I'm not sure what to think." Paul looked down at his coffee and swirled it in the cup. "I'm due back in New York on Wednesday. I have a plane to catch tomorrow. I'd heard the rumors about you and the basketball player before I saw you with him. People said you'd moved on. I didn't want to believe it. But then again, we're not even dating, so why should I care?"

"Would you like to meet him? Would you like to meet Pete? Would that help?"

"I don't have time right now. There's a lot of business I need to attend to before I leave tomorrow," Paul said. Then his forehead furrowed, as though he were rethinking her invitation. "Thank you. I'm sure he's a nice guy."

Ann sensed that Paul needed some time to think and that now wasn't the time for him to shake hands with Pete over a cup of coffee. All she could do was wait. Changing the subject, she asked about his job.

"The bureau brought me back from London two weeks ago because there wasn't much happening. Some in England are calling it the "phony war." I'm glad I was back in New York when I got the news about my grandma, though, or I wouldn't have been able to make it home on time for her service. I'll find out what my new assignment is when I get back to New York."

"Do you enjoy traveling?"

"I do. It's certainly more interesting than what I was writing about in Portland."

Ann already knew this, as it was something he'd written about in his letters. She was stalling for time and trying to ease the awkwardness of the conversation. "Well, thank you for meeting me here today. It's good to see you again, and I'm sorry it's not under different circumstances. I had tea with your grandma a few months ago.

Did she tell you that? She was a lovely lady, and it meant a great deal to me that she would be so kind-hearted toward me after what happened."

Paul's face relaxed, and a faint smile appeared. "Yes, she told me. I'll drive you back to the Sorrento now if you like."

When Ann said goodbye, she wondered if she was doing so for the last time.

***

On Valentine's Day, Ann did her best to pretend that it didn't bother her at all, seeing many of her friends receive flowers and candy when she didn't. She checked for new mail every day, but she hadn't heard anything from Paul since their meeting at the diner. When he dropped her off that day to say goodbye, he was polite but cool.

Ann was studying in her room when Helen entered, returning from her afternoon classes. "Here, I picked up your mail for you," she said, placing a postcard on the desk. It was from Paul. On the front was a picture of the Statue of Liberty. On the back was a short note scribbled in his familiar messy style.

Dear Ann,

They're sending me back to London for the next few months. I hope all is well in Seattle.
-Paul

That was it. Ann was disappointed. Helen, who was fixing her hair in the mirror, saw in the reflection, the disappointment on Ann's face as she dropped the postcard. She didn't ask her to explain. Instead, Helen put down her brush, opened a drawer, and took out a chocolate bar. She handed it to Ann with a gentle smile.

Thirty-One

Apple blossoms sweetly scented the warm spring air, and the white flowers drifted about like confetti. Ann was taking Noel for a walk around the irrigation canals on her first morning back in Wenatchee for spring break. It was hard to deny that her dog was slowing down with age. Their pace was slow, but there was no rush. The whole day was free.

It had been a busy semester, and Ann was tired. She had thrown herself into her classes and her volunteer work at the soup kitchen, welcoming any distraction, which helped her forget the ache she felt whenever she thought of Paul. After receiving his postcard, Ann hadn't written back. As little as the last note had said, the message had seemed clear enough. Paul had said goodbye. This time, most likely, for good.

As far as Ann knew, Paul was still in London. The reports from Europe were getting uglier with each passing day. Germany did not stop with the invasion of Poland. Norway and Denmark were now occupied too. But so far, England seemed safe.

When Ann circled back around toward where her father's truck was parked, she lifted Noel and put her in the cab. Her father had given her use of the vehicle today, and she had promised to practice her driving on the private country roads around the orchards he managed. She had been ready last summer to take her test, but those plans had been forgotten after she'd called off the wedding. Her driving skills were a little rusty, but it was time. She'd get her license this week while she was home in Wenatchee.

The engine sputtered a bit, and the gears made an awful sound when Ann had trouble shifting, but it didn't take long before she got the hang of it. Driving past her neighbor's house, she spotted Marty outside, sitting in a rocker on his porch. He waved when he saw her and grinned. Marty, who had always seemed old to Ann, was an affable, toothless giant of a man, and a perpetual bachelor. He was also a pilot.

When Ann was younger, he took her for thrilling rides in his biplane, a yellow De Havilland Tiger Moth he used for crop dusting.

Ann had loved the feeling of peering over the valley from high above, and she'd imagined herself as her Amelia Earhart, fearless and brave.

When she reached the end of the dusty road, she turned around and decided to stop at Marty's to say hello. It had been a long time. After parking the truck at the end of his long driveway, Ann got out with Noel and greeted Marty's old basset hound, Hank.

"Marty! How are you?" Ann asked, walking toward the porch.

Marty reached into an icebox that was next to him and offered a Coke to Ann. "Isn't this a nice surprise! I'm hanging in there, dear. Is college in the big city going well? How's life treating you?"

Ann gratefully took the Coke and settled into the empty rocking chair next to Marty. For the next hour, they sat together, gazing toward the road, catching up on each other's news. She told him about Paul, the broken engagement, letters, the misunderstanding, and the silence that had ensued afterward. When it was time to go, Ann hugged Marty and said goodbye. "I'll see you around," she said.

"I'm proud of you, girl. You're a strong one. You've always known what you wanted, and I've always thought you'd go far. Maybe you should think about sending that boy another letter. It sounds like bad timing has been part of your problems. Don't give up." Marty was never shy about sharing his thoughts. He patted the hood of the truck after he finished giving his advice, like a judge with a gavel.

***

Sophia, the new neighbor, popped over from her house next door and joined Ann and her father for dinner that night. They shared a chicken pot pie that Ann's father had prepared (he was becoming a much better cook in Ann's absence) along with some strawberry shortcake that Sophia had brought over.

Ann liked Sophia. She could tell her father did too. The woman's friendly chatter was a welcome addition to the dinner table. It soon became apparent that the two neighbors enjoyed Saturday evening meals together regularly. Sophia had been a teacher years ago, and Ann was interested in learning more about her experiences. The group lingered at the table long after dinner was over, enjoying each other's company. When it started to get dark outside, Sophia offered to take the plates to the kitchen and make some tea.

Smiling at her father, Ann told him she thought his neighbor was pretty. Embarrassed, he pretended not to hear.

***

Ann returned to Seattle the next week with a feeling of fresh resolve to finish the school year strong. With the extra credits she'd picked up last semester, she was past the halfway point to getting her degree. She was well-rested from her vacation, and she'd also managed to accomplish something she was proud of in her time away. Ann now had in her possession, a new driver's license. She was too frugal to spend any money from her trust on a car, even though her Aunt Rose had assured her it was fine. But she liked knowing she could if she needed to. The streetcars worked just fine for now.

The romance advice from her neighbor, Marty, had been considered, and Ann decided she'd write one more letter to Paul before giving up on the idea of a reconciliation. She tried not to think about the fact that this advice was coming from an older man who didn't seem to have a whole lot of experience in the romance area. She was ready to throw caution to the wind.

The outside terrace on the seventh floor at the Sorrento sounded like an excellent place to sit and write. It was a beautiful, warm, sunny day, so Ann gathered up her books, pens, paper, and sunglasses from her room before going upstairs to find a comfortable lounge chair. The only other person on the terrace that day was Peggy, who seemed to have had the same idea. Peggy was always writing letters to Joe, who was still stationed in Hawaii. They'd gotten engaged on New Year's Day that year, while Joe was home for a visit.

"Peggy, hello! Mind if I join you?" Ann asked.

Peggy looked up and smiled, patting the chair next to her. "Ann! Of course not, sit down!"

Ann wondered if Peggy and Joe had hit any bumps in the road throughout their long-distance romance, but she didn't ask. The two women sat next to another in companionable silence, each with their thoughts focused on the men they loved, who were thousands of miles away.

When Ann was finished writing, she said a prayer and hoped for the best. She wasn't even sure of where to send the letter. Paul might be in New York by now. She'd send the note there. Hopefully, somehow, it would reach him.

***

In May, Ann received a reply from Paul.

Dear Ann,

I'm writing to let you know that I'm still in London, but I received your letter. It was the best thing ever. I love you. My beautiful girl, you fill my thoughts always. Life without you is not a life I want. I'm sorry for not writing sooner. I let common sense get away from me, and I convinced myself after seeing you last time that the hope I had for us, for a future with you, wasn't real.

You told me I was wrong, and I believe you. Work has kept me busy. I miss you, and I eagerly anticipate hearing from you again.
With all my love,
Paul
p.s. Please send me a picture of you.

***

"One more week!" Helen plopped onto her bed with a dramatic sigh. The women had been preparing for their class finals, and they were all tired from the extra studying. It was Saturday night, and Peggy, Nora, and Ann were all crammed around the mirror in Ann and Helen's room, making final touch-ups to their hair and makeup before they all headed out together for the last dance of the school year.

Ann finished applying her lipstick and moved away from the mirror, making room for Helen. She was ready to go. Picking the newspaper off her desk, Ann scanned the headlines while waiting for her friends to finish up. She had been following the news in Europe more closely since Paul had been assigned to the AP London office. The mail service was excruciatingly slow, so staying current on world events was Ann's way to reassure herself that Paul was okay. He was embedded with the British Expeditionary Forces, who, until recently, hadn't seen a lot of action.

Ann hadn't heard from him in several weeks. In the last few days, some stories about a large contingent of B.E.F. and the French troops began appearing in the papers. It was less than reassuring. German forces trapped the Allied soldiers on the coast of France near a place called Dunkirk. Today's headline read, "B.E.F. Evacuation is Proceeding | Withdrawal Battle Raging." Ann prayed for the safety of those men (she prayed a lot lately), and she did her best to convince herself that Paul was working in London, or even better, on his way back to New York.

"Don't worry so much. He's okay," Peggy said, observing Ann. "We're going to have fun tonight!" Peggy's compassionate tone and smile offered some comfort to Ann. If anyone understood how she felt, it was Peggy.

"You're right. I'm sure he is. I need to quit reading the papers so much."

***

Ann's father was waiting in the lobby for her. He had driven to Seattle to pick her up from the Sorrento and take her home for the summer. Giving Helen a big hug, she said goodbye and looked around the room one last time. Knowing she was coming back in the fall made this departure a lot easier than the one she'd faced in the previous year. But the trade-off had been painful. She missed Paul. And she was still waiting for news that he was safe.

Ann stopped by the front desk one last time to turn in her key and check for any mail.

"This came for you, miss," the desk clerk said as he handed her a letter.

Relief poured over her. The bright blue and white border of the envelope told her everything she needed to know before she even saw the return address. It was from London—from Paul.

Her father helped Ann with her luggage, and he raised a questioning eyebrow when he saw the letter in her hands.

"I have a lot to tell you!" Ann said as she kissed him on the cheek.

In the car, Ann told her father everything. He didn't seem as surprised as she thought he'd be.

"I'm happy for you," he said. "I've got some news as well. Sophia and I are getting married before you go back to school."

"Oh! That's great! I knew it!" Ann felt light and happy. It was turning out to be a good day.

After some time, when the conversation had finally died down, Ann opened the letter from Paul and read it. It was dated May 2, 1940—an entire month ago. As usual, he downplayed the dangers of his location. He loved his job, he missed her, and he expected to come home for a visit sometime in September. Ann would have to try hard not to wish the summer away. She couldn't wait to see him.

Thirty-Two

For the rest of the summer, Ann worked with her father in the orchards. She picked and sorted cherries throughout June. It was tedious and hard work, which only made Ann feel more grateful for the opportunity she'd been given to go to college. She loved the valley she'd grown up in, and Ann enjoyed spending time with her father outside, but she could do without the aching arms and sore back at the end of each day.

Ann's father reminded her that she didn't need to be working so hard and that she could go home and relax, but she persisted. She tried to stay busy because it was the only way she could take her mind off the worry Ann felt when she thought of Paul being in a war zone.

By July, the peaches were ready to be harvested, and Ann got to work on picking those. The news from Europe was disturbing. Italy had joined the war with Germany. Norway, Belgium, Holland, Denmark, and France had all been occupied and were now under German rule. The Germans were dropping bombs on British ports. The "phony war" as some called it, was very real —and dangerous. Letters from Paul were few and far between. She treasured each one of them, keeping them in a box under her bed, re-reading them often.

In August, Ann busied herself by helping Sophia with the canning. Together, they pickled cucumbers, made peach jam, and chopped many tomatoes for sauce. Sophia was just as chatty as Ann. The two of them got along swimmingly, and Ann appreciated the distraction Sophia's conversation provided as the bad news from Europe continued to pour in. Ann also took great comfort in the fact that her father had found such a perfect companion to spend time with the rest of his days.

On a hot Saturday in late August, Ann accompanied her father and Sophia to the courthouse, where she served as a witness to their small wedding ceremony in front of the judge. It was simple but beautiful. Sophia wore a pale blue suit with a matching pillbox hat, and she carried a bouquet of pink roses that Ann had put together for her. Ann's father wore his only suit and a huge smile. Afterward, they all went to the Windmill Restaurant to celebrate.

The next morning, Ann returned to Seattle on the train. Classes were starting next week, and she was excited to move back into the Sorrento. King Street Station was a welcome sight. Ann stepped down onto the platform and observed the crowds of people with a sigh of contentment. She loved the city.

When Ann arrived at the Sorrento, there were already a couple of messages waiting for her. One was from Mrs. Delzer, asking her to come by for a visit once she was settled in, and one from Nora, letting her know what room to find her in. There were no letters from Paul. Was he already on his way home?

Quickly putting her things away in her room on the fourth floor, Ann surveyed the new space with delight. The setup seemed similar to the ones she'd had in the years prior, but being on a higher level meant an even better view of the city and Puget Sound. She felt lucky to be sharing a room with Helen once more. Helen's suitcase sat in front of the closet, waiting to be unpacked. Where could she be? Ann decided to walk over to the Delzer's house and see if they were home.

Barbara Delzer was in the front garden cutting flowers when Ann walked up and greeted her. "Ann! You're back! How nice to see you. Did you have a good summer?"

Just then, David and Sally spotted Ann too. Their hugs and excitement over seeing her made Ann feel good.

"My father married his neighbor a couple of days ago, so yes, I'd say that made for a good summer," Ann said.

"Oh? How romantic! She's someone you like?"

"Oh, yes. She's wonderful. They're both very happy. Other than that, I picked a lot of cherries and peaches."

"Here, let me pick some flowers for you to take back to your room," Barbara offered. When she finished, Ann followed her into the house and greeted the other children. Billy and Margaret were in the kitchen, washing and drying the dishes together. Barbara smiled with pride. "I've put them to work. They're a great help around the house, but the work never ends. If you want to take up your old job again, it's all yours. We'd love to have you back!"

"I'd like that very much. Thank you." Ann had missed seeing the children regularly last year, and they were growing so fast. The best part of working for the Delzer family was that they treated her like family. "When do you want me to start?"

***

Throughout September, Ann lived in a state of anxious expectation. Had Paul left London in time? That question invaded her thoughts persistently as she went about her days. London was now being hit with bombs daily by the German Luftwaffe. The devastation, according to radio and newspaper reports, was extensive. Even if Paul had left London for New York before the bombing started, his journey home across the Atlantic was far from safe. At the end of the month, Ann still hadn't received any communication from Paul.

Ann was walking through the arboretum with Rose on a crisp Sunday afternoon in October, enjoying the chance to catch up with her aunt and talk about school, books, and the latest movies they had both watched. The topic of Paul, and why he might be missing, was one that Ann tried to avoid. By this point, she couldn't talk about it without tears spilling or her voice shaking.

Rose must have known what was on Ann's mind though, because she eventually asked in a gentle tone, "Ann, honey, what's going on with Paul?"

"I think something happened to him," Ann admitted as she fought back tears. "And it's my fault. If I wouldn't have been so selfish ... if I just would have married him, he wouldn't have gone to London. He'd be working at *The Oregonian* right now. He'd be safe. I would have been fine."

"It's not your fault. And you don't know that something has happened. Paul could just be delayed. Did you ever stop to think that a little more time is what you both needed? Time to grow, time to find out who you are, what you want, and to have your adventures? You've both been doing that, and that's a good thing. You weren't made for a life that is just fine. You're made for more than that." Rose placed a comforting hand on Ann's shoulder. "You could call the *Associated Press* office in New York and inquire about Paul, if that would give you some peace of mind. You can make the long-distance call from my house."

Rose was an angel in Ann's eyes, always knowing the right thing to say and do, still watching out for her. Ann stopped and watched a squirrel scurry across the path, considering her aunt's words. "I'll do that. Thank you."

"Trust God's timing on this. If you and Paul are supposed to be together, then it will happen. Worrying won't change anything."

***

On Monday, Ann decided she'd take the trolley to her aunt's house and miss class so she could make that phone call. It was the first time she'd skipped class in all her years of school. If Ann wanted to reach Paul's New York office during business hours, there was no way around it. But when she came downstairs and into the lobby, Robert, the desk clerk, had a telegram for her.

Hands shaking and heart-pounding, Ann took the message into the Fireside Room to read in privacy. The short message was from Paul. He was hurt. He'd been in a hospital in London, and he'd been transferred to New York. Now he was on his way to Swedish Hospital in Seattle. She had no more information beyond that. Ann raced out of the lobby and up Madison Street to the hospital.

Checking in at the front desk, Ann was disappointed to learn that Paul was not there. The stern woman behind the counter squinted her eyes as she assessed Ann. "Are you a family member?" she asked.

"No, I'm a friend."

"Miss, I'm afraid I can only tell you that he's not here."

"Can I leave a number with you to call, so I can know when he arrives?"

"Not unless you're family."

Ann thanked the lady and walked back to the Sorrento. There was nothing else to do but go to class. She'd figure out something. Nothing was going to keep her away from Paul now, not when he needed her most. Nora and Peggy could help her. They were both in the nurse's training program, and they worked at Swedish. At dinner that night, Ann asked them if they could let her know when Paul arrived.

Two days later, Nora knocked on Ann's door after dinner. She looked serious. "Paul arrived today. I told him I'd bring you by to see him tomorrow during visiting hours." She paused and took a deep breath. "He's got some serious injuries, Ann. Some burns, some broken bones, and some hearing loss. His building was bombed."

***

The sight of Paul in his hospital bed nearly took her breath away. He was sleeping when she arrived. Bandages covered his arms, and his right leg was in a cast. Paul wasn't alone. His mother was seated in a chair next to him, knitting. She glanced up and nodded when she saw Ann, then motioned for them to step outside the room.

"He was asking for you," Mrs. Lewis said. She didn't seem upset about that. She seemed warmer toward Ann than she'd ever been before. "Go on. He'll be happy to see you when he wakes up. I'll give you some time alone. I need to get some breakfast." She rubbed her eyes, as though she needed a moment to collect herself. "He can't hear very well right now. We're hoping it's temporary. You'll find a pen and paper on the table. You can use those to communicate with him."

Ann nodded, gratefully, and said thank you. A few minutes later, Paul woke up. Seeing Ann, he smiled and reached toward her, taking her hand. She leaned down and kissed him. "I was so scared. But you're here now. You're going to be okay. I love you so much!"

A grimace of pain flickered across Paul's face. He knew she was speaking to him, but he couldn't hear her. Reaching for the notepad and pen, he took it and wrote something. When he handed it to her, it said, *You're the most beautiful sight I've ever seen. I wish I could hear you, but my ears aren't working right now. I guess a man can't have everything.*

She didn't cry until she left the room. The tears were from relief more than sadness. Nora was there, waiting in the hallway. Paul's mother was there too. Ann could see the love in her eyes and the concern for her son. The woman didn't always know how to show it, but Ann knew. She cared about Paul in her own way.

Throughout that week, Paul remained in the hospital. The burns on his arms required intensive and painful treatments. Other than the obvious physical limitations he was dealing with, he was the same old Paul. The doctors thought he was lucky to be alive. Ann thought about all the prayers she'd said while he was gone—asking God to keep him safe. Luck had nothing to do with Paul's return. God had protected him.

Thirty-Three

The burns were healing. The doctor had removed the cast, and Paul was leaving the hospital today. Ann carried his bag and a vase of flowers as she walked behind Mrs. Lewis and the nurse who was pushing his wheelchair down the long white corridor toward the entrance. A car was waiting to take Paul to his grandmother's home—only his grandmother was no longer there. Getting used to that would be hard. Paul's parents had inherited the grand old house after Elizabeth's passing, and they'd taken up residence there after selling their home in Tacoma. Gloria had prepared his old room for him and had hired a nurse, allowing Paul to finish his recovery at home.

Ann and Gloria Lewis had grown more comfortable around each other over the past couple of weeks, seeing each other often as they came and went from Paul's bedside. It wasn't precisely friendship, but at least there was more understanding between them.

Being careful to turn toward Paul so he could read her lips when she spoke, Ann said goodbye to him as the nurse helped him into the car. She promised to come over to visit as soon as she was free that evening. When she brushed his cheek tenderly, he took her hand and kissed it, then waved goodbye.

Hurrying down Madison Street toward the college, Ann did her best to make it to her next class in time. The last of the fall leaves were covering the sidewalk, creating a crunching sound as she stepped on them. Ann had missed a lot of classes lately, due to her frequent visits with Paul. But now, without the restraints of the hospital's strict visiting hours, she'd be able to see Paul more often in the evenings.

Ann knew Paul was struggling. He did his best to remain hopeful, but his hearing had only returned a small amount—and just in one ear. Paul had become somewhat proficient in reading lips if people were looking at him when they spoke. The doctors reminded them to give it time, but with each passing day, the hope he'd had faded a little more. Paul missed his work, and it made her sad for him when he'd been released from his position with the Associated Press. Even though it meant he was in Seattle with her, this wasn't how she wanted it to be.

The previous afternoon, when Ann had been at the Delzer house, she'd spoken with both David and his mother about Paul's hearing loss. David, though only a boy of eight, had some understanding of what Paul was facing, because of his own deafness. He might even be able to help Paul adjust to this new reality. She'd asked if she could take David with her to visit Paul sometime. Both David and Barbara had readily agreed, and David had offered to teach Paul some sign language. She'd broach the subject with Paul tonight. It was a sensitive area—that blurry place between hope and acceptance.

Sliding into her seat toward the back of the room, Ann took out her notepad and pen, ready to listen. She had made it to class with a minute to spare. The professor started his lecture, and Ann tried to concentrate. Before long, she found herself reading the other notebook she had with her. It was the same one she and Paul had been using to communicate each day in the hospital, and now it was nearly full. She read the conversations they'd had—his familiar scrawl alongside hers, alternating back and forth. Some of it was funny, and in other parts, Paul had described the terror of the bombing. It was a slow way of communicating, but Paul was a good writer, and she loved reading what he had to say.

***

Paul sent a cab to pick up Ann and bring her back to his house each evening so she could have dinner with him. He'd been advised by his doctor not to drive until his leg healed. Ann knew he was going stir crazy being stuck in the house all day. He was used to his independence, and he wanted it back. It was a cause to celebrate when on Wednesday night, a week after he'd been released from the hospital, Ann saw Paul pull into the front drive in front of the Sorrento in his red Plymouth.

"Look at you!" Ann was grinning. "Do you want to come in and see some old friends?"

He paused, then nodded. Paul was self-conscious about his hearing, and he was uncomfortable with speaking, but Ann also thought it would be good for him to start seeing more people besides herself, his nurse, and his parents.

"Hold on. I'll run upstairs and get Helen, Peggy, and Nora if they're around. They'll be so happy to see you!" Ann said.

When Ann came back downstairs with her friends, she found Paul sitting near the fireplace. For the first time since he'd been back, he seemed like himself—healthy and at peace. Facing away from her, watching the flames, Paul didn't know she was there. When she approached and said his name, he didn't respond. Of course, he didn't hear her. It caught her off-guard. He looked the same, but at that moment, she was reminded, once again, of the adjustments she'd need to make and get used to as they faced this new reality together. Would he really never hear her voice again? Would he never be able to listen to music or hear laughter? Her heart ached.

"Paul! Welcome back!" Helen said as she approached. Paul stood, smiling. He greeted everyone with hugs. It was a warm reunion, full of happiness, and even champagne. Peggy had somehow procured a bottle and some glasses, which she brought out for the group.

Nora raised her glass toward Paul and Ann. "To a couple that we all love, admire, and celebrate. Paul, happy homecoming!"

***

Paul was back in the hospital again that November for skin grafts on his arms. He rarely complained about the pain, but Ann could tell, it was brutal. She was by his side as often as possible. Focusing on her schoolwork was hard. Often, she'd bring her books to the hospital and read while sitting next to Paul's bed. It was the Tuesday before Thanksgiving when Ann was studying quietly by Paul's side when he started pointing toward a monitor next to him.

"Ann! I can hear the beeping. It's that machine. Say something!"

***

When the last day of school arrived before Christmas break, Ann was never more excited to be done with a semester. If it hadn't been for Paul's encouragement to keep going, she probably wouldn't have made it. "Don't slack off on account of me!" he'd say.

She only had one more semester of classes and one semester of student teaching to go. She was on track to graduate early, thanks to the full class loads she'd been taking. Ann and Paul had begun to talk more about their future together. But this time was different. They had both changed. They cherished each other with an intensity they hadn't known was possible before. They were treading carefully and taking it slow. Second and third chances weren't gifts to be squandered.

Ann dug through her closet and chose a beautiful blue dress for her evening out with Paul. They were going to the Terrace Room at the Mayflower as they had on their very first date. She gave herself a spritz of Bourjois, a perfume she knew was Paul's favorite before going downstairs to the lobby. He was waiting for her, looking like a movie star with his charming smile and perfectly tailored suit. He greeted her with a kiss. She felt like the luckiest girl in the world.

Over the salad course, she could tell Paul had something important on his mind. He put down his fork. "I need to work again."

"Okay." Ann chose her next words carefully, not sure if she wanted the answer to her question. "Are you going back to your last job?"

"No. I want to be with you. I'm going to find something here in Seattle. Is that what you want? Do you want me to stay?" His tone was anxious.

"I want you to be happy. But yes! If that's what you want, of course!"

"I should probably start searching for my place too. It's getting a little crowded at my folks' house."

Ann laughed at the image of that enormous house being crowded with three people, but she knew what he meant. The frosty relations between him and his parents had thawed somewhat, but they were still not the most comfortable people to live with. "Don't you need to find a job first?"

Paul smiled. "Not really. I *need* to work. The newspaper business is where I always wanted to be. It's an important part of my life that's missing right now. It's not about the money. My grandmother's estate was settled today, and as it turns out, she was a shrewd businesswoman, more than we ever knew, and she was very generous."

"The way you feel about the newspaper business ... I think that's the way I feel about teaching," Ann said, thoughtfully. "It's a part of me. I need it."

Thirty-Four

The Sorrento girls were hosting another game night in the Fireside Room on the first Thursday after everyone had returned from the holiday break. Ann had invited Paul with the hope of finally introducing him to Pete, who would also be there. Her friendship with Pete was not something she wanted Paul to feel uncomfortable with. Pete was important to her, and she figured once Paul got to know him, he would see for himself that they, too, could be great friends. The only problem—a snowstorm had rolled in that day. The roads were icy, and the authorities were telling people to stay off the streets. Nineteen-forty-one was bringing some of the coldest winter weather anyone in Seattle had seen in recent memory.

Ann was having dinner upstairs with Helen, Nora, and Peggy that evening, telling them about her plan.

"I don't know, Ann," Nora said. "You and Paul are finally doing so well again. Are you sure? What if Pete does have feelings for you?"

"I'm sure," Ann said with confidence, taking another bread roll and smothering it with butter. "Pete is like a brother to me. Paul will see that. But now, as much as I'd love to see him, I'm hoping he stays home tonight. I don't want him driving across the city in this weather."

After dinner, the women took the elevator down to the lobby. When the doors opened, both Paul and Pete were there, chatting amiably, backs turned away as they stood near the bar.

Ann nudged Nora, grinning. "Look at that. By the way, we need a fourth player. Want to join us?"

Without waiting for an answer, Ann grabbed Nora's hand and pulled her toward the bar to say hello to the guys. Nora had been asking a lot of questions about Pete lately, and he always blushed when she was around. Ann would do her part to fan that little spark she saw between them.

"Pete, Paul, hello! I see the two of you have already met," Ann said. "Paul, how on earth did you make it through all that snow?"

"Hi, Ann. Yes, we just met. I didn't drive if that's what you were thinking. I had an old pair of Nordic skis at the house that I used to get here." Paul's skin was flushed from the cold, but he had a big smile. He looked the healthiest she'd seen him since his return.

"That's a smart way to do it," Pete said. "I wish I had a pair of skis to get around on right now."

By the end of the evening, Ann could see that her plan had worked. Everyone was laughing and having fun together, and she was happy to see how comfortable Paul and Pete were together. Even better, arrangements were made for a double-date with Pete and Nora at the Black and Tan club the following weekend.

***

Sunday dinner at Aunt Rose and Uncle Gary's house was a new tradition that Ann anticipated each week. Today, Paul had come along too. The whole house smelled delicious when they walked in. A turkey was roasting in the oven, and the table had already been set with a bounty of mashed potatoes, Jell-O salad, deviled eggs, and buttermilk biscuits.

"Aunt Rose, you're spoiling us! Is there anything I can do to help?" Ann asked.

"You can pour some water in the glasses and see who wants wine. Thank you, dear."

"How was your week? Anything new?" Ann filled a pitcher with water from the sink.

"Ah, not much. I've been doing some preliminary research on a new book I'm thinking of writing and getting the garden ready for planting. How about you?"

"I talked to Mr. Ferguson, the eighth-grade teacher at Seattle Prep, who I worked with a couple of years ago, and it's all arranged. I'll be doing my student teaching semester for his class in the fall."

"That's great! I miss teaching some days." Rose took the turkey out of the oven and set it on the counter.

"Do you ever think of going back? Seattle College keeps growing in enrollment. I wonder if they're hiring."

"I do think about that sometimes," Rose said. "After dinner, what do you say we take the dog for a walk around the neighborhood? It's so nice outside."

After the large dinner that Rose made, a walk around the neighborhood was the only way anybody was going to be able to make room for dessert. She had baked a pumpkin pie, which looked terrific, so the group headed outside for a stroll.

"Do you mind if we walk by the Fairbanks house?" Ann asked, referring to the home her mother and Rose had grown up in. She hadn't seen it in a while, and she was curious to see if somebody had bought it.

"Yes, let's do that!" Rose said.

Paul and Ann strolled behind Gary and Rose, admiring the expansive green lawns and tidy houses along the block. Ann loved this neighborhood. When they reached the Fairbanks mansion, what they saw was horrifying. A rock had been thrown through one of the beautiful stained-glass windows. The railing around the front porch had been knocked down. The landscaping had been neglected so severely that the grounds now resembled an overgrown jungle. Ann tried not to cry. Who allowed this to happen? Rose gasped, staring at her former home in sorrow.

"Hey, the sale sign is still up," Paul said. "I'll write down this number and see if I can let the current owners know what has happened. Maybe they're not aware. It looks like there could be squatters living there." Sure enough, empty bean cans littered the grass, along with discarded cigarettes all over the front steps.

"Let's not stick around and find out. I don't want to run into whoever did this. I think that's a good idea to call that number, Paul," Rose said.

Ann was quiet for the rest of the day. She hated seeing that beautiful old house like that. Common sense reminded her that it didn't belong to her family anymore, but that didn't change her feelings of outrage. She'd never even had the chance to go inside and see it. And now, she was afraid to know what the vandals had likely done to the interior.

Paul wrapped his arms around her, doing his best to comfort her. "I'm sorry," he said. "I'll do my best to make this right."

***

"Will you push me on the swing?" Sally asked. Ann had taken the Delzer children to the park that afternoon.

"Of course, sweetie. Hold on!" Ann said as she gave the little girl a hearty push. "How was school today?"

"I got 100 percent on my spelling test."

"I'm not surprised. You studied hard. Good job, Sally!"

Just then, out of the corner of her eye, Ann saw Paul walking toward them across the grass.

He stopped at the basketball court to say hello to David, signing something Ann couldn't quite make out. Even though Paul had regained most of his hearing, he'd kept up with learning sign language so he could talk to David. It was just another reason Ann loved him so much.

"Hey, Sally! Hey, Ann!" Paul said. "I thought I'd find you here."

"Hey, what's up?" Ann was curious about both the unexpected visit and the suit Paul was wearing.

"I had to find you because I have some good news. I start work at the *Post Intelligencer* next week!"

"Oh, wow! Congratulations! That's wonderful!" She grinned.

"What's the *Post Intelligencer*?" asked Sally.

"It's a newspaper, Sally. It will be my job to write about what's going on in Seattle."

"I just read the comics." Sally jumped off the swing. "But when I get better at reading, then I'll read your paper." She ran over where Margaret and Billy were, by the slide, to tell them Paul's news. She liked being the one with information.

"We should celebrate!" Ann said. "Want to meet me at Jack Frost tonight after I get off work? My treat."

"I'd love to, but I have an appointment in a few minutes, and I'm not sure when I'll be done. That's why I came and found you. I couldn't wait to share the news. Mind if we do it tomorrow?"

"Sure. What kind of appointment?"

"Can't tell you until I know more," Paul said, grinning.

Ann raised an eyebrow in response. Now, she was more curious than ever. "I'll come by tomorrow at around seven. Sound good?"

***

When Ann returned to her room that evening to prepare for dinner, Helen was painting her nails and listening to Judy Garland on the record player. As usual, her roommate appeared effortlessly glamorous, even with rollers in her hair. Ann sat down at the vanity and made a face. Pieces of her chignon were falling out every which way. She took her hair down and started brushing.

"I don't know what I'm going to do after we don't live together anymore. You've been my person that keeps me from looking completely hopeless when it comes to what to wear and how to be presentable," Ann said.

"You don't give yourself enough credit. You know what you're doing. But I'm going to miss you too. I can't believe we only have three weeks left of living here," Helen said.

It was the last year the coeds would have use of Hotel Sorrento as their living quarters. The new dorms that had been under construction would be completed by the time the students returned in the fall. But Ann wasn't moving into those. She was going to live with her aunt and uncle while doing her student teaching. It was closer to Seattle Prep.

"Paul was hired at the *Post Intelligencer* today," Ann said.

"Oh, really? That's great! What's going on with the two of you? Are you going to get married, for real, now?"

"I don't know. I'd like to. Maybe I should ask him this time. After all, he already asked me once." Ann said it as a joke, but once she heard the words, she wondered. Would that be weird? Girls didn't do that. Did they?

"Hmm ..." Helen was thinking. "Yes! You should!"

"Well, I was just making a joke."

"It's not a bad idea. It's different, but hey, it's also romantic!" Helen removed the rollers from her hair and sprayed the curls. Now the room smelled like nail polish and hairspray.

Ann decided to change the subject. "Hey, are you going to be around tonight? If you are, we should invite Peggy and Nora over to the room. We haven't had 'girls' night' in forever."

"Let's do it!"

Ann powdered her nose and checked her watch. It was time for dinner. "Are you ready to go upstairs for dinner?" She looked at Helen, who still had a conspiratorial smirk on her face. The girl loved romance. "Hey, remember, it was just a joke!"

Thirty-Five

"Put down your pencils and bring your tests to the front of the room, please," the professor said.

Ann glanced up at the clock. The last hour had flown past. Relief, then pure happiness spread over her as she stood up and turned in her final test. She knew she had done well, and she could be proud. The only thing that stood in front of her and a degree now was one semester of student teaching.

As Ann walked down the steps from the science building into the sunshine, she thought about how much she was looking forward to finally putting the knowledge she'd gained over these past three years to work in a classroom. She would have to pack up her things in her room at the Sorrento for the last time, and she wanted to stop by the Delzer's house and say goodbye. Tomorrow, she'd be moving into the guest room at Aunt Rose's home.

Ann had decided to stay in Seattle over the summer and search for a job, hopefully something that paid a little more than her work as a mother's helper. As much as she loved working for the Delzer family, the money from her college trust fund was nearly gone. It was time to start adding something to her bank account. She didn't want to be a houseguest forever. The problem was, she had yet to find anything. There was always the option of going to Wenatchee and working for her father. But Ann wanted to be closer to Paul.

Yesterday, Paul had asked Ann if he could pick her up and take her to dinner tonight. He said he had something to show her. The excitement in his voice had made her curious. But when she asked what it was, he'd only tell her it was a surprise.

***

Paul was driving toward the Queen Anne neighborhood where Rose lived, but when they got close to her house, he drove right on. There was a picnic basket in the back seat. He had been quiet, but finally, he turned to Ann.

"I was able to reach the owner of your grandparents' old house," he said. Now they were on the same street as the beautiful old mansion. "His name is Mr. Anderson. He lives in California, but he has an agent here. He was appreciative of the heads up regarding the state of the property. The 'campers' have been removed, he assured me. I know you always wanted to see the inside, so I asked him if I could make an appointment with his agent so you could take a peek." At that, he pulled in front of the house and turned off the engine.

This was one of the most beautiful things anyone had ever done for her. "Really? Thank you!"

The house was overrun with weeds and still neglected, but Ann could see past those things. She had a good imagination. Following Paul, she excitedly got out of the car and walked toward a portly man, presumably the agent, who was waiting on the porch. The man threw the cigarette he'd been smoking on the front step and stubbed it out with his foot.

"Are you Mr. and Mrs. Lewis?" he asked. *Mrs. Lewis.* Ann liked the sound of that.

Paul didn't correct the man. Instead, he held out his hand for a shake. "I'm Mr. Lewis. And you're Mr. Jakes? Thank you for meeting us here."

"Go on inside. Take a look around. I'll wait out here." Mr. Jakes wasn't the friendliest guy. It didn't surprise Ann that the house had remained unsold for so long.

Ann opened the massive front door, and they stepped into a spacious hall. A grand double stairway led to the upstairs landing. Crystal wall sconces along the walls matched the large showpiece chandelier hanging from the tall ceiling. Thick dust had covered every surface, casting a shade of gray over everything. Empty liquor bottles and broken glass were strewn about the place. Pieces of the banister appeared to have been ripped out and were missing. But this was where her mother and aunt had grown up. Ann tried to imagine the room as it had been. It had obviously been lovely at one time.

For the next few minutes, Ann walked through the house, doing her best to take it all in and memorize the space. From the front hall to the left was what appeared to be a small library. Tall empty shelves reached to the ceiling. To the right of the hallway was a large drawing room. And straight ahead, through an open archway, Ann could see another hall that led to yet more spaces—the dining room, the kitchen, the game room, a conservatory, and a butler's pantry.

Upstairs were five bedrooms, a morning room, and two bathrooms. Up one more flight of stairs was a large attic and what was likely the servant's quarters. Some furniture—including a grand piano in the drawing room—remained, but most of the pieces were broken. It was sad to see, but Ann was still grateful for the opportunity to explore the place.

Standing on the front porch again, Ann and Paul thanked Mr. Jakes for his time. Paul walked Ann to the car and opened the door for her. When she got in, he smiled and said he had a question for Mr. Jakes. "I'll be right back," he said.

Ann watched as Mr. Jakes lit another cigarette and took Paul's business card, then shook his hand. Paul returned to the car. "Ready for a picnic? I thought Kerry Park sounded nice tonight."

"Thank you, Paul, for showing me my grandparents' old house. That meant the world to me."

When they reached the park, Paul carried the picnic basket over to a low rock wall on the edge of a steep hill. In front of them, they could see the whole city. He spread out a blanket for the two of them and began digging through the basket. He pulled out some cheese, bread, salami, blueberries, two glasses, and a bottle of champagne. They took in the beautiful view as they ate.

Ann shivered in the cool summer evening breeze and put on her cardigan.

Paul, who had been quiet, finally spoke. "So, I have a question for you." He reached into his jacket pocket and pulled out a small box. Ann could feel her heart beating faster.

"I thought I'd try this again. Ann, I love you so much. Your happiness means everything to me. If you believe you could be happy spending the rest of your life with me, I'd like to ask you to marry me. Will you?"

"Yes, yes, oh, yes! I wanted to ask you! I love you, Paul. I want nothing more." She took the ring he offered and placed it on her left hand. This time, she knew it was right. She kissed him long and passionately.

"Okay." He smiled. "Then I have another question for you. What would you think about buying the house?"

Ann was stunned. "Uh, can we afford it?"

"Yes, I'll show you the numbers. The owner and I have reached a tentative agreement, pending your approval. But as you saw, it needs a lot of work. We can also have any of the furnishings from my parents' house in Tacoma that we want.

They're selling that house and their furniture needs a place to go, anyway. If it's not too crazy, do you think you could oversee the project and plan a wedding over the summer? We could get married and move in by the end of summer, if you like."

That sounded like the best summer job ever to Ann. "Wow, I'm speechless. It's more than I ever dreamed. Yes, let's do it!"

"So, you were going to ask me to marry you?" Paul was grinning. "What were you waiting for?"

"I don't know. I just thought it somehow would seem fair, seeing how you've already asked me once."

Paul laughed. "I got what was coming to me. I completely steamrolled you on the big decisions we were making for our future. It wasn't right, and I don't want to do that again. Please, tell me when I'm not listening to you as I should. I want to know."

"We're both different people now. I needed to grow up some more. I needed that time. I thought I'd lost you, and it made me realize how much I love you. God brought us a second chance, and I thank him every day." She put her head on Paul's shoulder and admired the diamond sparkling on her finger. The happiness inside her felt like it was going to bubble over like the champagne in her glass.

Paul raised his glass. "To you, my love."

"To us." Ann raised her glass in return. Then she said one more thing that was on her mind. "My aunt let that house go because it required so much upkeep—and she didn't think she could manage that while working at the same time. I want to teach. How will we make that work?"

"Ann, my grandmother left behind more than enough. I'll show you. Money is not an issue. We'll hire the people we need to take care of the house, and you can teach. The house is back in your family where it belongs. It's going to be an adventure. We'll fill it with our own memories—and maybe some kids. I can't wait!"

"Neither can I." And she meant it, with all of her heart.

Epilogue

June 1942

"Here, everybody come over here to the front porch so you can be in the picture. Ann, you stand in the middle. Ladies, hold your diplomas up. Okay, everybody, look at the camera. Rose, I can't see you. Stand in front. On the count of three, smile. One ... two ... three!" Uncle Gary peered through the viewfinder and took several pictures, hoping for the best. It wasn't easy getting all those people in the frame. He almost fell over as he backed up, tripping over Ginger, the Lewis's new puppy, as she ran around his feet.

The lively party guests standing on the front porch consisted of the dearest people in Ann's life. They were all there to celebrate her graduation from Seattle College. Though she'd finished six months ago, the ceremony had happened earlier that day.

Ann took Paul's hand and looked around in wonder. "I can't believe they're all here," she said. Late last summer, they had gathered in the same spot for their wedding pictures. It had been a lovely day, much like today.

Her father and Sophie were content and settled into their new life together in Wenatchee. Sophie was good at convincing Ann's father to work less and relax more. For Ann, this meant she got to see them more often, as they now took more frequent trips to come and visit.

Aunt Rose and Uncle Gary were, once again, both teaching at the University of Washington.

After the U.S. entered the war, many of the younger male professors had left to serve. Rose's old job was suddenly available, and she had taken it—but not until she was given an apology and a hefty raise.

Mr. and Mrs. Delzer were there too. Margaret and Billy, now both twelve, were old enough to be a significant help around the house with their younger siblings. Their mother would need their support in the coming months, as Mr. Delzer had enlisted in the navy. He was leaving for Europe in two weeks.

Many of the Sorrento Girls were also present, gathered around in small groups on the lawn. Peggy, Nora, and Helen had also walked in the graduation ceremony earlier that morning, and this party was as much for them as it was for Ann. Helen would be sticking around, much to Ann's delight. She'd been hired to teach at the same elementary school the Delzer children attended.

Peggy and Joe were getting married in a week. Joe had been at Pearl Harbor when it was bombed. After recovering from some injuries he'd suffered, Joe had been honorably discharged for medical reasons. He was now re-adjusting to civilian life. They were moving to Olympia, where Peggy had recently started work as a nurse.

Nora was planning on offering her services as a nurse in the army. She would be leaving soon. Pete, sadly, wasn't at the party, as he had already joined the military. He had left for basic training a week ago.

The elder Mr. and Mrs. Lewis were over by the fountain, deep in conversation with Mr. Ferguson, who'd just retired. After Ann's semester of student teaching in his classroom, he'd announced his upcoming retirement and had recommended her to the school administration at

Seattle Prep. They'd offered her the job, and she had accepted. She would start in the fall.

Ann smiled as she watched Sally and David play on the shaded front porch of her home with a train set that had belonged to Paul. She'd rescued it from the attic of the house in Tacoma before it had been sold. The toy engine David was pushing along the tracks looked very much like the Empire Builder, the train that had first brought Ann to Seattle, nearly ten years ago.

That adventure had been the beginning of what had brought her here. She was grateful for all of it—her growing faith, her marriage to Paul, their beautiful home, the friendships, the lessons, the fun, the heartaches, and now, the diploma she held in her hands. None of it had been easy. It had required courage, honesty, and strength—along with the help of some good people.

Ann's life had been a great adventure, so far, and now, she was ready for the next chapter.

Coming Soon

Palmer Girl

The Historic Hotels Collection ~ Book Two
Preview

One

Elizabeth Nordeman realized it was too late to avoid being spotted. The last space on her dance card was about to be filled. Taking one last discreet sip from the glass she'd been holding, she set it on the passing silver tray of a uniformed waiter. Then she turned and smiled politely at the elegant woman and the young man who approached her. Elizabeth had seen them making a beeline toward her place at the base of the grand staircase where she'd paused to catch her breath after the last Quadrille. She'd been hoping to make an early exit and go back upstairs to her family's apartment without anyone noticing.

Drawing near was Bertha Palmer, their hostess, and judging by the determined look on her face, her motives were clear. Every high society woman of Chicago, minus the ones with marriageable daughters of their own, seemed to have united around her mother's cause, which was to introduce Elizabeth to every eligible bachelor of high social standing in the city.

Elizabeth could sense her mother watching the scene from across the Palmer House ballroom, as if to will her daughter to make an effort and maintain the manners she'd taught her. So far this evening, she'd been dutiful. Never mind, this event was the last place she wanted to be at the moment.

"Mr. Harold Pierce, I'd like to introduce you to Miss Elizabeth Nordeman. Miss Nordeman recently arrived with her family from New York. Her father, Cornelius, is a colleague of your father's." Mrs. Palmer introduced the eager freckle-faced man at her side to Elizabeth in an efficient and breezy manner that was mixed with a trace of a southern drawl. "Miss Nordeman, Mr. Pierce, is a student at Northwestern University. I've known his family for years."

"How do you do, Mr. Pierce," said Elizabeth, giving a curtsy, then extending her hand.

"It's a pleasure to meet you," he kissed her hand. "May I request the pleasure of your company for this next dance?"

Mrs. Palmer excused herself and moved along to her next guests. Elizabeth, having no other option, accepted his offer and followed Mr. Pierce.

The following song, a waltz, allowed Mr. Pierce the opportunity to pepper Elizabeth with unwelcome questions. He exercised a familiarity she was unaccustomed to from someone she'd just met. "What brings you to Chicago, Miss Nordeman?"

Ignoring his breach of etiquette, Elizabeth did her best to answer politely, while still focusing on the steps of the dance, which seemed different than any she'd learned before.

"The World's Columbian Exposition, sir," she answered.

"But that isn't happening until next year."

"Very true, sir, but my father works for the Exposition Corporation. There's much to be done before it opens." Elizabeth didn't elaborate any further on why her father had uprooted the family and brought them to live at the Palmer House for the next eighteen months. Anyone who read the papers already knew at least part of the story—or thought they did.

"Aha, I see. That's why Mrs. Palmer said our fathers were colleagues," said Mr. Pierce, stepping on Elizabeth's toe. "My father is responsible for bringing the fair to Chicago." Knowing this was an exaggerated boast, and that a great many people had contributed to the effort, Elizabeth merely nodded, thinking to herself the man before her was somewhat pretentious.

The look of approval on her father's face as she waltzed past him was apparent, and it strengthened her resolve to please him. Even if it meant dancing with Harold Pierce. When the waltz ended, Mr. Pierce offered his right arm to Elizabeth and escorted her from the dance floor. "May I offer you a refreshment, Miss Nordeman?"

"No, thank you." Elizabeth made a point of closing her fan, a sign most men in her circle would have understood to mean she wasn't interested in further conversation, but Mr. Pierce persisted.

"I regret this evening's festivities are already coming to a close. Thank you for the honor of your company with the last dance. I will call on you tomorrow."

"Thank you, sir, though I am not at liberty to accept that offer. You may ask my father." Elizabeth bowed her head toward Mr. Pierce, once again signaling the end of their conversation. At this, she turned on her heel and did not wait to hear Mr. Pierce's response. She was halfway up the stairs before she heard a loud voice call behind her.

"I'll do that!"

Elizabeth kept walking, pretending not to hear, and let out a sigh. *Oh, dear, I hope I didn't encourage him.*

***

The breakfast room smelled like fresh coffee and bacon when Elizabeth joined her father the next morning. Patricia Nordeman always took her breakfast in bed, leaving father and daughter to themselves for the first meal of the day. Looking up from his newspaper, Cornelius nodded his acknowledgment of her presence before asking, "Did you sleep well, my dear?"

"Yes, father." Elizabeth placed a napkin in her lap. "And you?"

"Good, good. You were introduced to Eugene Pierce's son, Harold, last night, I noticed. Nice fellow?"

"Pleasant enough, I guess, but I'm not interested in him if that's what you're hinting at. He might ask you if he can call on me. Please say no."

"No?" Cornelius frowned. "Elizabeth...his family has connections. We must be careful not to offend."

"Please?" She paused. "Enough with the matchmaking. I'll be careful. I promise." Elizabeth watched as her father put down his paper with a sigh.

"And what are your plans for today? More shopping?" asked Cornelius. She had been thinking of going to Marshall Field's to see what was new, but her father's disapproval of that idea was communicated, clear enough, in the tone of his voice. Elizabeth came up with a new plan.

"Of course not, father. I was going to take Sissy with me to the flower market. I wanted to put together some new arrangements for the apartment."

Since the move to Chicago, Elizabeth had been lonely. She missed Catherine, her best friend in New York. Though she knew it wasn't proper to form friendships with the help, Sissy, her lady's maid, was the closest person she had to an ally in the city.

"Very well, don't take the streetcar. Take the carriage. I'll tell Louis to get it ready for you."

***

Bertha Palmer and Elizabeth's mother, Patricia, were having tea in the Nordeman's apartment when she arrived home from the market that afternoon. An array of brilliant flowers, ferns, and grasses, wrapped in brown paper, weighed the women down as they walked past the front parlor. Peeking over the top of some yellow roses, Elizabeth smiled and greeted her mother and their visitor, and Mrs. Palmer laughed with pleasure at the sight of Elizabeth's shopping haul.

"I see you found the flower market, dear. I'm a patron of the Horticultural Society, myself. The perfume from those packages is wonderful. As soon as you unburden yourself, please, join us. I would love to know how you're enjoying our fair city so far."

"Elizabeth, let Sissy take care of those. Please, come sit." Her mother picked up the porcelain bell to ring for more tea. Elizabeth handed the flowers to Sissy, along with the hat she was wearing.

"Sissy, please put them in water, for now. I want to create a new centerpiece for the dining room. Oh, and make sure we have some fruit for the arrangement." She joined the other two women and sat on the settee.

"If you're interested in floral design, then you really must come to the garden show next week," said Mrs. Palmer.

"Elizabeth insists on creating all our indoor arrangements herself. She created this piece right here," said Mrs. Nordeman, gesturing with pride toward the display of pink chrysanthemums and ferns adorning the mantle.

"Well, it's quite beautiful, I must say!" Coming from Mrs. Palmer, this was a true compliment. She was a woman who was known for her good taste. The Palmer House, built by Bertha's husband, Potter, as a wedding gift to his bride in 1871, was a grand and splendid centerpiece of Chicago's social life. The city was still trying to prove itself to the country as being worthy of high esteem, in equal rank to New York or Boston, and the building was a point of pride for everyone. Sadly, the original hotel was destroyed only days after completion in the Great Chicago Fire. The current version was not only just as fine as the original, but was also said to be fireproof. Mrs. Potter was known to be as deeply involved in running the Palmer House as Mr. Potter and was responsible for many of its celebrated features, such as the elaborate floral arrangements which graced the elegant ballrooms, the lobby, and its restaurants.

"Thank you," said Elizabeth. "I would love to attend the flower show next week."

"Then you will come as my guest. I'll have my secretary send you the details." Mrs. Palmer took a sip of tea with an air of finality as if to say that settled the matter. Elizabeth smiled gratefully. She knew it was an honor to have an important lady like Mrs. Palmer take a particular interest in her well-being as a newcomer to the city.

"Before you arrived, Elizabeth, our guest was telling me about Harold Pierce." Mrs. Nordeman took a small sandwich from the tiered tray in front of her and paused when Annette, their housekeeper, entered the room with another place setting. After Annette placed the items on the table near Elizabeth and left quietly, her mother resumed the conversation. "I know his family contributed a great deal to the upcoming Exposition. Harold seems like a nice young man."

"Yes, I'm sure he is," said Elizabeth, wondering if there was a way to change the subject. Thankfully, Mrs. Potter had other matters on her mind. She wanted to discuss the Women's Building, which would be a highlight of the Columbian Exposition and would feature exhibits that celebrated achievements from women across the world. Mrs. Palmer was on the board of directors. Elizabeth listened with interest, silently hoping that Bertha's feminist sensibilities might begin to influence her mother, who was more of a traditionalist. Mrs. Nordeman's personal feelings on the topic at hand were hard to read, as Elizabeth's mother was a woman of unflagging composure. Her expression remained neutral, as always.

"It's time I must go," said Mrs. Palmer when the clock chimed on the hour. She stood and looked intently at the floral arrangement on the mantle while she waited for Annette to gather her hat and gloves. "Miss Nordeman, I believe you have great talent. How would you like to create an arrangement for the lobby downstairs?" Elizabeth's face grew warm with pleasure. Before she could answer her approval, Bertha added, "Of course, you'll be paid a tidy sum. We'll talk more."

Elizabeth's mother interjected. "That's not necessary. I'm sure Elizabeth would be delighted to offer her services gratis." Mrs. Nordeman walked into the vestibule with her guest toward the front door. Elizabeth knew her mother disapproved of the idea of her daughter working for pay. She didn't know whose will would prevail. Both Mrs. Nordeman and Mrs. Palmer were strong women.

When Elizabeth's mother walked back into the parlor, alone, she had a small pink box in her hands with a notecard. "A delivery for you," she said. "It was left at the door." Her left eyebrow arched with curiosity. Elizabeth took the card and opened it. *This candy is sweet, like your smile. Let's talk soon. -Harold.*

"It's from Harold Pierce," she said, not hiding her distaste for the man. Her mother opened the box and frowned. Chocolates. They were beautiful but unwelcome. Such a gift was too forward. Elizabeth knew her mother thought so also. As far as she knew, Harold hadn't even spoken to her father yet.

"They sure do things differently here," Mrs. Nordeman sniffed. Elizabeth nodded. She knew her mother missed New York. Their apartment at the Palmer House consisted of many beautiful rooms, and it was exquisitely decorated in the most luxurious of furnishings. However, it was not comparable in scale or grandeur to the magnificent Fifth Avenue mansion the Nordemans had left behind. It had been a sacrifice for Patricia Nordeman to come to Chicago and leave her New York life behind for her husband. "I'm going to go lie down before dinner. We're eating in tonight," Elizabeth's mother paused, then lifted a chocolate from the box. "By the way, Mrs. Palmer would like a large floral arrangement for the front lobby delivered by Friday. She said to keep the receipts for reimbursement and add something for your labor."

Mrs. Palmer is a good influence on my mother, thought Elizabeth. She liked her—admired her, really. Her mother looked tired today. Maybe that was why she hadn't put up her usual resistance. The steady stream of social activities hadn't stopped since they'd arrived last month. Every night they attended glittering parties, their grief masked behind beautiful clothes, a busy schedule, and good manners. Elizabeth was happy for a night at home. She hoped it would be just the three of them.

Acknowledgments

Thank you to all the trailblazing women who've gone first. Amelia Earhart and Lea Puymbroeck Miller are prominent examples of those who used their voices to spoke out for justice and equality, not only for themselves but for others. They're an inspiration to me, in life- and for this book. But those ladies represent countless more women whose stories may never be told. Your bravery has made this world a better place for those of us who've come after.

To my husband, Derek, thank you. You're my greatest encourager. You have helped make this book possible in more ways than I can list here. Thank you for listening to all my ideas and for applying your meticulous attention to detail to these pages. Our love story is my favorite one of all.

To my daughter, Grace, and my son, Trent, I love you. I'm proud of both of you, and I appreciate the love and support you give and the patience you have shown when my mind has been elsewhere.

To Maren Kreun and Darcie Wentworth, my very first readers- the practical feedback, and the time you spent answering questions meant the world to me. Thank you for your friendship and your kindness.

ABOUT THE AUTHOR

A graduate of the University of Idaho with a degree in elementary education, Dawn Klinge began writing online through blogging in 2005. She's a Pacific Northwest native who loves a rainy day, a hot cup of coffee, and a good book to get lost in. This wife and mom to two young adults is often inspired by true personal and historical accounts. Dawn is a member of the American Christian Fiction Writers Association and the Northwest Christian Writers Association.

Made in the USA
Monee, IL
19 June 2021

71737121R00225